I0672443

JAMIE DIBS

Dreadful Penny

Book 1 in the Penny Lee series

**TIME
Z⊙NE
PRESS**

First published by Time Zone Press 2023

This novel is entirely a work of fiction. The names, characters and incidents portrayed in it are the work of the author's imagination. Any resemblance to actual persons, living or dead, events or localities is entirely coincidental.

Jamie Dibs asserts the moral right to be identified as the author of this work.

First edition

ISBN: 979-8-9888236-2-9

Cover art by Daniela Bertua & Alejandro Colucci

This book was professionally typeset on Reedsy. Find out more at reedsy.com

For Mabel

Contents

Acknowledgments

The quotes from "Agamemnon" by Aeschylus is from the 1966 translation by Robert Fagles.

I

DUBAI

October, 2015

1

The comet

The light filling the Learjet's interior turned harsh, as unforgiving as the haze of the desert below. Penny was the last to put on sunglasses, as though she had nothing to hide.

"We've received clearance to land," the pilot said over the intercom. "Seatbelts, please."

She reached across the stocky torso of the man beside her, the man she fawned over, the man she aimed to ruin.

His cell phone seemed glued to his broad cheek; she was surprised it didn't leave a permanent indent. Whether or not he relished the non-stop dialogues, rare was the moment when someone didn't need to speak with the CEO of a multi-billion dollar oil company.

She plucked the seatbelt that Timur was ignoring and tried to secure its buckle. He swatted her away, nestled the phone in the crook of his barely visible neck, and tried to secure it himself. He was grinning, though, so Penny knew he still got a rise out of her attention.

It would have been a different story had she been his wife, but that woman was far away in a golden tower with an unbeatable

3

view over lonely mountains.

"I'm talking," he growled.

"Landings get bumpy."

He would soon tire of her, but not yet—not yet; she needed to keep him interested another three days.

She stuck her tongue in his ear.

He pushed her away, the gesture both playful and suggesting annoyance. His grin widened, though. Penny fell into the plush leather chair across from his. She wasn't just putting on an act with Timur. It wasn't that she liked him, exactly. More that she had come to dread the little silences, the in-between moments when she was left with nothing but her own thoughts.

The chaos of the past six weeks had kept her focused. That's how long she had danced in his orbit. Not like the parade of other celestial objects that got caught in the pull of his gravity: those he consumed and then flung back out to the starry nothing. Timur Buribaev was not the sun, but a king Jupiter, with his own constellation of pale, demur moon-faced girls and mistresses flashing perfumed rings.

Penny knew how to win the attention of Jupiter's raging eye. She had arranged for him to catch a glimpse of her at the Bolshoi on the arm of a competitor. Then at a private room at Café Pushkin, where he had been perusing its famous vodka menu when he saw her with a private-equity director.

Timur was Kazahk, not Russian, but he spent plenty of time in Moscow and Penny and her handlers had noted he tended to play the field with impunity. What with the wife away in Almaty, counting his oil money.

He was ready for her. Two weeks ago—September bowing to October in 2015, Muscovites taking the first snowfall in stride—she had crossed Jupiter's orbit at a cocktail event at Tretyakov Gallery. Timur hadn't recognizing her bright comet's tail for an incoming asteroid even as she whispered promises of supernova kink if he'd rescue her from incoming winter for his upcoming business trip to Dubai.

The private jet bumped and jostled on air pockets. She pretended to look anxious, leaning across the aisle to squeeze Timur's big hand. As though she weren't his extinction event.

Outside her window, Dubai's towers sprouted like a dark forest above the haze. Timur's plane was not landing at Dubai International, but at the newer al-Maktoum airport. Still surrounded by frenetic construction and a maze of concrete, it catered to arrivals preferring discretion.

Kasym Shokay, seated opposite his boss, addressed Timur in the sonorous Kazakh language while keeping his inky eyes on her. He was still trying to lasso her comet's tail and spin her in a different direction. He'd been there at the gallery when she insinuated herself into Timur's conversation, and as soon as she began to flatter the big man with Russian endearments, he'd switched the conversation to Kazakh.

She didn't understand a lick of their native tongue, but words weren't necessary to decode Kasym. He looked at her with unfeigned distaste, and murmured a protest to the chairman.

Initially Penny hadn't needed to retaliate. She was pretty sure that Timur Buribaev, chairman and president of the thirty-two-billion-dollar KazPetro Corporation, didn't take to having a lieutenant question his personal lifestyle.

But having won her place on his trip to Dubai, she knew she was now on borrowed time. Grow too familiar and she might stop amusing the chairman.

She cut off Kasym's quiet stream of protest. "You're not going to leave me alone all weekend, are you, Timur?"

Timur scrolled on his phone, inscrutable behind his Ray-Bans. "You will enjoy, Veronique."

The Learjet's cabin could comfortably seat twelve but today it contained only five passengers, plus a stewardess: chairman and CEO Buribaev, executive vice president Kasym Shokay, two bodyguards, and the woman whom they thought was named Veronique.

The Learjet banked. The landing strips were huge and surrounded by half-built towers, beyond which stretched flat desert, featureless other than new crisscrosses of roads. The glitzy business capital of the Middle East: work in progress.

They were down with a bump.

"Welcome to Dubai World Central al-Maktoum International Airport," said the pilot, repeating it in Russian.

Russia had imprinted itself on Timur's existence. Kazakhstan had once been part of the Soviet Union and Russian was still a fact of their lives, welcome or not. Even ethnic Kazakh elites like Timur had to walk a tightrope tied on one end to the ex-mother country. Timur's bodyguards and security personnel were Russian-speaking, Moscow-trained Kazakhs; Penny wondered if he trusted them, or if he had even hired them.

Kasym stood to open the luggage bin. He pulled out a pair of shiny black carbon-fiber briefcases. One of them contained their passports.

She leaned forward and touched Timur's knee. "Darling, how long before we get there?"

"Fast. Always fast with me, is it."

"I know," she replied with a smile. "I just want to make sure you don't miss that call you told me about."

"No, no," Timur said, pushing his Ray-Bans up his thick

nose.

Kasym watched her stretch to collect her handbag from the overhead locker. She wasn't sure how much of his hostility was jealousy.

Penny was wearing all white: a polo and a sporty skirt, with scanty gold sandals, and the outfit showed off her healthy limbs and her taut waist. A dose of sun gilded her skin, but the essential creaminess of her color was thrown into relief by her black hair. Her eyes, obsidian scimitars bared beneath luxurious eyebrows, were the variable that enabled her to blend nearly anywhere, just as her blood was a blend of East and West. Depending on the outfit, the language and the posture, she could be French, Japanese or, at a pinch, any of the tribes in between.

She pulled down her handbag and the big puff coat that she would no longer need. As she assembled her winter things, Kasym got in her face, that mustache of his almost kissing her brow.

"Don't forget your scarf," he hissed, "you won't be staying."

"Says who?" she said, louder.

"You think you can whore your way—"

A bimbo would have accepted that with nothing more than a squeal of protest. Veronique Goetzle was not scripted to be an airhead sex toy. Penny slapped him. Kasym paused, as though considering returning the gesture, but merely whistled a lonesome note.

"Enough!" Timur's bellow had a way of concluding the moment, leaving Penny and Kasym with an enforced armistice. Their eyes traded silent bombardments over their demilitarized zone.

The bodyguards adjusted their ties and their aviator sunglasses before opening the exit. Bright heat assaulted the interior. The pilot was the first to disembark and the outside's glare seemed to obliterate him. When he returned a moment later, he was already perspiring. "Passports, please."

Kasym opened one briefcase by touching a button on the top of the handle. The briefcase frame was made of Madagascan ebony, or so he had boasted. She had been more interested in how it opened, noting the button only recognized certain thumbprints. Kasym pulled out five passports, four of them bright azure, and one Swiss red, an expert forgery.

Penny declined the stewardess's drink; she didn't want to have to pee later. She uncrossed and switched her legs, a gesture noted by Timur with the passivity of ownership. Kasym's eyes burned a little darker.

She looked ghostly on her passport photo. Today the forgery's quality didn't matter: the customs officials probably didn't bother to even look at Learjet passengers' paperwork. The pilot returned with their documents all stamped with the United Arab Emirates' immigration mark, and handed them back to Kasym, who locked them in the briefcase. He took the extra measure of pulling a cord from the case's top and securing it around his wrist. Penny would have to figure out a way to get Veronique's passport if she was going to get out alive.

Timur, summoning his gentlemanly side, gestured for her to step out first. He filled most of the corridor and she brushed against him as she advanced, lingering just long enough to remind him why she was there.

The light on the tarmac was blinding and the air was like syrup, humidified by the haze from the nearby Gulf. A quartet of white-gowned Emirati officials waited for them by a limousine.

"Welcome to the United Arab Emirates, Mr. Chairman," said one.

"Hot," Timur grunted as he ducked inside the car.

"Welcome, *ahlan wa sahlan*, welcome."

The arrivals packed into the limo, Timur flanked by the bodyguards, the three big men comically stuffed into the rear facing the slender Penny and Kasym enjoying plenty of room in the opposite seat.

Beyond the rows of private jets emerged the city in a panorama of cranes, diggers and the skeletons of towers-to-be.

The driver, one of the Arab envoys, came on the speaker. "This is Jebel Ali, part of Dubai World Central," he said, "a new concept city dedicated to logistics and aviation. The construction you see will soon house nearly one million people servicing al-Maktoum International Airport, here, and Dubai International. Imagine, the equivalent of the entire population of Stockholm or San Francisco will soon live and work here, at the largest international airport in the world."

Timur made a grumpy gesture and the speaker fell silent.

They passed by the control tower and then across the apron fronting a vast hangar. A jumbo Airbus 830 rolled past like a brontosaurus. They drove on to a landing area for helicopters. One was descending now.

The bodyguards got out on either side of the limo, scanning the helipad. Satisfied, they gestured for Timur to follow them, trailed by Kasym and Penny. The Arab officials escorted them toward the helicopter as its skids touched the tarmac. It was a Eurocopter, a twin-engine light utility chopper with an enclosed fantail. Penny had never piloted one of those, but she

9

knew the design was meant to provide a more stable, quieter ride. She always had preferred vehicles with speed and a little danger.

Inside the cockpit the Arab pilot, dressed in military garb, tracked the party as his rotors calmed to lazy circles.

"You are going to have the most amazing tour," said one Emirati. He focused on her. "This is your first time to Dubai, yes?"

"Yes," Penny said.

"No," Kasym said, catching up from behind. "We are not tourists. This is just transport, you understand? Only transport."

They reassembled in the helicopter without the Arab minders, this time Penny sitting beside Timur, leaving Kasym to scrunch between the two bodyguards. The seats were expensive leather. The engine was still loud so they donned clunky headphones attached to the ceiling.

"Everyone buckled up?" asked the pilot into their headphones. Veronique was the only one to nod. The Emiratis closed the chopper's door and backed away.

The Eurocopter lifted off. They cleared the construction around al-Maktoum and sprinted over a grid of brown residential streets and beige courtyards overlaying desert. They flew low enough for her to see cars and even people, until they reached the hard blue of the Gulf. Below, a thick spit of land lengthened and fanned out, all of it recently reclaimed and shaped like a vast palm tree across the water.

"Below to your left is Palm Jumeriah," said the pilot, his voice diamond clear in their headphones. He went on a bit, but the chopper was veering east, and the Palm faded from view, replaced by the bland cobalt of the sea.

Several minutes passed. Timur stared out his window with an expression as blank as the Gulf. The bodyguards gazed out on either side. She felt Kasym, stuck in the middle, staring at her legs—until he panicked, his voice lost in the noise of the chopper but his finger protesting to something out the window.

The chopper banked sharply toward land. As they skimmed in low, the pilot said, "We have a surprise request from Chairman Buribaev to give Veronique a special look at beautiful Dubai."

Penny smiled girlishly and squeezed Timur's hand. She leaned over to kiss him, but the edges of their headphones knocked.

Kasym slumped in humiliation. Timur hadn't informed his deputy of this little detour, any more than he had revealed she'd be joining them for this trip. Ever since Veronique Goetzle crashed the chairman's party at the Moscow gallery, posing as the marketing chief for a Swiss engineering company, Kasym Shokay had lost one battle after another. She wasn't like the usual grasping women hurling themselves at the chairman, and Kasym had no way to counter someone who turned shop gossip into pillow talk.

It felt good, putting the factotum in his place.

More low-rise homes rushed below and above loomed the new city center, a phalanx of ambitious glass towers. The urban cluster emerged from the desert like a sci-fi dream, an army of glass rockets launching from the red sands. But they were dwarfed by the spaceship in their center: Khalifa Tower, named after the country's most powerful emir.

"Ahead is Burj Khalifa," said the pilot. "Named after our country's former president, Sheikh Khalifa bin Zayed al

Nahyan, it is the tallest man-made structure in the world."

The sheikh's tower was a knife of obsidian in the bright sky. It rose up as a series of slick tubes resembling minarets, black glass winnowing to the wispiest of tendrils.

The Eurocopter gained altitude as they headed straight for the skyscraper. She winced. The flash of terror surprised her, but for six weeks she had been wearing Veronique Goetzle's fake skin, six weeks of pirouetting lies to get into Timur's bed, six weeks of resolutely ignoring everything that could expose her.

This isn't going to work. The thought had been buried in her gut and now bubbled up like bile.

The chopper hoisted itself above the final spire and Penny felt the needle's presence, poised like a blade eager to open her from chin to belly, to let all the secrets coiled within her slither out.

The helicopter headed back toward the water. It didn't have far to go. Their destination: Burj al Arab, Arabian Tower but known by foreigners as the Burj. Only the incredible height of the Khalifa skyscraper could make the Burj appear petite. White sail-shaped struts girded its curvy glass body, making the Burj resemble a fantastic dhow prowling the coast. The hotel stood on a triangle of reclaimed land. One bridge, well policed, connected it to the city.

It was one of the most secure buildings in the world.

But not secure enough.

Stack and Lev were already there, registered as guests. She had worked with Stack before…well, maybe 'conspired' was a better word for it. She knew he was extremely capable but that didn't engender trust. The opposite, maybe. Lev was new to the organization, a young black hat who had boasted about doing time in an Israeli jail but was coy about the details of his release.

"Welcome to our destination, Burj al Arab," the pilot said. "It is the world's tallest hotel, rising higher than the Eiffel Tower. It has been called the world's only seven-star hotel. On behalf of the management, Mr. Chairman and guests, we wish you a most luxurious stay."

The Eurocopter circled the hotel once before alighting on the green helipad that jutted improbably from the Burj's crown. From there stairs zigzagged along the roof, all white save for a red carpet that rolled toward a door. Clambering up the final set of stairs to meet them was a dark-skinned man in a black suit, black tie, and white shirt with French cuffs.

"Your butler is here to greet you," the pilot said.

The butler was soon joined by two more, also Arabs kitted out in black tie. Their movements and demeanor appeared impervious to the blistering sun.

As the passengers removed their headphones, Penny kissed Timur on the cheek. "That was wonderful. Thank you, darling. *Rakhmet.*"

Timur grunted amiably and moved past her to exit the chopper.

The butlers hauled out their luggage, including two huge Louis Vuitton steamer trunks upright on wheels. The sun imposed itself and Penny shielded her eyes. She indulged a final glance at the desert city standing proud across the narrow waters, shimmering in the heat; the spindly reaches of Burj Khalifa were lost in the haze. The wind snarled her hair into rebellious black asps and billowed the men's suit jackets, revealing the holstered sidearm that Kasym Shokay carried.

He buttoned his jacket over the gun and made a pistol of his thumb and pointed finger, aimed it at her, and with a wink, pulled the trigger.

2

Flies and honey

One week ago, Penelope Lee had stood on Fuad Chamoun's terrace overlooking the lush, deep valley. The sun was descending beyond the mountain and the greenery was coming alive with comforting domestic lights. Smoke from the kebab grill scented the air with cumin and pepper.

"Here," Fuad said, "have a glass of wine. It's Syrian, Domaine de Bargylus. This may be the last case we'll get for a while. The jihadis are closing in on them, poor bastards."

She accepted the glass and raised it in salute to Fuad's brother, Etienne, who was tending to the kafta. Their father had favored both Arab and French names. So: Fuad and Etienne. "To whatever you're cooking that smells so good."

Etienne replied with a shy smile as he fanned the kebabs with a palm leaf. He was the artist in the family, awkward but intense.

The wine was delicious and Penny drank more, looking over the darkening valley. "He's going to Dubai."

"We know," Fuad said.

"How?"

He shrugged. Fifty-something with only a bit of paunch, his leonine hair going from black to pearl, he maintained the commander's indifference.

"Physical security," she began, "I need—"

"What happened to you in London," he said, "has happened in this business many times before. Enough pointless talk."

Let him think she had botched the job and paid the price, end of story. "A honey trap attracts flies, got it."

"You should be glad, Penny. We are near the end. The hardest part is already done. You must get Timur to take you—not any of the others, just you—and we're going to have him exactly where we need him. And you won't be alone," he said. "We're sending Stack. He'll be in position in two or three days' time."

Stack had been with her in London. He had told Fuad about the attack, ran the footage, and kept quiet about what had really come after.

"All right," Penny said, non-committal. Stack was another subject she'd rather not get into with their boss. "When do I get my money?"

"Once my client confirms receipt of the data. Buribaev is meeting the Chinese in Dubai at the Burj al Arab."

"You're sure of that?"

Fuad nodded in the gathering dark. "It was confirmed this morning in Beijing. The meet is nothing official. There won't be any minutes or records. Just Buribaev and General Liang, two men sitting down to dinner to see if they can do business together. But Buribaev won't leave Almaty without a laptop. You've observed his security measures?"

"Biometrics on all the hardware. Fingerprint and retina scan. That laptop is practically glued to his fingers."

"But he's never met an evil maid like you." Evil maid attack, hacker slang for physically accessing a computer while its owner was away—such as the apocryphal maid in a hotel, cracking the computer while the guest was absent. "There's something else I want you to find out."

The smoke from Etienne's kebabs was making her mouth water. "Is this errand for your client," she asked Fuad, "or for you?"

"I'd like to you to find out why the meet is in Dubai."

"China's hungry for energy supplies," she reasoned. "Kazakhstan's a producer. Dubai's neutral." She assumed Fuad's client, the one that had bankrolled her for the past two months, was in the oil game, eager to understand or disrupt whatever KazPetro or the Chinese were up to. But Fuad never revealed client names to his operatives. "What's it to us?"

"We've picked up chatter that the meet was originally to take place in Beijing."

"And Dubai's a party town."

"The chatter," he said, "involved a sudden burst of communications between KazPetro and Enimash in Moscow." Enimash was an oil services company owned by a Russian tycoon pal of Putin's.

"You think Timur's going behind Russia's back?" Which could mean a juicy opening for Fuad's client...or extra intel for Fuad to sell to someone else.

"Maybe, or maybe doing Moscow a favor. See what you can find out." The waft of spiced meat was irresistible. "Etienne, those smell ready. Are you hungry, my dear?"

They passed through Fuad's kitchen, a surprisingly antique affair with a small wooden stove in the center. The Chamoun compound had been here for centuries and the kitchen's medieval wooden counters and brick hearth preserved some of that memory. The rest of the house was indistinguishably modern, straight out of an American suburb.

Two of Fuad's cousins, Jamal and Isa, were hustling to get the rest of the dishes out to the dining room. They came from the shorter and rounder branch of the family, Jamal sporting a shaven head and Isa a bushy mustache. These two were the muscles of the organization, the hands and feet, the fixers and handymen and odd-jobbers. Fuad's spy ring was a family business.

Only his sister Daliyah was absent, and she never informed others of her comings or goings, and no one ever dared ask.

Fuad pulled out a chair for Penny at the table as his cousins covered it with one plate after another: mezzes, hot and cold, along with sausages, giant baked pita bread and, delivered by Etienne, the beef kafta. Etienne smiled at her as he placed his handiwork on the table.

"It smells wonderful," she told him, and Etienne blushed with pleasure.

The men were convivial, and she relished the food after a month enduring clumsy chunks of boiled horsemeat and sour milk; despite his wealth, Timur's culinary tastes didn't stray beyond what his mother had raised him on.

She reached for the wine but got only dregs. *That* had gone fast.

"We must have arak," Fuad said, pouring the liquor into everyone's glass.

"Absolutely," Penny said. She added water to her drink and it turned a milky white.

"For good health, *fi sehatkum*."

Everyone clinked rims. The arak tasted like aniseed. It was

good and she downed it in one, nodding her empty glass at Fuad to give it a refill.

"You drink like we're in a saloon," he said.

"Five weeks in Moscow and Almaty has a way of building a girl's tolerance."

"You'll get fat," Fuad said. "You already have some under your chin."

She slammed the glass. "Pour, dammit."

"I...I think you're..." Etienne could barely speak to her without stammering so he turned to his older brother. "Fuad, leave her alone." Etienne was endowed with the impressive Chamoun jaw, but a moonier face, pasty skin and ringed eyes. He was blessed with nimble fingers and a reservoir of patience. Even the CIA, the SRV and Mossad struggled with faking identities. In the digital age, it was becoming difficult and expensive to furnish passports, credit cards, online histories, legends. But Etienne pursued his craft in the family compound's basement, a den of chemicals and materials and printers and dyes, serenaded by banks of servers humming in the cold dark.

Quasimodo to her Esmeralda, beast to her beauty—the poor sap.

Etienne's comment elicited a look of anger and for a moment she thought Fuad might explode. He relented into a sneer. "When, little brother, are you going to talk to women like a man?"

Etienne looked at his precious hands as the cousins guffawed.

"For Penny, he'd have to get in line," Isa said.

"There's quite a queue," Jamal added.

She'd been tolerating, even enjoying, these lame jokes for

years, like some kind of valediction. But things had changed. London, she supposed—events she didn't like to think about. The cousins' banter about her supposed availability made her bristle.

Penny walked around the table and bent over Etienne and kissed him. He quivered like a man shot. The cousins crashed into silence. "You boys got something to say to me?"

"Enough," Fuad snapped. "There are certain lines in this family, Penny, that you do not cross."

"Sorry, *dad*."

"There was a time, not so long ago, when you said I was just as good as a father."

The jibe resurrected a sudden idea of her true father; the fierce feeling of protectiveness of his memory was a recent emotion. "You're no father," she blurted.

Fuad had filled the void of her vanished parents with a sort of rearing that for a time she had embraced, relished, devoured. If it was unconditional love she craved, though, she'd have to get a puppy.

Fuad saw her budding rage and decided to change the subject. He snapped his fingers at the cousins. "I think we could all do with something sweet."

Jamal made for the kitchen.

"And espresso," Fuad told Isa. Etienne moved to follow the cousins.

"Etienne."

The brother cringed.

Fuad said, "Penelope should not have done that. Perhaps she cannot help herself. It is how she was born, how I made her, how she helps us. But I forbid you to touch her."

She sneered, "Oh, now I'm some kind of witch?"

"You are an amazing human being," Fuad said. "No agent of ours has gotten as far as you."

"You mean survived."

"Perhaps tonight's dinner invitation was a mistake."

She was about to agree when the door from the kitchen swung open and the cousins began covering every square inch of the table with dessert plates, the clanking of china putting an end to the conversation. Etienne mumbled excuse me and shuffled into the kitchen. Fuad looked at her as though to dare her to taunt his younger brother some more.

Another emotion gathered itself into a wave. Not grief, as memories of her father might trigger. She felt a powerful awareness that this would be her final assignment for the Chamouns.

She wasn't hungry and just pushed things around with a fork while the men tucked in and Jamal filled everyone's glasses with more arak.

"Penny, you're not eating," Fuad said. "Try the mamaal."

"A minute ago, you were accusing me of getting fat."

"*Ya lahwy*," Fuad sighed.

Jamal and Isa began to clear the table. She got up before she said something she'd regret, and took an empty plate into the kitchen. Fuad could afford an army of servants, but the family compound was off limits to most people, and the men liked doing the chores together, as if they were just a normal family. Etienne had his hands in the sink, suds up his arms. She put a plate in the water. The cousins headed out to retrieve more from the table but she heard Fuad tell them to see to the dogs.

"I'm sorry if I embarrassed you," she said in French.

He sponged a plate methodically, but she could sense his tremors.

21

"I'm...I'm working on a new one. German. Very difficult."

She sighed. "I don't need another passport."

"It should be done by the end of the year."

"Etienne, you need to stop. Fuad's right."

There was dignity in his glance, though. "You never know."

"The Japanese one cost how much? Two hundred thousand dollars?"

"Can't you see, it's a work of art?"

"And I'm your muse."

"I don't care what my brother says."

She took a kitchen towel to one of his cleaned plates. "Etienne, I'm never going to use all of these identities. It's a waste. Not to mention a security risk."

He ran the water. "You might, one day, you might..."

"What?"

"Want to run away and never be found. By anybody."

"What about you, Etienne?"

He froze. "What about me?"

"Could you still find me? You could, couldn't you? Trace the credit cards, track the phones' digital footprints. Your creations, your secrets."

"Fuad couldn't. Nor Daliyah. Nor the targets out there, all the people you've burned." For the first time that night, he looked her in the eye. "Only me."

"You shouldn't fall in love with me, Etienne. You've seen what happens."

"Am I one of your assignments?"

"No. Never. But...I...wouldn't know what to do with someone who wasn't."

Back to washing. "The German encryption is really very difficult."

She returned to the dining room where Fuad spooned his empty espresso cup. "Go outside," he said in a tone that suggested he had been weighing his resentments.

He didn't get up, so she took this as an instruction, not a suggestion. She walked alone through the hallway to the front door and out to the compound's walled enclosure. The air was sweet and crisp with fir and cone. The two rottweilers immediately accosted her, nearly toppling her over. They were trained to snap and tear, but right now they just wanted licks and kisses.

"Down," barked a command in gravelly Arabic. Penny made out the woman's silhouette in the dimness of the night, the soft lights along the wall illuminating her strong-willed hair and her tall, mannish body swathed in fine Oxford Street pinstripes. Her cigarette glowed.

Daliyah Chamoun spun the webs for the network's small army of hustlers, hackers and honey pots. She caught them, trained them, ran them, cocooned them, and ate.

"Etienne is brilliant, but weak."

"Spying on your own family now, Daliyah?"

"You're not my family. No matter what my brother says." Penny followed her in a slow walk across the compound, the dogs dancing around them. "It's time. Get Buribaev in your bed and make sure you're so good he takes you with him to Dubai."

"I understand."

"He will be vulnerable alone with you in Dubai. Sedate him. Use his body to access his laptop. Contact Stack and follow his directions for the decryption."

"How do I get out?"

"Find a way to the safehouse in Deira for exfil. We're looking at exit routes by sea."

Exit routes, still looking. Since the horror in London, she had been all about *who* and *why*, this new Penny hatching from a chrysalis of numbness into a cold wokeness. Tonight, though, she wanted to know *what* and *when*. "What do I need to do?"

"Place his thumbprint on his laptop. Hold open his eyelid and make sure the scan succeeds. Stack will be two floors below you, with a new programmer."

"A new one?"

Daliyah ignored her lament. "Buribaev's laptop is protected against Internet hacking. You will install a keylogger, allowing Stack and Lev to capture his encryption key. They will then be able to unlock the disk drive. It won't take long. Thirty minutes."

"Nobody leaves Timur alone for thirty seconds."

"They'll leave him alone if he's in bed with you."

"What do I sedate him with?"

"We've prepared a midozolam gel. It will look like a contact lens. Don't stick it in your eye, it'll kill you."

"Midozolam—can't we just spike his drink?"

"The stomach absorbs too much, especially when it's diluted in a liquid. A big man like Buribaev, he might not even notice. Max didn't." She smiled as the rottweilers tussled over a big fallen tree branch.

"Max? Your dog?"

"He weighs 130 pounds, that one. I gave him half the dose we'd give Buribaev. Nothing happened."

"So use something stronger."

"We need his pupils to look normal. For the scan to access the keylogger."

"I can't bring a syringe with me. My cover doesn't make me

a diabetic. Even if it did, his security guys wouldn't allow it. Kaysm Shokay goes through my stuff all the time."

"No syringes. No capsules to empty into his drink. The most effective administration of midozolam, other than sticking a needle in his rectum, is buccal."

"Buccal—what does that mean? Bucco, mouth?"

"Cheek."

"Cheek," Penny repeated.

"The drug must be on something that he will put in his mouth and suck on. Vigorously, so the capillaries inside his cheeks absorb it. You understand?"

"Okay," Penny said, "he has to suck on something. What, I give him a lollipop?"

"Don't be stupid."

She thought it over. She could put it on her finger, but how to get him to suck on that? Then she realized what Daliyah intended. "My breast."

"It seems the most likely instrument."

She wondered how long Daliyah had spent concocting this one, and if she had gotten a rise out of it. Probably.

"But if I smear that stuff on my nipple, it'll knock me out—or worse."

"If untreated, you would be paralyzed, catatonic, and maybe dead."

"You could say it with a little less enthusiasm."

One of the rottweilers jogged over and put his nose between her legs, tail waving. Penny had to push back against his weight to keep from toppling but was glad for the distraction. "What a good boy, such a good boy," she cooed, digging her fingers into his thick hide.

"Max, not now," Daliyah clucked. "Stupid dogs. Here, go

25

play." She picked up a branch fallen from the great cedar inside the compound. Max jumped in anticipation and followed the stick's arc toward where Fuad parked his Audi, a Jeep and his collection of Ducati motorcycles. Jamal had come outside, a cigar lit between his blubbery fingers. The cousin kept Max distracted so Daliyah and Penny could keep talking.

"So how do I keep this thing from sending me into a coma?"

"The gel reacts to water—to saliva. If placed dry on the skin, it will take time to permeate the cells and affect the nervous system."

"How long?"

"Ten minutes."

"So I smear this stuff on my breast and I have ten minutes to get him to suck it off."

"Otherwise, depending on how much longer it stays on you, you will suffer anything from drowsiness to paralysis. But we suggest you do not put any midozolam directly on the nipple. Put it...here." She traced a finger on Penny's breast.

Daliyah knew every millimeter of her and wanted her creature to remain in awe of her Creator's omniscience. The surety of Daliyah's words also told Penny that this wasn't the first time the Chamouns had attempted this particular snare...should she be grateful she hadn't been the guinea pig?

She batted Daliyah's hand away. "What if Timur doesn't all of it lick it off? Or what if it takes me more than ten minutes to get him where I need him?"

"There is an antidote. We have adapted flumazenil into a topical cream. It will be inside your hand lotion container."

"Flumazenil. That only works when it's injected."

"No, this cream will do it. But you need to apply it no later than ten minutes. Use it right away."

Penny used to deal with these absurdities by remembering why she kept doing this job. The money was good but just a means to an end. For a time, libertine living had been enough. *Beats getting an office job, right?* The answer had always been yes, but Penny had forgotten why.

"Etienne is preparing everything for you: the midozolam in a contact lens case, the flumazenil in a hand cream container, small enough to take through an airport."

"How do I let Stack know when Timur's unconscious?"

"Veronique's Tinder account. Stack will be in close proximity. He'll go under the Tinder handle Majaplaya." She began to spell it.

"I know how it goes." Daliyah's handling of the slang was too clumsy to bear.

"Swipe right when you're ready. Then he'll hack your cell."

"What if they don't let me take my phone?"

"You'll need someone's phone, anyone's phone, to log in."

"That's not a security risk?"

"We can't control everything, Penny. You must access a smartphone. Use Buribaev's, if you have to."

"Okay," she sighed. "Is there any way for me to contact Stack otherwise? Can I Tinder him, swipe the other way?"

"Not without blowing your cover."

"But what if I need to call for help?"

Daliyah crushed her cigarette beneath the toe of her high heel. "For two hundred and fifty thousand dollars, *ma petite*, you don't get to call for help."

3

Vodka and Bordeaux

The Burj al Arab looked solid from the outside. Inside, however, it was a pyramid of space, with duplex suites—no mere single rooms at this hotel—crowded around a vast atrium.

Penny followed Timur to the entrance of their suite on the twenty-fourth floor, near the apex, accompanied by three Oxford-accented Arabs in black tie.

"Welcome to the most amazing hotel experience in the world," intoned a butler as he threw open the double doors.

It was as garish as it was vast: anything capable of gold plating was plated gold. Everything else—the carpets, the pillow cushions, the marble tabletops—swirled in primary-color arabesques, and the stairway sweeping upwards boasted gilded rails.

A blond European man in a trim suit waited inside to greet the chief executive of KazPetro. The welcome was profuse and Timur, bored, waved him to silence. The manager bowed out, gesturing to a table adorned with a magnum of Ruinart Blanc de Blancs, a box of white truffle chocolates and a box of Romeo y Julieta cigars.

"Vodka," Timur said.

"Of course, Mr. Chairman," a butler replied. The full-service kitchen's freezer was stocked with Belvedere, Grey Goose, and Snow Queen, the vodka brand of Kazakhstan; the hotel had done its homework.

Veronique ran agog—*honey, look at this* and *baby, look at that.* Penny was recording every detail of the layout, lingering an extra moment in a side room decked out as an office. Herman Miller chairs, green leather baize over the table...Apple computers.

"There is also HDTV," a butler said, "and an iPad."

Even the iPad was gold-plated. Penny lifted it. The frame made it heavy as a textbook.

Stack and Lev, the new programmer, would be in another suite on a floor below, taking turns to monitor their screens, waiting for her to make contact.

"Let's see upstairs," she suggested.

A butler led the entourage up the winding staircase. Against the high wall was projected a digital clock, reminding her that time was running out.

The upper level's rooms were a complex arrangement around an H-shaped corridor. The master suite was an apartment unto itself, with a kitchen and dining rooms; the closets could have housed families, but for now just secured the Louis Vuitton steamer trunks and a panoply of striped hotel robes that suggested, somewhere, a safari park was missing a few big cats.

The en suite bath really was a *bath*, in the old Turkish sense, a *hammam*, with a deep Jacuzzi tub surrounded by marble pilasters and framed in back by a thick scarlet curtain, held open by gold tassels.

Opposite this wound a counter with his and hers sinks, each guarded by a phalanx of products for skin, hair and teeth. Penny needed both hands to pick up a heavy dispenser of Bulgari, which probably contained more scent than her neighborhood cosmetics store.

Everything was covered with marble that knew no shame: desert yellows, mountain whites, meadow violets. Blood red marble columns surrounded the shower at the end of the tubular chamber. Metallic-colored mosaics smothered any lingering emptiness.

"If you'd like me to pour your bath, miss, please just let me know," the head butler told her.

"Wouldn't that be fun?" she cooed into Timur's ear but he just grunted.

They returned to the master bedroom. Dominating the scene was another panorama. From this height the Gulf was not in view, and only glowing sky filled the room.

The bed was so high she'd need a stepladder or a running jump to get in it. It was draped in the purple of a Roman emperor's toga, with a canopy stretching over the top.

Within the canopy's roof was raised a mirror. Its frame and dimensions were human-sized, and it was tilted at a minor angle, to maximize the viewing pleasure of anyone whose head lay in the vicinity of the pillows.

"Interesting detail," Penny purred, sliding into Timur's arm. His wide face remained passive, but he regarded the mirror for a few seconds, long enough to register interest. She gave him a peck on his jowl and wandered to the windows, to see the non-view, and to clear her mind.

Her white skirt had pockets, just big enough to hold a smartphone. Penny took out her iPhone. The WiFi worked.

Veronique liked to surf fashion and sport sites. A decade's worth of Facebook profile had been constructed for her: friends, a mother and an aunt, clean-cut former boyfriends, girlfriends whose backstories she knew by heart—a slice of upper-crust Switzerland.

"And I take that," Kasym said, plucking the phone from her fingers.

She hadn't noticed him slip behind her.

"Hey!"

Kasym thumbed the screen. "It will be safe, along with your passport." He seemed disappointed not to find anything alarming and switched it off.

"That's my phone!"

"Yes, it is," he said, putting it in his own pocket.

"Give it back."

"Is security risk."

"Timur!"

But Timur had wandered off, a sure sign that he had accepted Kasym's whispered warnings about digital threats.

Kasym smirked with mock sympathy. "You are here for pleasuring of Chairman Buribaev, not to entertain yourself."

She considered a retort but opted for slyness. "Can I have it back if I'm good?"

His fingers seized her chin. "What did you say?"

How had she let this one creep up without detecting him?

"Nothing."

He released her. "Many girls hold his interest, for a time. A very short time."

"I'm not a girl."

"You play good game," Kasym said. "Maybe you might have made something of your life other than...whatever is you really do, Veronique Goetzle."

She forced herself to subdue the alarms ringing in her brain. Kasym glided across the stateroom toward his own quarters. She had to assume he'd dissect her phone's memory and its catalog of Veronique's friends, history and tastes. Penny's legend had to hold up for just three more days.

Timur was downstairs in the office, where a bodyguard was setting up KazPetro's own computer terminals. Timur was murmuring into a cell phone that was practically lost inside his big hand. This was a working holiday. The chairman of a thirty-two-billion-dollar oil company didn't have holidays of any other kind.

"Honey, why don't you work upstairs," she said. "It would be so much more comfortable."

He waved her off, but she draped herself around his back. "You could mix business with pleasure," she whispered.

Timur paused his flow of Kazakh into the phone.

"Set up your laptop in the bedroom," she purred. "Maybe you don't need to go out. We'll get one of those butlers to fill the Jacuzzi and then..."

"Later," he grunted.

Veronique accepted this with delight and smothered his thick neck with kisses.

Kaysm entered. "The chairman is busy now," he snapped.

She retreated upstairs, her playful smile reverting to a studied frown. She locked herself in the suite's bathroom and opened her toiletry bag. She took out her contact-lens case to reassure herself that the poisonous gel was still there. The hand lotion, too—a salve unlike any other.

Penny caught her reflection and saw how her body was angled over the counter and a memory surprised her, for she imagined she saw the man named Viktor standing behind her.

After what he had done to her in London, she had exorcised him from her mind. She'd taken her revenge and was determined to never feel the way he had made her feel, ever again. But Viktor had popped up several times in the past few days, usually the night when she lay beneath Timur, as if to mock her attempts to convince the chairman of her pleasure.

"You don't scare me." Saying it like she really meant it.

She brushed up her lipstick, her mind still foisting images of Viktor behind her in the mirror. *Stack knows...* Full-bore self-gazing in the mirror. *Penny Lee, you've got this.*

The door latch jiggled. An impatient knock.

"It's occupied," she called.

"Do not lock." It was one of the bodyguards.

"I'm using the bathroom," she protested, moving to the toilet and lowering the seat.

"Open or I break."

She flushed the toilet and crossed the long bathroom to open the door. "Satisfied?"

The bodyguard smirked. "You know rules. Next time I break."

"I'm a woman. I need some privacy."

The broad-shouldered man turned away and continued his scouting. The two bodyguards were trained to be constantly sweeping, and the confines of the hotel made them restless. Cooped up in the suite, they burned calories by double, triple-checking anything within their reach.

She wandered back downstairs. She could hear Timur speaking in Kazakh. The briefcase with the laptop lay open on the table in the main living room. He was on a secure videoconference. Timur saw her but turned his back on her.

"Why don't you go out," Kasym suggested. "There's pool, gym, anything you want."

She changed into a bathing suit. It was a chocolate Roberto Cavalli monokini, held together by a ring around her neck and the connecting fabric that covered her bellybutton down to the spaghetti ties on either hip. The suggestive design made a string bikini seem frankly dull. Timur and his men were listening as another man's video image on the laptop screen droned over a flowchart. They all fell silent as she paraded past.

She pirouetted toward Timur, making a scene of interrupting his work. The other men indulged in the break by ogling her. Timur let her twirl into his embrace.

"Go play," he told her.

"It's more fun with you." She checked the laptop screen. "Besides, if that guy thinks oil prices will climb above seventy dollars, fire him."

"You're right." Timur turned to the screen. "Gregor, you're fired."

The figure in the video image cringed.

Timur smacked her on the bottom, sending her toward the exit. "You are smarter than clowns I have here, but now you go."

The men laughed nervously and she repaid them with a wagging finger, oh you naughty boys. Timur began shouting at the man on the laptop screen. He sounded like he really was firing the guy. Good, Gregor probably deserved it.

Penny covered herself in a long gauzy wrap and slipped into flip-flops. She exited the suite with the happy knowledge that she could have done that jock's stupid analyst job ten times better, except she didn't want to trade her freedom just to become some brown-nosing executive vice president slaving over other people's emails.

At least that's what she had always told herself. It seemed true when she was released from duty, hopscotching from one playboy's yacht to another.

Penny took the elevator down to the outdoor pool and did laps beneath the greedy eyes of fat men smoking shisha.

Timur took her to dinner that evening at a restaurant up top and opposite the helipad. They had a table by the long window to themselves, but the view, facing the Gulf, was monochrome black. The bodyguards kept an eye nearby. Kasym had chosen, or had been told, to eat elsewhere.

She wore a dark, low-cut evening dress with a sapphire suspended just above the crevasse of her breasts. Timur had given it a cursory glance and buried his nose in the menu. The staff crawled around them like cockroaches. Would the Chairman like a suggestion regarding the wine?

He ordered a 1973 Pomerol to go with his steak and her lamb, but then also a bottle of vodka to go with his Bordeaux. Veronique tried conversation and she tried holding his fingers and smiling at him. He grew animated when he started complaining about KazPetro's business.

She tried dropping something she had picked up from her research. "I heard from our CEO that the Arab Gas Pipeline's going to close again." The war in Syria was disrupting the regional industry, and outside oil giants like KazPetro were always scrambling to secure supply.

"Will stay open," he said.

"How do you know?"

Timur grunted and poured another slosh of vodka.

"C'mon, Timur. How do you know?"

"Never mind," he said, taking a long draft. His eyes had dulled. "*Oristar*," he sneered, and she picked out the Kazakh word for Russians, followed by something that sounded impolite.

Then he clammed up. Penny knew she could press him when he fell into one of his moods, but delicately. She shifted to inconsequential banter, laying the pathway back to serious talk. Timur refilled his heavy glass to the brim.

Later he collapsed in the vastness of the bed, snoring before he could rip off her clothes. Penny lay gazing at their reflections, Timur on his belly, a meaty sprawl, and herself, a slender slice of dessert trapped beneath his arm. In the dark she could make out only the faintest outline of her face in the mirror above the bed. The mirror was big and solid enough to kill them if it fell.

Would that be such a tragedy? Viktor asked.

4

Time to die

Do it now.

Timur was stretching his toes in bed, emerging from his grog. The laptop was across the room, not yet having drawn his attention.

Which is where she found him once she had returned wearing nothing but a smear of knock-out drug on her tit. He had draped himself in a furry zebra-striped robe that made him look like a primordial beast of the Asian steppe. He acquiesced to her kisses and happily pawed her until his phone rattled.

She tried to distract him from its buzz by burying his face between her breasts, twisting her torso to aim the toxin at his mouth. *Take it...*

Kasym's trademarked one-two-three knock prompted him to push her aside. "Dress," Timur commanded as he moved toward the door. Veronique pouted as she retreated to the bathroom and locked the door, so that Penny could scramble for the hand lotion with its flumazenil antidote.

She hadn't hesitated to contaminate her flesh. But now, as she saved her own life by kneading the lotion against her breast, tremors seized her hands. She caught herself in the mirror, obsessively covering her entire torso with cream.

Beats the desk job, right? Viktor smirked.

"Shut up."

She breathed until her heart stopped racing and contemplated her failure.

Jupiter might spend the rest of the day relaxing in the duplex, drinking in one of the cafes, or luxuriating at the spa, but he would not be alone. Kasym and the bodyguards and the butlers would resume their orbits.

Penny couldn't stand the idea of wasting the day in the suite, watching the hands of the clock projected against the stairwell crawl from minute to minute. Veronique told Timur she was bored, and he permitted her to go out so long as one of his bodyguards kept her company.

She donned a wrap over her monokini and slipped into sandals. The bodyguard, still immaculate in his white shirt and blue suit, stood behind her in the elevator, smelling of cologne. She could feel his eyes checking her out from behind his aviator sunglasses, but he wouldn't dare lay a finger on her.

The lobby occupied two levels at the bottom of the hotel's vast atrium beneath a gauntlet of dancing fountains and aquariums flashing fancy fish. The Burj al Arab couldn't risk boring the guests even during the mundane moment of standing on an escalator.

The bodyguard remained two steps behind her.

Veronique approached a tall red ottoman where attendants gestured for her to wait as they fetched a golf cart to ferry her across the causeway. She regarded a middle-aged Black man in a beige linen suit and an open-necked shirt, sitting with his legs crossed, twiddling a mobile in his fingers. The red-rimmed glasses and the bracelet of prayer beads suggested an eccentric playboy.

Stack.

She blithely followed the hostess's gesture and sat beside him. The bodyguard stood in a military pose of rest nearby, endlessly scanning the crowd.

Stack glanced at her, with the casual interest that men routinely took in her, but he otherwise preserved a polite distance. Timur's bodyguard took no further notice of the man in the linen suit, and a moment later she followed a smiling bellboy toward a golf cart. The cart would now take her—and the bodyguard, always—across the bridge to the Burj's private beach.

Bumping into Stack was a coincidence. It posed a risk. But Penny was quietly delighted to see him. It reminded her that she wasn't entirely alone. She didn't give him the slightest acknowledgment as she made for her golf cart.

The day burned away and after lounging long enough in the heat along the Gulf waters she eventually made her way back. Uniformed men at the approach to the causeway confirmed Veronique's identity and the bodyguard's. There were dogs, too, in case a car needed to be sniffed.

Busting out of the Burj al Arab on foot would not be an option.

Timur elected to host his Chinese guests in his suite. He told her to get dressed. Veronique picked a navy cocktail dress that was corporate but didn't hide her curves. Timur wore a suit with a KazPetro pin in his lapel and a Vacheron Constantin watch on his wrist. It was the one he had been wearing in Moscow when she first angled into him. Trying to impress her, Timur had told her the watch had cost more than his two

Ferraris.

Kasym ushered in three Chinese men. The boss, General Liang, looked the part, with a humorless buzz cut atop a square face and a barrel chest. Despite the Chinese man's grumpy demeanor, Timur, himself usually taciturn, came to life. He was in his element now—his big broad face lit up with a welcoming smile, his arms spread wide. The two CEOs warmly embraced and exchanged pleasantries in broken English as they arranged themselves around a table prepared by the butlers. One of the Chinese men handed out presents of expensive Maotai whisky as he complimented his hosts in fluent Russian. Veronique shook hands with the guests, and kissed cheeks with the Chinese boss. "Wah! Such a beauty!" he proclaimed in English.

"Thank you," she said. "So many powerful men in this room, I don't know which way to turn."

"That way," Kasym said, gesturing toward the double doors.

Timur nodded to her. She left. Kasym closed the dining room's double doors on her with a smirk.

"Would miss like to eat in the living room?" a butler offered.

"I'm not hungry."

She sat on a sofa opposite the grand stairway. The projected clock's seconds hand seemed to slow to a complete halt.

The voices behind the door maintained a steady drone. Occasionally a butler would come and go, his silver platter ferrying food and drinks, the open door letting out a burst of animated talk before quickly clicking shut.

Finally, the negotiations wrapped up, and the double doors parted.

Penny jumped on Timur, wrapping him in her legs and arms, as Kasym ushered the last Chinese officer out of the suite.

The meeting must have gone well enough because Timur was relaxed, and had drunk enough to be in a good mood. He responded to her shamelessly in full view of his men and the butlers.

"I'm bored, Timur. You've kept me waiting too long."

The shine in Timur's eyes lightened his earthy face and his fingers dug into her flesh. She giggled as he hoisted her and took to the stairs. He was a little too old for this to be a good idea, but Chairman Buribaev was also determined to show off his strength.

"Like bull," he said, pausing halfway up to catch his breath.

"Or a stallion," she said. "Fast Kazakh stallion."

He led her into the bedroom and she used her suspended foot to slam the door. The briefcase with the laptop was still on its chaise, closed tight.

"Now wait here," she said.

"No." He grabbed the collar of her dress with both hands and began to rip.

"My dress!"

"Buy new one."

They squirreled her out of the remains of her clothes. "Now your turn," she said slipping her hand inside the fold of his shirt. She gave it a good rip and buttons rained on the carpet. He laughed as his hands groped and squeezed and the only way to slow him was with a languorous kiss. He tasted like boiled beef and Arabian spice.

His fingers fiddled with hooks. Penny squirmed out of his embrace, leaving his two hands holding her bra. He was too astonished at her escape to protest. "Girl stuff," she said, pirouetting into the bathroom.

She ran to the contact lens container and smeared herself

with the last of the gel, with a spritz of the Bulgari for good measure. A single phone call could be enough to distract Timur, but she resisted the urge to run to him. Seduction should be fast but not rushed.

Veronique wrapped a leg around the door frame. "Mr. Chairman."

Timur was still hers, leaning bemusedly against the bed, wearing just boxer shorts. His torso was square and hairy, and his stout belly was hardened stodge rather than flab. If her escape had surprised him, Timur returned the favor by grabbing her with unexpected reach. She was on the carpet, squeezed beneath his bulk, and he was devouring her with his mouth. "That's it...yesss." She levered his head toward her breasts, feigning erotic joy as she tried to breathe.

Savagely she tilted his head aside and used her feet to push him into a roll. He was too engrossed to be surprised by her deft manipulation of his mass so that she was on top. She bent her lips to his ear. "Bite me...oh, please bite me...yes..." Pain electrified her body and she couldn't stop her feet from kicking, but it must have sparked some dark desire in him because he practically devoured her breast. "Use your tongue...like that."

The pain wasn't anything like her fear of what would happen if he stopped. Every time he tried to sample her other nipple, she found a way to steer him back, until his fondling hands slipped away, and his jaw went slack.

She straddled the unconscious chairman.

Five, maybe six minutes before paralysis imprisoned her.

The iPad with its gold plating was heavy in her hands. Getting a Wi-Fi signal ate up a long thirty seconds. Another forty-five seconds to navigate her way onto the hook-up site. Veronique's Tinder account found Majaplaya, fronted by a ragamuffin of a little Black boy.

One crazy Arabian night, he messaged.

Aladdin's not my type, she replied to his pre-arranged code.

Laptop ready?

Opening chat.

She messaged him with the iPad's phone number and reached for Kasym's briefcase. It was heavy and she carried it with both hands over to Timur's side. The chairman began to snore.

She opened Signal for encrypted chat and in a minute it murmured with an incoming call. She opened a screen, propping the iPad upright. Stack appeared in the window. Then Lev, boasting a hipster beard, stuck his head in the camera to have a look. "More girls on Tinder should look like you," he said.

Penny didn't have time for this amateur. "I have three minutes," she hissed.

"Get back to work," Stack said, pushing Lev out of view. "Chairman ready, Pen?"

She raised Timur's hand and forced his thumb onto the obsidian button on the handle of the briefcase. The locks were silent but when she pressed Timur's thumb down, the lid cracked open. She removed the laptop, displaying it for Stack to see, and powered it on.

Penny glanced at the bedroom door. All clear.

"So how much time I got?" Stack asked, keeping his voice low.

"About twenty minutes," she said.

"Thought it was thirty."

"I'll need time to escape before he wakes up." Starting with: get the antidote.

43

A black-and-white QR code popped up on the laptop screen. She twisted Timur's arm around to press his forefinger against it but the position was awkward. When they had been fooling around, she had used his own energy to spin him over. But now he was just dead weight.

Stack waited with eyes wide behind his red frames. "Clock's running, Pen."

She pushed Timur's finger onto the code.

"Retina," Stack said.

She grabbed Timur's hair and lifted his chin onto the keyboard, then used both hands to pull open the lids of his right eye. Using her knee and elbow to maneuver the laptop, she waited for a laser embedded in the camera above the screen to run its ocular test. His face twitched.

"It's waking him up," she warned, stifling the bile of panic in her chest.

"It's just a reflex," Stack assured her. "Lev, you reading it?"

"Yeah, I'm making my way in," Lev said off-screen. "Penny, I'm going to need you to do some typing now. All right?"

She checked the laptop's clock. Two minutes left. No margin. She jerked around. The light emanating from the crack beneath the bedroom door—it bisected.

Someone was on the other side of the door.

Veronique let out a playful groan.

Whoever was there didn't move. Perhaps he was enjoying what he thought he heard: Kasym was a deviant worm. She cooed a series of yeses, eyes pinned on the divided crack of light. The intruder left.

After a moment, Stack said, "Do that one more time, Lev might faint."

"Next step," she snapped.

44

Lines of code ribbed the laptop screen.

Lev appeared in the Signal screen on the iPad. "Type in control function five."

She pressed the three keys. The lines of code sped across the laptop.

"We're in!" Lev whooped.

She had to get to the bathroom. Now.

The line of light below the hallway door remained unbroken—clear—

An unusual sound came from the Signal link, as if someone had struck the microphone with a pillow.

"Hey," Stack shouted, "what the—"

She stopped. Looked at the screen.

Stack's head darted out of view, as if an invisible cane had yanked him off screen, and something viscous and cloudy obscured the camera.

"Stack?"

She heard Lev off camera: "No, please, no!"

The cloud half-blocking the screen moved, or oozed, further down the Signal window. Was that blood?

This isn't happening.

The striking-pillow sound again. A shadow flitted in the Signal window's background and she identified the long cylinder of a gun's suppressor. Lev's face filled the Telegram window— or what was left of it. Someone had blown most of it off.

Stack and Lev were gone.

A white man dressed in a butler's outfit put his face into view. Wide, Slavic cheekbones, big lips and gray, joyless eyes. An almost pretty face marred by a harelip that scarred the flesh below his nose. He saw her nakedness without interest. "Penelope," Viktor said. "Time to die."

5

Midnight in Dubai

Once again, the line of light beneath the bedroom door was broken in two.

Whoever was out there had come back.

She sprang at the bedroom door.

Threw her shoulder against it, slamming it shut as the intruder was pushing it open. Turned the lock, rolled away on her shoulder. Three holes appeared around the doorknob; the bullets nicked the bedposts, spangled one of the great dark windows.

Penny made for the en suite. She drew the door shut and locked it. It wouldn't stop the intruder but would buy her—

Time.

The mirror revealed red bite marks on her breasts. They stung when she smeared on the hand cream.

She stepped into the Jacuzzi, out of the doorway's line of sight. Two *bams*. The doorknob jolted in place; another bullet whinged off a marble column, destination anywhere.

The door withstood the first kick, giving her enough time to step back onto the floor. She needed space.

46

Assuming the antidote was working.... If not, whoever had come to kill her wouldn't have to do anything more than wait.

The bathroom door gave way, slamming into the wall and ricocheting back. The butler extended a hand to still the door. He was dressed like a butler, anyway, black tie, cufflinks, polished shoes. White guy, though, or perhaps like Penny, of ambivalent stock, a bloodline that could pass for anything from black Irish to Persian. The other hand raised a handgun that seemed small in his palm—a choice of concealment over power. It was fitted with a suppressor to muffle the sound, but indoors, it would still make a bang.

The man pointed his gun at her.

She didn't look him in the face. Never look at your opponent's face. Never raise your hands in an obvious martial pose. Two basic rules of Shimura's aikido. The third never: wait for an opponent to strike.

Penny launched herself toward him and to the side. The silencer in that marbled room couldn't suppress the gunshot's scream. Something yanked her right upper arm backward but did not stop her. The gun's rack opened, popped its magazine. He moved a hand behind his waist to retrieve another clip but she landed beside him and folding his gun hand in her two arms.

Astonishment. She pressed into the fold of his elbow, letting his own movement spin him around.

Now she reversed her arms, going against the grain of his bones. *Crack.*

He bellowed. She released him and kicked the ball of her foot into the back of his knee. Down he went. She wasn't through with him. Penny grabbed both of his ears and smashed his face into the corner of the sink counter. *Crunch pop.* Screaming—

47

both of them screaming their lungs out. In the mirror the remains of his left eye oozed to a dangle. His blood adorned her skin.

Not all of it was his. Her right arm was soaked.

I'm shot. She couldn't believe her own eyes.

Torn nerves. The pain made her a quick convert.

Penny ran the faucet. The blood was coming out rapidly, unstoppably, but the wound looked superficial—a glancing hit. She rotated the arm, which hurt more, but nothing precious was damaged.

Did the wound even matter? Viktor Gubinov was here. *Coming for me.* It seemed incredible, and she might have freezed right there, if not for the awkward splay of her feet around the corpse of the gunman she had just...mauled.

All of those cold mornings in Shimura's dojo. For self-defense. That's what she had told herself. For warding off handsy rich men. Not for...

Breathe.

She had actually killed someone.

You're alive!

Each inhale brought a new hotwired pain. Yeah, she was alive all right.

The washcloth couldn't stem the bleeding. She opened her toiletry bag and removed a tampon applicator. She pulled out the tampon from the plastic tube and, gritting her teeth, stuffed it into the trench made by the passing bullet, the string hanging loose. The cloth turned crimson and expanded beneath the pressure of her fingers, and she felt dizzy. She tipped forward and puked into the sink.

Penny gulped water and tried again. The tampon seemed to have done the trick and staunched the bleeding. The bullet hadn't hit an artery and it hadn't struck bone.

Think.

Penny ran to the closet outside. She grabbed her silky La Perla thong and tied it around her arm, to fix the tampon in place. Next, sensible things: khaki pants, T-shirt, linen blazer, rubber-soled slip-ons. She returned to the bedroom. Timur still lay unconscious, the laptop still on, its screen unspooling coded gobbledygook.

She returned to the bathroom to take the assassin's Smith & Wesson M&P22, plucking the magazine from his belt. Penny reloaded and with a washcloth unscrewed the hot suppressor, which went in a blazer pocket, followed by two more tampons. She gulped a fistful of aspirin.

Get to the safehouse in Deira, the industrial part of Dubai across the creek. That was the plan, right? Wrong. Everything was blown. There was not going to be any exfiltration. If she was going to escape the country, she'd need Veronique's Swiss passport.

Locked in Kasym's briefcase.

She crouched by the bedroom doorway leading to the hallway. Where was that worm? Kasym must have had a role in this...this catastrophe.

"Penelope, time to die..."

She prowled toward Kasym's room, gun first. She reached his door and the wall exploded beside her ear. She couldn't hear a thing but knew the shot had come from the stairway. Another flash burst from beneath the projected hands of the clock.

Midnight in Dubai.

A second man in a butler's black tie, thick eyebrows like dashes on his bald white skull.

49

Kasym's door wouldn't open. She returned suppressing fire, turned, shot the lock. Waited as more bullets raked the hallway from below. Push-kicked the door in. Tumbled in on her good shoulder and bullets sang above.

Kasym cowered in the furthest corner of the room, his mustache quivering like a wounded snake.

The Penny who had never killed anyone before was gone. This new Penny didn't have time to care. "Passport. Now."

"Wh-who are..."

She pointed the armed pistol at him. "Shut up."

He moved to a settee where the other briefcase case lay open, its lid facing her.

She kept her back to the wall and her body down. Two more bullets flew inside. Straighter angle, hit the far wall, and Kasym trembled. Faint tang of urine in her nostrils.

The second gunman was on the other side of the door.

And Viktor was a minute away.

"Hurry up."

Kasym's face transformed into a look of a drunkard's courage. His pistol had been inside the case, and he brandished it now, a small snub-nosed Beretta that fit into his slender, shaking hand.

She didn't hesitate. Her bullet smacked him in the collar.

Penny ran toward his briefcase. Inside, three bundles of cash, each banded by a currency strap: U.S. dollars, Russian rubles, Emirati dirhams. She stuffed them into her opposite inner breast pocket along with Veronique Goetzle's passport.

"You..." hissed Kasym, bleeding on the carpet.

He was clambering to his knees, the Beretta still in his hand. She had had enough of Kasym Shokay. She spun a roundhouse kick that knocked him unconscious, his weapon arcing across

50

the room, but as she completed her spin she stopped cold.

The second gunman had entered the room, death delivered in black tie.

She pulled the Smith & Wesson's trigger.

Nothing.

—The empty cartridge laughed up at her.

Or maybe it was the assassin who was laughing, his eyebrows knotted in an X.

Idiot should have shot her instead; she flung the gun at his face.

The man deflected her missile with a raised forearm, but it was enough. His shot, wide, blistered a window. She raised the briefcase and rolled on her shoulder, spinning behind her shield. Kasym's Beretta lay on the carpet. A bullet whacked the briefcase, its force tearing it from her hand. She was on her knee. The assassin ejected his magazine and fluidly rammed in another. He resumed his firing stance and took careful aim, but by the time he was ready to squeeze his trigger, a red spot coughed out of his chest, ruining his fine white shirt.

He looked down in surprise. She fired the Beretta again—not much recoil from such a light gun—and blew a hole in the side of the butler's cheek. He wasn't dead, but his hands jerked and he shot a chunk out of the chandelier. Glass crackled onto the carpet. She waited as he teetered. He was struggling to get his gun to stop shaking. Penny kicked the weapon free of his hand. She leveled the Beretta at his head.

The assassin's eyes trembled. The veins in his throat bulged, stark against the tattoos rising from beneath his bloody shirt.

She was pointing a gun to execute a man.

...the remains of his left eye dangling in the mirror...

She should have just done it, but her mind had taken her out

51

of the moment, escaped the pumping of adrenaline. She and the assassin stared at each other, blue eyes to black. Human to human. He raised his shaking palms in supplication as blood surged from where his cheek had been.

Dammit.

She had to get out of there.

The Beretta was stainless steel. Penny slammed the butt against his head. He wasn't out, but he was down, whimpering into his hands. She grabbed the gunman's weapon, another Smith & Wesson, and took off for the stairs.

The first of Timur's bodyguards lay sprawled at the bottom. The two butler-assassins had taken the sentinels out quietly: the garrote wire still clasped the man's neck. Another horror to process.

She jumped the corpse and made for the front door. The other bodyguard lay sprawled by the side table, the wires protruding from the back of his neck tied like a pretty bow, his dead hand draped across the box of cigars like a final wish.

Two Russian-trained bodyguards assigned to protect the chairman of KazPetro, eliminated so efficiently. She should be dead, too. Beginner's luck. And what about Timur, why wasn't he joining the body count? Had they assumed the prone chairman was already dead?

Penny didn't think so.

The assassins hadn't come for Timur Buribaev.

She planted the Beretta against the flat of her tummy, beneath the T-shirt. Then she opened the door, the second Smith & Wesson in hand, and peeked out. The corridor ran along the open atrium. Empty. She stayed in a crouch but risked inching her eyes over the railing.

A commotion about three floors down—staff, butlers, maids,

hotel security, men in suits on cell phones. The sound of gunshots would have quickly drawn attention. Lev and Stack's bodies were in there. Further down, all the way down to the lobby level, security men and cops converged.

No way she'd be leaving through the front door.

Keeping low, she scurried toward the elevator bank and a fire stairwell, which she had checked out earlier in the day. She opened the door to the stairs and looked down, Smith & Wesson first. Concrete steps. She paused to quietly shut the door behind her and listen. Footfalls echoing, something jangling. But she couldn't see beyond the two sets of stairs connecting her landing to the other levels.

Nowhere to go but up.

Viktor and his men would have known they'd make a commotion. They had come in messy. There was only one way to escape from the Burj al Arab beyond the causeway linking it to land. It must have been how Viktor had arrived.

The helicopter pad was only two flights up. She sprinted the stairs. Below her she heard the same door open, close. Someone was following her.

She burst into the corridor along the hotel's top floor, where there was a waiting room for the helipad.

A hotel concierge, a heavyset woman bundled into a crisp uniform, seeing her—the pistol, the blood, and who knew what in Penny's eyes—screamed.

Penny didn't have time for this, and she was getting pretty good at delivering a pistol whip. She stepped over the silenced woman.

The helipad awaited at the far end of the hallway.

The door to the waiting room opened again. Two men. But not what she expected.

Elderly white men, one tall, the other medium height, both slender and elegantly dressed in matching tan suits with silk striped ties, pocket squares and boutonnieres, marigolds pinned to their lapels. The shorter one had a square face and haphazard gray hair, and his lips pulled on a cigarette in a long holder, like an aristocrat from another century. The tall one was bald, with professorial wreaths of hair around his ears, and wore the sort of glasses an accountant might squint through. He leaned on a cane, his arching frame sheltering his smaller colleague.

"I say," said the tall man with glasses and the cane.

"Indeed," said the other, the cigarette never leaving his mouth.

Penny ran past them. Something caught her ankle. The floor rose up to smack her in the chest. She looked up and behind her.

"Ever so sorry," said the tall man, freeing his cane from her ankle.

"We do apologize," said his companion.

Viktor emerged at the far end of the corridor, his crisp white shirt patterned with someone else's blood. His wide, Slavic face seethed redly and the harelip burned like a white slash.

6

Skybound horses

The heavy door slammed behind her as she charged up the rooftop.

Bullets pinged as she ran to the top of the stairs.

The Eurocopter was there, waiting in the center of the lights, its three-bladed rotor spinning, the engine whining. The passenger door was open, inviting, and the pilot was too slow to realize she was a threat.

Penny jumped into the chopper.

"Go. Now."

The pilot turned and stared at the mouth of her gun. He was an Arab. Maybe not part of Viktor's organization, just rented. He looked scared.

"You will die," he said.

"I'm already dead. What about you?"

She slid the door shut as a bullet punched the Eurocopter's flank.

The pilot protested in Arabic but his hands gripped the controls and the chopper lifted. Viktor ran onto the helipad, followed by a second man—the wounded butler she had left behind in Kasym's room. Flames leapt from their fingers, and a syncopation of bullets struck the chopper as it veered over the abyss.

The pilot shrieked.

"What? Keep going!"

They were in space. The neat squares of streets were etched in orange. Ahead loomed the dark glitz of skyscrapers.

The pilot mewed and the patchwork of streets below blurred as the chopper gyrated. She stuck her head forward but all she saw of the pilot was his back, slumped over, his hand frantically reaching for something.

"What is it? What's wrong?"

"I'm hit!"

Blood smeared the Plexiglas beside him as he kept up with his furtive motion.

"Give me control," she said.

"I'm shot!"

"Join the club." She pushed herself into the co-pilot's seat and straddled the cyclic. The pilot sobbed. As she strapped on her harness the chopper entered a spin. They were falling.

She searched for the control switch.

The pilot wailed a prayer in Arabic. She found the switch and pushed her feet on the anti-torque pedals while her hands gripped the control joystick between her legs.

"Where's the collective?" The pilot didn't reply.

The spinning had slowed and she muscled the joystick against the direction of the rotation. But they were still falling.

"Is this it?"

No response. She pulled on the lever. The chopper buckled and began to ascend. Suddenly the towers were before them. She rammed the stick as they avoided a skyscraper.

The black tower was lit like an impossibly tall set of cylinders, each illuminated from below in ever narrowing increments. She was hurtling into the Burj Khalifa, in a macabre replay of the chopper tour with Timur.

She jerked the collective as hard as she could, pushed the stick to the left, and pumped the anti-torque pedals to set a new direction. The obsidian façade of the great tower filled the cockpit's view.

That sound she heard was her own scream.

The cabin whispered past the smooth glass wall, but as the chopper turned, its fantail clipped the edge of Burj Khalifa and jerked them into a tornado. She worked the pedals, found the collective, nudged the chopper up while Dubai whirled below, Burj Khalifa winking on and off in her view like a blinking black knife.

The helicopter was going down—she didn't need the flashing dashboard alarms to tell her that. Her stomach filled her mouth. She tried to arc toward the darkness of the desert. Glass towers zoomed up around her. She saw airplanes and lamp-lined runways, and made one final adjustment to veer away from everything and towards empty land.

Then she shut off the engine to the main rotors, RPMs dialed all the way, velocity fading. She pitched the nose up until she was facing the blank night sky. The tail whacked the ground first and the skids landed with a bang. The nose touched the earth and she burst forward.

The seat belt held her an inch away from kissing glass.

Stillness.

Penny checked her limbs. The bullet wound burned, but she didn't seem to have added new ones. She patted her torso and ribs. Nothing broken.

57

The landing had likely smashed off the skids because the cabin was now snogging the ground. The craft was tilted so that she was low, almost buried, with the dead pilot hovering above her, strapped to his chair. She heard the patter of blood from his wounds drip onto her blazer. She undid her buckles and moved back into the main cabin. She checked the pistol, pocketed it, and used her good hand to open the door.

The hardscrabble ground was aligned on an angle. She hopped down and fell. Everything was trembling.

Scrubland stretched into blackness, but after a moment she realized there were a series of metallic posts in the distance. Some kind of fence. She picked herself up, found her footing, and peeked around the wreckage. She beheld an array of lights, giant warehouses, forklifts and airplanes.

She was probably at a distant corner of al-Maktoum International Airport, judging from the scale of the compound and the visible lights of nearby skyscrapers. Penny hadn't gotten very far.

Ambulance lights flashed.

She closed the chopper's door, entombing the pilot's corpse. She had to hope the ambulance crew would assume he had flown alone.

Penny scampered away from the chopper on a diagonal, keeping to the dark. The ground was hard. She forced a jog as the first fire truck drove up, its beaming lights casting the shadow of the helicopter's carcass across the desert.

She made her way toward the biggest building among the cluster. It was six stories tall. To one side, atop a concrete apron, rested a trio of commercial jetliners. Crews of men and forklifts were hauling cargo between the planes, piles on the tarmac, and the broad, open mouth of the building.

At the sharp line between darkness and illumination, she observed the comings and goings of the workers and the stream of cargo containers. Of the three jets, two seemed to be disgorging cargo, while the other one was accepting it. And the logo on its tail was exactly what she wanted: a green cedar tree between red banners. Middle East Airlines, the Lebanese carrier.

She glanced back at the crashed chopper, now pierced by more emergency lights.

Penny didn't have much time. She edged around the darkness toward the MEA plane. It was a cargo jet, probably bound for Beirut. If it were carrying perishables, it would be controlled for air pressure and temperature.

She saw ground crew riding a bulky car that looked like an overblown golf cart, pulling a tall, wheeled container. The vehicle paused near the ramp leading into the MEA plane's belly. Three men in white and blue uniforms climbed out of the car and walked around to the container. When they opened it, Penny knew this was her only chance. The three handlers escorted out of the container a pair of beautiful chestnut-colored racehorses and walked them up the plane's ramp.

Penny strode into the wide mouth of the building, away from the knots of men hauling big icy packs of frozen lobster out from another airplane.

The outer wall of the cargo terminal was a honeycomb of capsules, filled with cargo containers carried around a network of rails by men and robots. Clusters of men in jeans, T-shirts and yellow hardhats heaved bulky containers between the planes and the cargo hall's web of rails and platforms.

Nowhere to hide.

Bearing a confident posture, pretending the filth caking her skin didn't exist, she walked a straight line across the mouth of the apron toward the MEA plane. The workers, men hauling boxes in and out of planes, were Indians or other South Asians, migrant laborers who weren't paid enough to care about her.

The ones minding the horses were Arabs. They wore uniforms, blue overalls pulled over white shirts. They were probably employed by the owner of the horses.

If the horses were important enough to warrant special attention, then, she guessed, the attendants would be along for the flight.

She walked up to one of the uniformed Arabs. He was leaning against a wall, concentrating on reading something off a clipboard. He raised his eyes and gulped.

She smiled. "Can you help me?" she asked in shaky Arabic. "Bathroom?"

Before the man could think of a response she had moved to his side. She needed to take him out of view. Penny cocked her head. "Girl's room? Toilet?"

The amazed man gestured toward a glass-encased office.

"Show me?" She knew it might be dangerous for a woman to touch him, so she pointed at the door and tried to look confused. The man nodded, still too surprised to think.

He walked her past the office and pointed at a pair of heavy steel doors. They were unmarked so if they were indeed toilets they were unisex, or no women worked here.

She pushed one door open and turned to the man. "Thank you."

He was too far out of reach. He was starting to realize she didn't belong there. The man held up a laminated ID card dangling from a lanyard around his neck. He wanted to see hers.

60

"Oh, my pass," she said, pretending to check her pockets, resisting the urge to aim either of her pistols at him. Instead she shrugged and smiled stupidly. The man released a low stream of unfriendly Arabic. His eyes noticed her dirt and blood.

She grimaced and touched dried blood on her bad arm. She went weak-kneed. The man moved forward to try to catch her.

Ushiro, the term used in aikido for an attack from behind. She clasped the man's wrist and turned him into the door. With the man in front, she used her own weight and flow to guide him into the bathroom: toilet, urinal, steel sink beneath a mirror. *Aringinate*, "lift and project". She spun him around the room, leaning forward, not letting him go. *Kubishime*, "choke".

It all happened in seconds. He squirmed in her armlock. Her wound bled. But he had no leverage. His hands flailed at her grip until he slumped over, and she eased him onto the toilet.

Five minutes later she emerged from the bathroom in the white shirt and blue overalls. Guns, cash, passport and pistols bulged from her pockets. She had replaced the tampon covering the wound with a clean one and retied the silk thong tourniquet. Penny walked past the office with the clipboard in hand. She hung back as the final pair of horses was led up the ramp into the Lebanese airplane.

The last of the uniformed handlers went up with the horses. She waited as cargo strongmen followed with mundane containers and boxes, but the horse handlers all remained on board.

A few cargo workers jogged down the ramp. One of them exchanged words in what she guessed was Hindi as he passed her. He looked at her quizzically, but her uniform protected her.

61

The man was headed for the toilet. He was about to be surprised.

Penny made for the ramp, trying to keep the clipboard from shaking.

Airport ground crewmen wearing bright pink nylon vests jogged past her carrying glowing sticks. The plane's engines whirred and then whined.

She reached the ramp as it was ascending. Someone waved a glowstick at her. The plane engines drowned out the shouting, but as she reached the entrance, she dared to glance back and saw an animated crowd by the bathrooms.

Penny hurried into the long tube. It was dark here, but ahead there were lights and she could see shadows moving around six horses standing in specially designed paddocks. Their smell was intense, six huge living things amid the rest of the inanimate cargo, snorting amicably as they sniffed at their luxurious bedding of hay.

The plane started to move, but the presence of the horses ensured the pilots maneuvered with maximum grace. She found a niche in the shadows where she hoped no one would come wandering.

How soon would it take for the authorities to request the pilots to turn around?

The Emerati police weren't the real problem.

How had Viktor found out about what she and Stack had done to him? And how had he known they were in Dubai? The only other people who knew were the Chamouns. Her bosses, her mentors. It didn't make sense.

The one thing she could count on, though, was that her escape from Viktor was temporary.

He had called her Penelope.

He knew her name.

II

BEIRUT

7

City of martyrs

Fever. Burning up. Were these flames real or a hallucination? Faces danced beyond the fire: Viktor, observing her with the dead eyes of a shark. Fuad, compassionate smile melting into a sneer. The sister she hadn't seen in ten years, bridal embroidery defiled with blood. Penny's fingers cupped a man's ears, and in the reflection of the mirror, his eyeball, dangling by an obscene cord of flesh, found her.

Infection. The word penetrated the smoke and heat like the bullet had pierced her skin. She was shaking but not from panic. From chills.

She was freezing.

They had crossed the desert, over blasted lands...of oil wells, arid riverbeds, bomb craters, chemical cities...or wrack, ruin and refugees. At the end they would have skimmed over snowcapped peaks before the land dropped precipitously into the green gorges of the Bekaa Valley and undulated down to the Mediterranean Sea, to Beirut. To home, if she survived long enough to reach it.

Some impulse, part training and part ineffable drive—the

thing that made her heart beat—got Penny out of the plane when it landed. The snort of horses, the commands of their handlers. Stumbling into containers and boxes. Somewhere losing the Smith & Wesson, but the Beretta still tucked into her waist. She emerged with her arm on fire and her spine turning to ice, wearing a janitor's ill-fitting trousers instead of the blue overalls.

Veronique Goetzle took her final bow at Lebanese immigration, doing her best to ignore her awful appearance and the way she must smell. She kept herself alert calculating the odds that the Emirati authorities had connected all of the dots. She had left them no shortage of clues, not to mention generous splatters of DNA samples.

No matter now. Struggling to simply remain standing and awake, she walked to the immigration desk and handed over the passport and an entry form. The officer gawked at her— filthy dungarees, unholy hair, sallow and drawn skin, black eyes glazed instead of bright, but the computer accepted her passport and, with a curt wave, he let her in.

So the United Arab Emirates had not put out an alert about Veronique. Eight hours after violence had overtaken the country's landmark hotel and the escape vehicle clipped the world's tallest skyscraper. Someone, maybe high up in the Dubai government, was opting for silence: don't worry, oil barons and foreign dignitaries, there's nothing here to concern you.

She knew how to keep herself out of the hands of the Emirati police. Viktor was another matter.

Penny crossed the arrivals hall, the dingy space mostly empty—it was only turning six a.m.—and headed for the exit.

Infection? If the bullet wound was exposed to sepsis, and

her blood had carried it to any vital organ, she was a goner.

Taking a taxi was a risk. She could be easily tailed. And Beirut was an unstable place: a lone, weak woman could make for easy prey, particularly as she passed through the Palestinian and Shia slums. But Penny was too feeble to follow the usual drawn-out precautions. She considered directing the taxi driver to Fuad's compound in the mountains. But her strength was leaking out of her in measurable quanta. She wasn't ready to face the Chamouns.

"*Shari* Gemayzeh," she told the driver. She gave him the street's number before slumping against the window. She didn't feel the engine start or the tires crunch against the pavement.

The taxi ambled through the maze of access roads before reaching Ouzai Highway, which made a straight line along the coast into the heart of the city. To her right reared Mount Lebanon, now a dark hulk beneath a brightening sky. City lights cascaded from the mountain's sharp heights down to the edge of the sea. The Mediterranean was as wine-dark as Homer had advertized.

The sun scaled the mountain ridge and the heat and light brought her back to some kind of reality. The morning haze turned orange and she registered the piles of city clinging to the mountain's skirts. Then they plunged into a tunnel and emerged into a third-world mess.

This land had once hosted orchards and farms. History's dispossessed had long since turned the pastoral into slums: Palestinian refugees and Shia camps, prime recruiting grounds for Hezbollah. But this was Lebanon, a country of infinite factions. As they left the underpass behind, she passed banners and flags representing Amal and Hezbollah, rival Shia political groups, but also images of Bashar al-Assad, the dictator of war-torn Syria, as well as more obscure imams; anyone with a coterie of AK-47-armed zealots could make a claim to political relevance.

And everywhere loomed the images of martyrs, in posters and on banners, their names and images spread across bridges and overpasses, presiding over this city of ghouls. Men and boys killed by the Israelis, killed by the Sunni, killed by the Christians, killed while fighting across the border in Syria.

The mood changed once they emerged in West Beirut, the prosperous stronghold of the Sunni Arabs: tower blocks that could have been in Miami, the green hillocks of universities, official-looking buildings surrounded by soldiers.

They drove slowly through Lebanese Army checkpoints into the center of town, the old Green Zone that once divided Muslim from Christian. The old boundaries of the civil war had given way to a vista of cranes and construction equipment. This was Beirut as a phoenix, rising from the ashes with plenty of financing from the World Bank.

Penny spied groups of men in muddied clothes huddled beneath new overpasses, but these unfortunates weren't Lebanese. They were Syrian refugees, a new phenomenon created by their own civil war.

The taxi reached a broad intersection of boulevards centered on a giant mosque; it, too, was new, built as a mausoleum for a recently murdered Christian president. But this somber landmark was at the heart of a young, rowdy Beirut. One road leading off the square into Eastern Beirut, the oldest and most established part of the city, was named for the French general who had once conquered this country. But everyone used the road's Arabic name, Gemazyeh. Its narrow, byzantine path threaded a gamut of shabbily elegant buildings, a reminder of the old days when Beirut was called the Paris of the East. Its innards gasped with cafes, coffee shops, bars and nightclubs. From sundown its crumbling sidewalks were filled with fashionable people—Christian men in hip-hop garb, Muslim women in high heels and short skirts. The narrow streets would echo with the laughter of people desperate to bury the past and forget the present.

But this was no country for anyone who wanted to imagine the future. The future was a luxury no one had time to afford. Perhaps that's why Penny had felt so at home in Beirut.

It was early morning now and the revelers had gone to sleep. Penny directed the taxi into a side lane and up an incline surrounded by houses and apartment buildings. She didn't have Lebanese lira, only the money from Kasym Shokay's stash. The driver happily pocketed her forty American dollars.

Penny did a full turn as the taxi meandered off. The neighborhood was quiet. A small parking lot filled the corner of the bent lane. Ali and his sons were always here, ready to park or fetch a resident's car, spending the hot afternoons hosing the cars clean of the city's dirt. There was no sign of a tail, but she had done such a poor job of covering her tracks that it would be easy for anyone now to keep an eye on her undetected.

The sky was blue and a gentle breeze rustled the great ficus trees that lined the alley, survivors of a bygone garden, harking from the days when the city's best neighborhoods had been pleasantly spaced. Beirut had always been a magnet, however—for Arab playboys and European chancers, more recently for refugees, and the city groaned beneath the buildings and towers to house them all. Eastern Beirut still had room for some livable quarters, though. Squint and it could be a slice of

71

bohemian Europe.

White-haired Ali said good morning, but his alarm was obvious. She knew she looked like a survivor in a slasher flick.

"Ali, no key," she told him in her tourist Arabic. She had never found the time to nail the language. "Key?"

He blurted a stream of Arabic which she took to mean, *What the blazes happened to you?*

"I'm okay."

He brought her the spare, politely ignoring her lie. Of all the deceptions in her world, this was the most benign. Penny knew, taking the key, that she was opening the door to lies she couldn't fathom, including her own.

Penny walked up the winding steps that led to her apartment on the third floor of a broad, six-story building. She had bought the apartment six years ago, at the start of her career, when she got her first taste of money. It had proven a sound investment, as the rebuilding of the city and the influx of Gulf cash had since driven property prices higher than the ficus trees. She had done so well that she had felt free to blow every last dollar on partying during her summer days off, because there was no better way to avoid memories than getting high on a banker's boat along the Amalfi Coast.

It was Fuad who had suggested she make Beirut her base— close to the Chamouns, in a city whose politics were too chaotic for any one group to ever dominate. That meant it was too gridlocked to get anything done, but this also enabled something like freedom to prevail. Lebanon was not directly in the oil spots that obsessed her clientele, but it was near enough, on the edge of the Middle East—of it but different, open and cosmopolitan, lawless but refined. The Syrian war and the rise of Daesh, the Arabic term for Islamic State, were testing every sinew in Lebanon's factional truces. But for now, in the autumnal days of 2015, it was holding together.

She punched the code to her apartment and passed through the gate. A corridor turned a corner to the stairs and an old-fashioned elevator girded in wrought iron. She stepped onto the landing and unlocked the heavy door to her home.

The first thing Penny did was cross to the bathroom, where she kept a store of first-aid medicine and a variety of prescription drugs. She found the Vancocin, legal but considered an antibiotic of last resort, lethal to bacteria and sometimes to vital organs. She'd need to be alive for that to become a worry. She swallowed two of the fat, nuggety pills.

The bullet had passed through her upper arm, stealing some of her flesh. Her skin bordering the wound was red and testy. The likely scarring might be a problem for her looks, but she was lucky and she knew it.

She shed her clothes and put the Beretta and the cash on the rim of the sink. Showering was a slow and delicate process. The hole bled again and burned. She wrapped it in gauze, not sure how else to treat it until she could get some proper help.

The flat came with three guest bedrooms, one of which had become her wardrobe, if such a term could dignify that mountain of Hermès scarves and Oscar de la Renta suits for day jobs, Fox & Rose lingerie for evenings, stacked boxes of Manolo Blahnik and Jimmy Choo shoes, and for the serious work, items from Pleasurements, sourced from visits to the Amsterdam shop where she could have the slightest bits of silk or leather tailored exactly to her curves. The treasure room had devoured most of her earnings, although she had no idea how much cash she had spent on these things. What she did know, despite the clutter, was exactly where to reach for her favorite Olivia von Halle silk kimono.

Tying it around her waist, she felt the wound open. She slipped her arm and shoulder free and hurried back to the bathroom.

The pistol had slid into the bowl of the sink.

That's when the shock hit her: the sight of the gun in the wrong place. The normality of her apartment and the quiet charm of the morning lost their ability to soothe. The madness of the blown operation crashed around her. The killers hadn't come for Timur or Shokay. They weren't interested in KazPetro.

Viktor had come for her.

The weight of the head in her hands as she broke it on the counter corner like a coconut.

But somehow the unease of that moment seemed too far removed, too abstract. The guilt felt forced. Or maybe it was just her way of trying to be normal. Normal people would feel...bad. She felt incredibly, amazingly, alive.

And throw-up inducing scared. Now she knew why they called it getting the butterflies. She wanted to rip out her stomach and shake it free of the damn bugs.

Police and intelligence agencies would be poring over countless images of her. They didn't know anything about Penny Lee. But it wouldn't take long for the UAE's intelligence services to realize Veronique Goetzle didn't exist. Penny didn't have any official records that could be linked to Veronique; Fuad always maintained firewalls, Etienne was scrupulous with his fake identities. But even if they never tied Veronique to her or to Fuad, Penny's life in corporate espionage was probably over.

Which she'd welcome, if it didn't come with a death sentence.

Had Viktor come on someone's orders? Or had he gone rogue, on a personal mission of vengeance? Neither answer offered even a crumb of solace.

How had he known to find her at that moment in Dubai?

Fuad. Had Fuad discovered what she and Stack had done, ratted his errant spies to the Russians?

She laughed for everyone in the bathroom to hear as she cleaned and bandaged the wound again. Look out, it's Penny Lee: evil maid, honey pot...killer.

She had been weeping. But not because of that man whose face she had crushed.

She forced herself to stop and steady her breathing. She focused on Viktor. Hating him was a palliative for the shakes he had induced. Being scared in her own home, here in Beirut, made her angry. This place was her only refuge. Viktor had robbed her of it.

Yeah, better to hate him than to let him scare her.

But she was terrified.

Breathe, Pen.

Because you're not going to live like this. They've taken so much from you...

But she had taken something from them, too, hadn't she?

No. Not like this. Didn't compare. Not even close.

You're not going to let them take any more.

She put the gun and the bands of cash into a safe that she kept in the second guest bedroom. She had converted this room to a library, all shelves groaning with books acquired as compulsively as her clothes. She locked the safe and hid it behind her growing collection of ancient Greek plays, her latest jag.

Hunger replaced the tremors with a different kind of urgency.

There wasn't much to eat in the apartment other than cereal and crackers—her teenage penance at a Swiss finishing school had taught her about cuisine but had failed to instill any desire to actually make it herself. But her maid had recently replenished the bananas and oranges in the bowl on the kitchen counter.

Penny boiled water to make green tea and ate the fruit. The bananas sated her for now. It was still hours before the coffee shops would open. At a loss, weak and exhausted but wanting to plan her next move, she sat on her couch and sipped the tea. The leather cushions swallowed her, and the hallucinations returned.

Flames.

Viktor's hollow gaze: the foulness of his breath on her face, the disgusting bacterial stink of his saliva that lingered on her skin.

Her sister, an intrusive memory—her sister on TV, Penny's idea of a joke gone horribly wrong.

And the joker, Stack, smirking even in death.

When she woke, she didn't know what time it was. She only knew that she wasn't alone in the apartment.

8

Smoke and ash

She opened her eyes in time to witness the sun checking out for the night. It glanced off the Mediterranean, out past the jumble of buildings and the commercial tankers and the United Nations warships populating the bottom of her window.

Her living room was graced with lots of those tall windows. The last gasp of daylight allowed her to see its contours: the coffee table, the ottoman, the dining table, the mountain bicycle propped against a wall.

The tiled floor was cold against her feet. There among its patterned squares materialized an oblong square of yellow light. Someone had turned on the light in the adjacent TV room.

The Verconin had worked. The fever was gone. The raw stiffness in her arm was a natural feeling of pain, not of infection.

She was tired, but she could move.

Penny heard noises from beyond the TV, in the kitchen.

She snuck off the sofa carefully so as to not disturb the leather. In a crouch, she hurried crablike to another exit, which

77

connected to the central hallway. She peered through the open entrance toward the TV room and the kitchen light. No one was there, but she heard the glug, glug of the water cooler.

Heading in the opposite direction, toward the apartment's rear where the bathroom and the bedrooms were, she crept into the library, to the hardback edition of Homer's *Iliad* that obscured the safe box.

The hallway light blazed on. A slab of light from the library's doorway illuminated one wall of the book collection. Penny, in the shadows, punched in the six-digit code. The lock made a loud WHIRR.

Footfalls. Someone approaching.

Penny reached inside. Her fingers found stainless steel.

My home. The bitterness clouded her focus, but she was helpless to block it.

Penny thrust the Beretta into the hallway and prompted a screech and a crash of glass on the tiled floor.

"Maliha!" Penny gasped.

Maliha, a middle-aged woman in heavy shoes and a hajib half-covering her gray hair, let out another cry. She raised her palms and dropped to her knees.

Penny lowered the gun. "I'm sorry, Maliha, I'm so sorry." She repeated this in Arabic as she helped the trembling woman back up. "What are you doing here?"

"I was late, ma'am, my son is in hospital. I stayed with him all yesterday and today. But I wanted to clean your flat. So that when you came back from your business trip you would be pleased."

"Maliha," Penny cooed, relieved and feeling ashamed. She put the Beretta on a bookshelf and helped the maid into the living room. "You shouldn't ever feel obliged to come here at night."

"I'm busy with the other customers all day, tomorrow and the day after," Maliha said as she pulled the scarf down around her shoulders, using a corner to dab her wet eyes.

"Sit down, let me make you some tea," Penny said. "I'm sorry I frightened you. But you really scared me."

"You said you would be gone at least two weeks."

Penny adjusted her kimono. "Business didn't go so well for me."

She moved to the kitchen and put the kettle on a burner.

"I hope Japanese green tea's okay," she called. "What happened to your son?"

"Traffic accident, ma'am. Right on Hamra Street. All of those people, everyone saw him get hit, but no one saw the car that hit him and sped away."

"Is he going to be all right?" Penny brought the maid her tea and sat with her on the sofa. Her own stomach growled. She needed to eat and then contact Fuad. She had slept through the day. That had been stupid.

"*Inshallah* he will make a full recovery."

"I'm sure he will."

Maliha took a sip. She didn't seem to like it. "And so did you see the man today?"

Penny froze. "What man?"

"He told me he would come see you today," Maliha said.

"What man? When was this?"

The maid was taken aback from the urgency in Penny's voice.

"I don't know what man," she said. "A man. I came yesterday to do the cleaning. Last night, I mean, because I had spent the day with my son."

"So you were here last night? What time?"

79

"Late, ma'am, after I had made dinner for my family."

Penny guessed that meant nine or ten o'clock. About the same time bullets flew in Dubai.

"What did he look like?"

"How strange he looked! Like a European, blond hair, but with the eyes of a Chinese."

"Big or small? Tall?"

"How tall he was!"

"What was he dressed like? Anything remarkable?"

"No, ma'am, just clothes."

Penny cupped Maliha's coarse hands. "What did he say to you?"

"I told him you were away on a business trip. He could leave a message if he liked."

"And?"

"He said...he said he was your boyfriend."

Penny squeezed the woman's fingers. *I don't have boyfriends.*

"...and that he would...find you...when you were back."

Viktor knew her name. He knew where she lived.

It was time to run.

"Maliha, wait here a moment."

She returned to the safe and pulled out a thousand dollars. That amount of money would go far for someone of Maliha's means. The maid had retreated to the kitchen and was busying herself washing the teacup, the fruit bowl.

"Maliha, I can't employ you any longer," Penny said.

"Ma'am?"

"I'm sorry. I have to leave Beirut. I'll miss you."

"But, ma'am..."

"Take this." Penny forced the money on Maliha.

"No, what is this thing? I cannot take your money."

"If not for you, then take it for your son. Please."

Maliha eyed the money suspiciously. Then she accepted the notes and folded them into a pocket. "Why are you going?"

"I can't tell you. But you have to go, too. You have to leave here right away."

"But..."

"Maliha, you have to go now. I'm sorry, but this apartment is no longer safe. Do you understand?"

"That man?"

"Yes, that man. Don't come back."

Maliha nodded, once. She understood. Beirutis of her generation had endured things that Penny didn't want to imagine.

"*Fi Amanullah*," the maid said, may Allah protect you, and she let herself out the front door.

Penny entered her wardrobe, beheld her legacy of splurging. Did it matter if she never saw any of them again? She loved beautiful clothes, the flash of elegance of a de la Renta off her shoulder, the elevation in her legs and extra edge to her ass from Christian Louboutin shoes...the feel of money on her skin.

Money transformed into drapings, that's all these things had been. Without hesitation, she changed into traveling clothes: jeans, T-shirt beneath a leather biker jacket, and Patagonia hiking shoes. She grabbed a red backpack and began to fill it with anything she thought she'd need: some of her medical stash, cosmetics and toiletries, a change of underwear and sensible socks. Baseball cap, just one watch – not the Jaeger-LeCoultre, but a sporty Rolex Yacht-Master – and, her one touch of refinement, a Hermès shawl patterned Jaguar green that could double as a headscarf.

Her bedroom was as austere as the wardrobe was overstuffed:

just a wide, low bed, a nightstand with a laptop and chargers, and a generous window overlooking the garden.

She added the chargers to the red backpack and placed the laptop on the floor. She used a kitchen knife and flashlight to smash the computer to pieces. She transferred the remains in the bathtub, doused them with butane and lit a match. The smell of burning plastic infested the apartment as she collected her six passports, credit cards and cash, all courtesy of Etienne Chamoun. She chambered the Beretta—one bullet left—and tucked it in her jeans behind her back.

The final contents of the safe: five back-up iPhones, each snuggled inside black Faraday bags, thick sleeves that would shield the phones from external electronic snooping, and a clutch of paper documents.

Penny walked into the bathroom, now illuminated only by the fire in the tub. The flames were greasy blue with melting metal.

She had always held onto these snippets of paper. All through the worst nights at the finishing school in Switzerland, or in Shimura's dojo, she would flirt with the fantasy of giving it all up, rejecting the tutelage of the Chamouns, to return to America. To find what remained of her family and reclaim who she had once been. To never see Fuad or his demented sister again.

The yearning rarely lasted more than a bad night or two, but it had never quite died. And since the horror in London, it had been pulsing within her more frequently. Tonight she was going to turn it into ash.

A perforated square, yellowed with age, proof of a US Social Security Number. A birth certificate. Melody Tang, RIP.

The documents fluttered from her fingers. It seemed wrong

to let them burn in that horrible blue flame; mingling them with the stench of that melting computer was a violation. Penny sobbed. She knelt and tried to rescue the bits of paper that hadn't yet caught fire. The flames scalded her fingertips and she pulled back. It was more than a dream being turned to smoke and ash.

She had finally killed herself.

Penny stood and wiped her cheeks dry.

Of all the spaces in this roomy apartment, there was only one room she needed to bid goodbye. If the wardrobe bursting with fripperies were her id, this final room was her ego, empty— she had even removed the pendant light—save for the twelve tatami mats, imported expensively from Japan, and a single wooden staff, about five feet long, propped against the wall.

Jikishin kore dojo nari. She whispered the words. The dojo lies within a pure and true heart.

Penny bowed. The emptiness of the room had been her anchor. Every day when she wasn't training in Japan or on an assignment, she would work here: knee walking, practicing with the *jo* stick, tumbling, balancing, dancing. The clutter of the other rooms were just stuff: the half-read novels and Greek dramas, the plants on the balcony that only Maliha had kept alive, the everyday things that had let her pretend she could lead a mundane life in an acceptable city. Even as she had raced through her playgirl lifestyle, the barren dojo had been her lifeline, her temple to sanity. In this room, she erased herself; amid the strenuous practice, she was at ease.

But she knew now that Penelope Lee could never return to this apartment. Her primordial life as Melody was lost forever, and this one as Penny was burning to a crisp. Whatever she was going to do with Penelope Lee would have to be invented far away from here.

Through the pain and weakness in her body was the anguish of abandoning this place. Anguish...and anger.

First, though, she had to see Fuad.

To get some answers.

And to get someone to stitch up her arm.

Penny shouldered the red backpack and opened the front door. The hallway's light was broken and the stairwell was dark. She moved to press the button for the elevator and froze.

Soft footfalls below.

The light on her level didn't work, but the light on the ground floor did. It wasn't on.

Padding up concrete steps.

She retreated back inside the apartment and carefully pulled the door shut. The lock clicked. It was a tiny sound, but she knew it would be heard.

Which meant she was trapped. Penny cringed. The right move would have been to creep further up the stairs outside.

Too late. She waited by the door. She could feel the hairs on her scalp standing at attention, pulling her skin taut.

Someone was on the other side of the door. Perhaps it was the subtlest shift of his body. She wasn't breathing. Maybe he wasn't either. But she sensed him there, like a shadow.

Did he sense her, too?

A key slid into the lock.

A key? Where did he get a key?

That's when she knew that Maliha was dead. Someone had followed the maid until he could corner her in a convenient place; Gemayzeh Street was pockmarked with shadowy alleys and unlit nooks.

The blond man with the Chinese eyes—for who else could it

be? —turned the key in the lock.

Penny retreated to the living room. She could move swiftly knowing the intruder would respect caution. That gave her a sliver of time.

She crossed the dark to the door leading to the outside balcony. She paused and heard the man gently close the front door. He was inside the apartment.

There would be a sound when she moved outside. She paused. The darkness buzzed with silence: a high-pitched tinny noise of nothing. Each one of her senses strained to catch a clue.

The man seemed to know the layout. He moved softly through the hallway, attracted perhaps by the embers in the bathtub, the only thing giving off light. Or maybe he thought he'd find her tucked in bed, because everything was dark. She perceived him in the doorway leading from the living room to the hallway. If that shadow stopped to look her way, he would surely notice her silhouette against the windows. But he moved down the hall, toward the bathroom and her bedroom. She counted to three and slid the balcony door open. It moved efficiently.

With a squeak.

She quickly skirted the balcony that wrapped around the apartment building. Beyond the tumble of smaller houses glowed the lights of Gemayzeh's cafes. The branches of ficus trees brushed against the far end of the terrace. The parking lot was a thirty-foot drop.

The terrace's railing consisted of decorative concrete pilasters. Penny inserted her free arm through the backpack's strap and hoisted her legs over by the tree. The gauze around her upper arm's wound shifted with a painful tug.

The man was coming through the balcony door just as she

85

lowered her body into space, clinging to a concrete pillar with both hands, her legs dangling beneath her. The man was leaning over the balcony opposite the door. He looked down.

He saw her.

She swung her legs forward and let go.

The shocking bang from a pistol shot came as her feet crashed into a rocking chair on the balcony below. Penny couldn't control her trajectory. Her body sent the chair skidding across the tiled floor. She landed on her ass, feet in the air. The backpack probably saved her head. Her spine was jolted in painful ways, but she rolled to an upright position on one knee.

The family on this level was watching TV in their living room. She heard them stir. Penny considered going inside, but if the killer were already running back to the stairwell, she'd never make it. She went to the balcony and looked up.

The man wasn't there.

He'd be rushing down the stairs.

The balcony door opened. A skinny boy was there. He wore a bright T-shirt and held a soccer ball. She could see the whites of his eyes widen. "Papa!" he called.

9

Imprinted

A year ago, another autumn, when Penny's life had settled into a rhythm as seemingly natural as the turning of the leaves, Fuad gave her an assignment in London.

He sent her, via a Parisian madam, to sleep with the managing partner of a hedge fund called Geneva Partners Capital Management. The target was a German forty-two-year-old named Manfred Ingerholz who had spun his PhD in chemistry into a career mastering the trading floors of investment banks.

She was not required to know anything about the target, but her quarries were often prominent men, easily searchable online. Ingerholz was occasionally quoted in the financial press and his bio was available on the Geneva Partners website. He sat on the boards of several international charities. He lived in Geneva alone with his American wife, having sent the three children to play Harry Potter at snobby boarding schools.

The last detail had stuck in her head. Penny knew what those kids were going through, although she doubted Herr Ingerholz would send any of his daughters to the Institut Château-Montclaire, cultivator of the wanna-be aristoclass.

No, that was for young women aspiring to social status. Her father had placed her there to give his beautiful daughter the kind of polish that she was unlikely to acquire in Sante Fe, the sort of elegance that her mother might have bequeathed had she still been alive. Penny—Melody—had hated the place, the other students most of all, but she had thrown herself into the tennis and horseback riding and skiing. It had felt like a holiday while her younger sister and everyone else back in America had to slog through stupid old high school.

Only recently had she begun to wonder why her father hadn't tried to put her into an engineering or math program. Or anything normal. He had been a scientist, for crying out loud. Had finishing school for breeding elite ladies really been Jonas Tang's idea?

Anytime her thoughts strayed to her father was a moment of danger, of distraction. She returned to the here, now, London, Ingerholz. She didn't know what Fuad intended to do to Mister Hedge Fund Manager, but it probably involved blackmailing him with a video of his exploits with Penny at his room in the Ritz. Fuad in turn was merely serving a client that had its own reasons for wishing Ingerholz harm: to betray his company, or enter or break a contract, or run some other dirty corporate errand. But these things rarely ended well for her targets, or ended at all. Blackmail respected no gentleman's agreement. Ingerholz was probably worth tens of millions of dollars— today. After Fuad was done with him, less. A lot less.

Kids, I've got news for you. Public high school in America, after your pampered years at Hogwarts, is going to be a blast.

The trader was cautious in almost all of his dealings, but no matter how discreet the service, no matter how many carats plated its reputation, Ingerholz should have considered other procurers to satisfy his sexual urges. The madam in Paris was not above betraying the odd client to Fuad's network; the Chamouns had some kind of leverage over her, too.

Ingerholz liked to stay at the Ritz Hotel in Piccadilly, sur-rounding himself with the great and the good of London society. His suite commanded corner views of Green Park and the rear of Buckingham Palace. He had become a frequent customer of the madam, who arranged suitably elegant young women to accompany him to dinner or the theater. Ingerholz wasn't particularly interested in speaking with his date, but his absolute need for propriety forbade him from simply bringing a prostitute to his room. He had to first go through the ritual of an evening out, a fantasy that his companion was expected to maintain, as if to hoodwink the hotel's employees. They might retire to the Rivoli Bar to sip a cocktail beneath its gilded ceiling domes, as though to advertise that Ingerholz knew how to attract a beautiful woman. Only then would he sign the bill and take her to his corner suite. His weakness wasn't his physical urges. It was his tightly held, secret sense of shame.

Fuad did not have access to the hotel or its staff. Penny didn't know if he had tried to bribe his way inside the Ritz's organization. Best not to, with well-run institutions: keep the number of people involved to a minimum. But once Ingerholz returned with her to his room, they would need a way to record it.

Stack accompanied her to London. The Ritz was his kind of place—luxurious and snooty. He'd be staying in the room downstairs from Ingerholz's suite, which Fuad had booked under an alias. Stack dressed in a suit and tie, had the hotel staff polish his shoes, and availed himself of the Ritz's basement club—a casino for guests only. He'd play down there, whittling away Fuad's advance, until the evening.

Penny wasn't stationed at the Ritz, but at a grimy three-star hotel near the tube station in unfashionable Hammersmith. She was here on a Canadian passport as Julie Belroix, born in Montreal, who had made her way across the Great White North one strip club at a time.

Her cover wasn't to be rich or to enjoy easy living. Julie was a college dropout who turned tricks and whose looks and poise had gotten her into the most exclusive lists. Madam's escorts were meant to be smart and cultured enough to keep a client engaged over dinner, but preferably by getting the client to show off how he was even smarter.

Penny took a black cab to the Ritz. It was her first time there. She dressed in a tight scarlet cocktail dress with an aggressive slit up the front, with a smart purse in hand and a fur cover-up to keep her warm. The top-hat-and-tails doorman pointed her toward the Rivoli Bar. She slid onto a barstool and ordered a glass of Bollinger.

"Hello, Julie." Ingerholz wore a conservative suit, tan sweater but no tie, with slightly funky glasses, milky white frames that segued into his salt and pepper hair. He seemed at ease, as though they had been seeing one another for a long time.

"Manfred," she said, exchanging kisses on the cheek. "You surprised me."

Ingerholz smiled. He wasn't bad looking, and his body was a marathon runner's trim. He was a confident financial dealmaker and public benefactor, with a charming family...and a compulsive taste for high-end prostitutes.

"Another glass," he instructed the bartender.

They swapped pleasantries. He complimented her, just

enough to convey his pleasure without compromising his own self-belief. She did the same, readily. This was a part of the job she enjoyed. Some targets were duds, but this one was handsome, treating her to champagne in the poshest hotel bar in town. He was playfully indulging the fantasy of a hotel encounter with an exotic beauty. Work required the exhibition of passion and excitement, and nothing engendered that more than a man who knew what he was doing. She always fooled the targets and didn't mind occasionally fooling herself.

He arranged for a hotel limousine. "I hope you enjoy theater," he said. Julie nodded enthusiastically. Penny didn't mind either way, but she'd have to pay attention.

The limo swung through Green Park to Westminster, past Big Ben and over the bridge. The London Eye held them in its sights but the limo kept going, determinedly navigating the narrow, cluttered streets of South London.

"I don't know this area," she said.

"Southwark," Ingerholz said. "You know the Old Vic?"

Julie wouldn't have a clue. "Uh, is it famous?"

The theater wasn't much to look at outside, but the interior was a multi-tiered, gilded spectacle. She was relieved he wasn't into musicals, but his tastes were perhaps too intellectual. "Eugene O'Neill," she said, reading the pamphlet. Heavy stuff, although Julie Belroix wouldn't know that either. Still, Ingerholz was showing class.

"This is serious theater," Ingerholz said. "Not *The Lion King*. You will get an education."

They settled into the old, uncomfortable seats in the orchestra section. Penny had a feeling Ingerholz would want to quiz her on this cultural expedition. It might not matter, he'd sleep with her either way, but it would be better if he thought his date could prove how much she appreciated his tutelage.

The actors were a mix of Americans and British. The main character was a fireman named Yank, of all things, working on a cruise ship. He was an agitator: proud member of the working class and all that. Julie checked her cheap quartz watch.

The fireman caught the eye of a young society lady on deck. She found Yank an intoxicating change from her waxwork of an aunt, until she accidentally found him at work, stoking the engines, covered in soot. Penny couldn't understand why the audience should sympathize with the fireman after the girl had fainted at the sight of him. What kind of schmuck thought a high-priced bitch like that would fall for a guy who shoveled coal?

The depressed Yank decided to terrorize rich people in the name of the working class. He got jailed in New York, but after joining the union, they threw him out too. Spurned by the snobby girl, cast out by the union, he finally tried to free an ape at the zoo, his gesture against the world, expecting some gratitude from the enslaved, only to have the beast crush him. The end. The guy in the ape makeup thumped his chest when he took his bow.

"Kind of weird, right?" Penny said as they went to dine at a nearby restaurant. It had been a grueling two hours of theater-going.

"O'Neill was trying to express his sympathy for the working class," Ingerholz said. "But he also recognized that socialism and unions were unsuited to helping people achieve dignity."

"I guess we're all on our own." She wasn't sure where Ingerholz wanted to take this. "When you think of it like that, I guess I can see why some people like socialism."

"I'm a capitalist," Ingerholz said. "I despise socialism."

"So why did we watch that play?"

"To gloat."

Penny didn't know what to say. She faked a smile, but his response had been creepy. Maybe it was German humor, rendered badly in English. But he didn't seem to be joking. She almost asked him about the charities he helped, but Julie wasn't supposed to know who he was. To her, he was simply "Manfred", a wealthy customer staying at a swanky hotel.

The restaurant was expensive but modest and quiet. It served Spanish food, and she sampled the *jamon* and the *rio tinto*, careful not to overindulge. She'd need to be ready for exercise. Ingerholz was jocular until his phone buzzed. His face darkened as he scrolled through his messages.

"Everything OK?"

He put the phone away and stared at his plate. Then he snapped out of it. "Shall we get the bill?"

Ingerholz escorted her back to the limo and the driver returned them across the Thames to the Ritz Hotel. Penny expected some banter that would turn towards what he'd want in the bedroom. Some targets were like that. But Ingerholz's mood hadn't recovered. Any buzz she'd have to fake.

He bought her a final drink at the Rivoli. Not for conversation, because he remained inward, but to play out his ritual. She tried to use the lush surroundings to get back into the mood.

"You're so handsome." She put her hand on his.

"Everyone is ugly. Everyone."

She leaned in. "Even ugly people like to..."

"Excuse me." He moved for the men's room. Not fast, not escaping. Just...mechanical. Yeah, tonight was looking like a bore. Now she hoped he'd be quick so she could sneak out of there and catch a decent night's sleep.

She pulled out her iPhone and messaged Stack. *Going up.* When Ingerholz returned she was checking her makeup in her pocket mirror.

"Are you ready?" he asked.

"Absolutely."

He signed the bill and she followed him to the lift. The doormen bid him good evening.

"I have an arrangement," he said. "You understand. An arrangement for this sort of thing."

"All right. Whatever you like, honey."

He pressed his electronic key to the suite's door.

"Do you like me like this?" Penny asked. She pulled the fur down from her shoulders. Trying to get a read on this guy. "Or any other way?"

"It really doesn't matter."

He opened the door.

The suite was classically decorated. The living room boasted a fireplace topped by a gilded mirror, facing a large painting depicting a scene from mythology, gods and cherubs. A sofa and chairs, upholstered in floral patterns, surrounded a marble coffee table. They faced a giant TV screen and a wet bar to the side. Floor-to-ceiling windows, divided by sweeping curtains, overlooked the darkness of the park.

Ingerholz's laptop and briefcase occupied one chair. He gestured for her to sit in another, his finger scrolling down his cell phone.

She looked around, clutching the purse with both hands as she looked for the best sites to place the cameras. She'd need a few minutes alone, here and in the bedroom.

"Do you, um, want a drink or anything?" she asked, sashaying to the wet bar.

Ingerholz shook his head and raised the phone to his lips. *Sie hier*, he said. German for 'She's here.'

"Who...who's that?"

"My, uh, colleague."

Telling his colleague that she's here? What the hell was this? She put the purse on the coffee table and tried to embrace him. "I'd hate to be interrupted. Once I get started, you know..."

He pushed her away. "I need to check my messages."

It was as though the man had abandoned any sense of charm, let alone sexual interest. Or as if his charisma had been drained out of him by some cosmic wound. Ingerholz moved to the bathroom and shut the door.

Sie hier.

She opened her purse and removed a delicate fish-eyed camera at the end of a three-inch long thread of a cord as thin as a strand of hair. She put it on the mantle over the fireplace, snuggling the worm-like contraption in the crevasse beneath a little platform upon which rested a vase. She touched a plate behind the camera's eye, noting its movement. It was activated and sending a Bluetooth signal to Stack, lodged in the floor below.

She moved into the bedroom, a circular room on the corner of the hotel. She placed another camera amid a bouquet of flowers on a sideboard, wedged between the windows overlooking the park and an illuminated Big Ben. But it wouldn't take in the entire room, and definitely not enough of the bed.

Outside, Ingerholz flushed the toilet. She had maybe ten seconds. Penny ran back, grabbed a chair and hauled it beneath the chandelier. She got up and clenched her eyes against the bulb's bright glow. Ingerholz turned the doorknob. She wrapped the camera around a spoke amid the lamps, using her thumb to ensure the lens was pointing downward, and jumped off the chair.

The doorbell chimed and she almost yelped.

She had a feeling it wasn't room service.

She dragged the chair back to its original position and walked into the sitting room.

A man had joined them. He was not big, just a little taller than Penny, but he moved with catlike precision. He had broad, Slavic cheeks and a tasteless mullet of blond hair. His eyes were brown, almost gray, and revealed nothing. His lips were sensuous, and he might have been handsome if it weren't for the blemish connecting his nostril to his mouth: a cleft lip. He must have had surgery, for it was now an angry line, but it looked as though the doctors had struggled to make the flesh whole. In a child it would have inspired pity, but in this man, it repulsed her.

"Honey, who's this," Penny asked, keeping her voice neutral.

"This is, uh, your date for tonight," Ingerholz mumbled.

She draped himself on Ingerholz. "A threesome. Well, that's fun!"

He pulled back. "No, just you two."

"I don't understand."

The intruder sized her up. "It's very simple." His accent didn't sound German; it was something sensuous, maybe Russian or Ukrainian, but with the lisp it was hard to tell. "Manfred works for me." He had trouble with consonants. *Manfred works for me.*

"Manny's the one who hired me. I don't just switch customers."

"The money's the same," Ingerholz said. But that wouldn't mean anything to Penny. No video of Ingerholz, then no blackmail...and no payment from Fuad.

"Manny," the man chuckled. "That is very nice, *Manny*." He moved to the wet bar and poured himself a drink. He didn't ask if anyone else would like one.

"Manfred, seriously, what's going on?"

"I kept you occupied until he could get here." He was annoyed. "Dinner and a show. Cocktails at the Ritz. What more do you want?"

"This is...like...a thing you guys do?"

The intruder's cell buzzed, and he swiped his passcode. "Shut up, you two." He glanced at whatever message had come through and put the phone in his pants pocket.

"It's just making the mood, uh, kinda weird."

"But isn't it exciting," the intruder suggested, "not knowing what to expect?" He threw the liquor down his throat and poured another.

She wasn't going to get paid for doing this guy. And he was not someone she'd ever want to touch. The job could be fun. It could be boring.

Right now it was just scary.

"Expect the unexpected," she said, trying to sound like she was going with it.

The man approached her.

She said, "The thing is—"

He slammed her face-first into the wall. She could have resisted, fought him off, but that would go against her cover, and besides her head was swimming. He dragged her to the bed. Ingerholz must have wanted to creep away, but the man snapped, "No, you watch." He didn't bother to remove her dress, just hitched up her skirt and yanked her panties down. It was awful and it hurt. Her mouth was coppery with blood, his skin was clammy and his breath rotten. She just breathed, telling herself it would end, this grunting and stabbing.

When she thought he had finished, he bound her hair in his fist and made her lick his harelip. After what they had been through it was nothing physically, but she knew it was his way of imprinting himself, like a logo. Rape as a branding exercise.

The evil man lurched to the bathroom, leaving his pants spooled by the bed.

Ingerholz, reduced to a mere pimp, had gone into the living room. Being present at such a seedy scene might be enough for blackmail. Maybe not enough. To hell with it. She chopped the back of Ingerholz's neck and he fell unconscious on the sofa. She knelt by the stranger's pants. Her rapist, perhaps arrogant in his thirst for power, had been foolish enough to leave behind his Android phone. She held it up to the cameras for Stack to see, hoping he had caught the man entering his passcode.

The force of his nostrils exhaling on her tongue.

Her own cell phone pulsed once. Stack's message: *Four three six eight.*

She swiped the code on the evil man's Android. No time to look over her shoulder. She went straight to settings and turned on his Bluetooth. That would be enough for Stack to hack everything. By the time the stranger returned, she was running through the hotel hallways a bloody mess.

10

Cold confessions

Penny, behind the wheel of her Mini, ignored the kid with the soccer ball and faced the blackness of a Beirut night. She peered over the railing, wondering if she could engineer another jump down. A thick branch of the ficus tree skirted the edge of the balcony.

From inside came a crash and a woman's wail.

The killer was breaking in.

Penny leaned to grab hold of the branch, punching through the canopy of leaves. It seemed sturdy enough. She lifted her feet onto the balcony railing.

More chaos inside.

Something banged into the small of her back and she heard the timpani of the football bouncing on the tiled floor. She turned. The boy stared at her, moonlight catching the water in his eyes. He had kicked the ball at her, as if to demand her help against the invader.

The killer was in there, punching up the people in his way, because of her.

Sorry, kid.

Penny jumped to the tree's limb. Hands grabbed branches, shoes found solidity. Spears of foliage tried to fob her off as she inched toward the trunk. She was making a lot of noise and the whole tree was shaking, but she counted on darkness and the canopy to hide her position.

Bang. Leaves whistled.

She wrapped herself around the trunk and let gravity take her.

From above, a woman's cry. Its anguish wormed through Penny's spine.

The last five feet or so were a clear drop. She rolled to a crouch within Ali's parking lot. One of Ali's sons emerged from the little shack where they passed the time playing dominoes. He halted in surprise.

"Keys," she said in Arabic. "Fast."

Ali's son looked up at the source of the gunshots. He must have decided to obey her, because he retreated into the shack and emerged with car keys in his fist. He jogged to the Mini Cooper, ready to back it out of the park as he always did. But Penny shook her head. "Give me."

She got into her car, tossing the red backpack on the passenger's seat, and turned the ignition. Not the headlights. She reversed so abruptly she nearly ran over Ali's son. The white-haired old man now came out of the shed to see what was going on. Penny turned the wheel furiously. Something pounded on the roof of the car and for a second she thought Ali or his son had banged on it. Then she saw the soccer ball careen into the darkness.

Penny paused and stared after the ball. Ali craned his neck to look up at the apartment building.

Don't think; go.

She twisted the car into the narrow lane and gunned it. Switching on the headlights that illuminated obscure lanes, she raced for the highway that followed the coast. The traffic congealed and she kept checking the mirrors and looking around for any threat. The gunshot wound ached as bad as ever. Blood escaped the bandage.

She finally got the car on the highway dominated by banners of martyred Christian politicians, past the bend where once militia had pulled over drivers and murdered anyone Muslim. She shouldn't feel sorry for herself in such a place.

But right now, she was feeling plenty sorry.

She drove into the Armenian quarter, one more patch in the city's fabric. Keep going and she'd follow the coast through the self-satisfied Christian heartland, to the casino and the red lights of coastal nightclubs, among the villas owned by Gulf sheikhs, and onward to ancient seaside towns. But that wasn't her destination. She turned inward and began the ascent of Mount Lebanon. The roads narrowed and morphed into switchbacks. The Mini Cooper's steering required some muscle, and every turn aggravated the gunshot wound. Blood squished, depleting her of another thimbleful of life, but the pain kept her awake.

She followed the signs for Beit Mery, a Christian and Druze enclave atop the mountain. The city glowed beneath her and the Mediterranean lay flat like a supple strip of velvet. She pulled onto a narrow shoulder of road.

Penny kept an eye out for signs of a tail. If they had enough people and were organized, she'd never spot one. But subtlety didn't seem to suit Viktor's style.

No one seemed to be following her. She restarted the car and headed for the far side of the mountain. Here Mount Lebanon was honeycombed with hamlets. They all looked the same: rustic stone houses amid a maze of small country roads. She took an indirect route down to the valley around the Lebanon River. The landscape quickly changed from Mediterranean coastal beiges to the dark greens and browns of a thick pine forest. It was like a different country. It was also relatively empty. By the time she reached the valley basin, her car was almost alone on the road.

Fighting to keep awake, she headed up the far side of the valley to the tallest reaches of Mount Lebanon. She nearly crashed into a small pod of people, two women herding a pack of children. The women's eyes glowed with fear beneath their headscarves and the kids looked sullen and feral. Syrian refugees. Over the next set of peaks waited the Bekaa Valley, a Shiite-dominated land of vineyards, orchards and hashish that was struggling to absorb war refugees. Climb its heights and she would overlook blood-soaked Syria.

But Mount Lebanon was still tranquil. This was the timeless heartland of the Christians and the Druze, a Muslim Shia offshoot, and families such as Fuad's had safeguarded it for centuries.

She turned near the village of Arsoun and took a tiny side path through walls of pines. She emerged in a clearing. The Mini bumped over a log bridge spanning a creek and came to rest outside a series of walls of stone piled up the side of the mountain.

Penny cut the engine and opened the car door. She would remember standing up.

* * *

"Penny, can you hear me?"

The man's voice penetrated the gray and white fog.

She felt utterly relaxed.

"Penny?"

"Allow me, monsieur."

Gray and white. The light mild and welcoming. A sense of warmth, of contact.

Viktor's dead stare. Fire. The assassin's head in her hands, his eye swinging from its cord. Blue-tongued flames and the smell of melting plastic. Hurtling at a wall of glass.

"Shh, shh."

"It's okay, my dear." They spoke in French.

"Lie back down."

"She'll tear the stitches."

Her panicked breath was ragged. Hands firmly lowered her head against a pillow.

"Etienne," she said.

"Yes, it's me."

The other she didn't recognize. A middle-aged Arab with a mustache and round glasses.

"Who are you?"

The man smiled. "I'm not sure Fuad would approve of an exchange of names. I'm a doctor from Clemenceau. There, I've already said too much."

"Doctor…" She saw the IV tube disappearing into her wrist, and the fresh gauze wrapped around her right upper arm.

"You have lost a lot of blood," the doctor said. "But you are very fortunate. The bullet missed the subclavian artery and the brachial plexus—this is most lucky."

"See," Etienne said. He held a metal pan and tweezers. He plucked out a dark ingot. So the bullet had done more than just dig a trench in her arm.

The doctor shook a small bottle of pills. "I've got you on a schedule of antibiotics, because the possibility of infection can linger."

"Hungry," she said.

"I'll see what we can get you," the doctor said, putting the pills on a nearby table and taking his leave.

She was in a cavern-like room with a domed ceiling. Beneath the curving stones stood her bed, a desk and a set of chairs, and a coffee table that had been shoved haphazardly into a corner. Framed black-and-white photographs hung from the slate walls. Penny recognized the space as one of the chambers Fuad's ancestors had carved out of ancient caves, which he now used as a reading room.

"I'm so...relieved," Etienne stammered.

"Thanks," she said, letting him hold her hand, her arm sleeved in a cloth she didn't recognize.

Several blankets covered her body. She could feel the cold of the room on her nose and cheeks. The window overlooking Fuad's compound glowed with bleached light. The day looked wet and grim. Only her red backpack, resting on one of the chairs across the chamber, had any color.

"How long have I been out?"

"About ten hours," Etienne said.

"And this?" She released her hand and showed him the sleeve.

"It belongs to my sister."

She resisted grimacing at the thought of touching anything belonging to that woman. "Is Daliyah here?"

"No," Etienne said.

Of course, that meant the brothers or the cousins had

undressed her and put her into the gown. Whatever.

"You'd better tell Fuad I'm awake," she told him.

"I know." Etienne shuffled toward the wooden door, couldn't resist a backward glance, and left.

Penny swung the covers off. Yep, it was just the sister's dress and nothing beneath. After what she had been through, being prissy about being undressed seemed weird, but this wasn't a job, or a fling...this was the Chamouns. She removed the IV needle from the back of her wrist. A dot of blood followed and she pressed the opposite sleeve there to staunch its path. She tried moving her bandaged shoulder and it seemed okay, just a little stiff with a dull ache. She wasn't sure if that was because the wound was healing or if they had her on painkillers. But her head felt clear.

She put her bare feet on the wooden floor. It was cold. She walked to her bag. Her things were arranged on the coffee table: the cash, the passports, the phones in their Faraday sleeves. Her personal effects had been neatly folded and returned to the red backpack, including yesterday's clothes, which had also been washed. Her shoes waited beneath a chair.

Only the Beretta was missing.

She resisted the urge to stuff everything in the backpack and take off.

The door creaked open. "Should you be up?" Fuad asked in English. He wore slacks and a sweater. He had let his silver locks grow and looked like an aged Lothario. She couldn't believe it had been only ten days since she was last here.

"I feel fine."

"I think that's the doctor's decision to make."

"Fuad, I'm okay."

"A few hours ago you were almost dead." He closed the door

behind him.

"I don't suppose I could change now," Penny said, gesturing at her backpack.

"Give me your version," he said, ignoring her request.

"Viktor Gubinov murdered Stack and Lev while they were downloading Timur's laptop."

"The man who..."

"Raped me in London, yes, that one. He showed up in Dubai at the moment we had broken into Timur's laptop. He took care of Stack and Lev, and sent two men to kill me. They may have infiltrated the Burj because they were all wearing butler uniforms, like the staff there. Or they might have dressed that way and come in by helicopter."

"Timur's alive," Fuad told her. "Back in Almaty, trying to bury the whole thing. Needless to say, your mistakes have completely exposed us."

"*My* mistakes?"

"Tell me everything."

They sat down and she related what had happened.

"There were also these weird Englishmen," she said, describing the dandy pair. They had been easy to remember.

If Fuad knew who they were, he didn't let on. "I'll look into them," he said. "Go on, tell me about the helicopter."

Penny went through the story several times. He made her repeat it, asking questions from different angles, forcing her to admit what she remembered clearly and what was a hunch or perhaps a faulty recollection. No matter, she retold the events with confidence.

"The man may have killed my housekeeper. Blond, with Chinese eyes. That's how she described him. Has any sign of her turned up?"

"I'll look into it," Fuad said.

"You'll look into it."

He leaned forward. "I owe you nothing, Penny. You have put my client in danger. Me, and my family, this house, in danger. You shouldn't have come here."

"I checked for tails."

"In your condition, I wonder if you were aware of anything at all."

The floorboards felt like ice now.

"I...I'd really like to change into my clothes," she said.

He shook his head. "We're not done here. Why did this man, this Viktor, why did he come after you? At such professional risk?"

"I don't know," she snarled, "it seems to fit his personality."

"What did you do to make him do this." It was a question phrased as a command.

"I..." She threw her hands up. How did Viktor know she was in Dubai?

"Stack was involved, wasn't he?" Fuad demanded.

"Dammit, Fuad."

"No, Penny, no dammit Fuad."

"You know what Viktor did to me. You saw it."

"Now you're trying to justify yourself. What did you and Stack do to Viktor to make him ruin my operation?"

The door opened and Etienne walked in carrying a tray covered by a silver lid. Penny's stomach rumbled at the sight of food, but Fuad shouted in Arabic, "Not now, get out!" and Etienne backed out of the room and closed the door.

"We robbed his organization," she whispered.

Fuad's face turned purple. "You what?"

She braced herself. "We stole twenty-three million dollars

from the Russian mafia," Penny said.

11

Stealing from thieves

A month after the attack in London, Penny received an un-expected visitor at her apartment in Beirut. A month of self-loathing, of obsessive showers and douches, of quivering in her home.

This is part of the job. You know the risks.

Then I can't do this job anymore.

So what are you going to do? Work in an office? Count widgets on a spreadsheet? Keep the boss happy with a blowjob?

She had counted the savings she had amassed, plus the value of the Beirut apartment and the house in Japan, and put that against the price of a first-class ticket to Ibiza or a shopping weekend in Paris. The gaps were sobering.

The anger didn't fade. It smoldered and occasionally erupted. Maliha sensed something had gone wrong, but the one time she attempted an inquiry, Penny shut her down with a curt word. With others the venom flowed: the stupid barista at the corner café who added milk, the dimwit kid handing her a zaatar-flavored flatbread too hot to handle, one of Ali's sons after he got mud on her car.

Her only solace had been reading and she had found her-self enmeshed in ancient Greece, the old stories full of men and women demanding blood and justice. That afternoon Aeschylus had been her seducer. His Oresteia trilogy sparked something in her with its tale of the conqueror, Agamemnon, returning from the rape of Troy only to be murdered by his wife, Clytemnestra, who never forgave him for sacrificing their daughter to win the gods' favor before his campaign.

This is one badass woman, Penny mused. At one point, Clytemnestra trapped and killed the king with an axe. Penny underlined the passage:

> So he goes down, and the life is bursting out of him –
> great sprays of blood, and the murderous shower
> wounds me, dyes me black and I, I revel
> like the Earth when the spring rains come down,
> the blessed gifts of god, and the new green spear
> splits the sheath and rips to birth in glory!

Penny closed the book and meditated on that.

And I, I revel.

The doorbell made her jump. She wasn't expecting a visitor; she never had any. Barefoot, she padded silently to the kitchen and retrieved a long Japanese kitchen knife. Holding it behind her back she peeked out the eyehole.

Stack.

She couldn't believe it. How did he even know where she lived?

Was this some kind of trap?

"Penelope, honey, I know you're on the other side of this door," he said. "I'm alone."

She opened the door without releasing the chain.

He held up a laptop. "I come bearing gifts." He looked

at ease, the usual Stack: graying African curls, lean frame dressed in a tan linen suit, Buddhist prayer beads on one wrist, fashionable eyeglasses folded in his breast pocket.

"What are you doing here?"

"Ask me inside and I'll tell you."

She undid the chain, but as he stepped inside he had to halt because the tip of the knife was touching the bottom of his jaw, where his skin was beginning to sag.

"I'm not in the mood for surprises," she warned him.

"One zero nine, seven six six, four nine zero."

She didn't lower the blade. "What is that supposed to mean?"

"That man who assaulted you? His name is Viktor Gubinov and that's the number of his account at Banque Rothorn. Surprise."

She hesitated, her knife against Stack's throat wavered, and a tiny dot of blood formed on his skin.

"I checked it out," Stack continued. "It's in a delightful Swiss canton near the Italian border. The staff deserve their reputation for discretion. You gonna put that shiv down, sweetheart? I just had this suit dry-cleaned."

Penny lowered the knife. "Come in."

"Thank you." He wiped his hand against his pricked skin. "Dope pad you got here, Penny."

She shut the door behind him and locked it. "So to what do I owe this call, Stack?"

"We're going to clean him out. His pork is prime for barbe-cuing." He waltzed into the middle of her apartment. "Don't suppose you have anything to lubricate the conversation."

Penny sighed and went to the kitchen, putting the knife back in its sleeve. She removed the Belvedere from the freezer and poured him a tumbler with a splash of orange juice. She found him in the living room, eyeing her notations of Aeschylus.

She handed him the drink. "I'm out of weed."

"This'll do," he said. "Heavy stuff," he added, meaning the book. "I didn't take you for..."

"A bimbo who can read an old play?"

"...for a connoisseur of tragedy." He put on his red-rimmed glasses. "Mm-hm. You are well down the path of revenge. You know this Clytemnestra bitch could summon the Furies?"

"I haven't gotten that far." She tried to hide her astonishment that Stack knew all of this, let alone could pronounce 'Clytemnestra'.

"The Furies, well now, they are wicked-ass *putas*. The king, whatsisname, had a mistress, Cassandra? She was an oracle who unleashed a curse on Clytemnestra. And the curse was a Fury, who was gonna pursue our queen to the grave. You know how?"

He paused for a response, as if daring her to not be impressed. Penny caved. "I'm amazed, Stack. You actually know this play?"

He affected a nasal whitebread tone. "Darling, I was a New York hedge-fund pimp before you were a glimmer in your daddy's eye. Charity balls, private fund-raisers overlooking Central Park. This country boy got cultured up, better believe it." He took an appreciative slip of his drink and threw the paperback at her. "Anyway. You're thinking revenge, and that's good, because that's why I'm here."

She sat down beside him as he opened his laptop. "So why did you give it up? I mean, if you were getting rich on Wall Street. Did you lose it in a crash?"

"No, my algorithms never lost," he said. "Which made it

even worse for some of those greaseballs. The idea of a black man making all the money...you think they were going to sit back and let it happen?"

"What'd they do?"

"It's not what they did," he said.

"Cryptic."

"There was one man there, genuinely the only white man I ever met who didn't see the color of my skin. The only color he could see was green. Chuck Wisner, head of fixed-income sales trading. I never touched Chuck's bank account."

Meaning he had raided his colleagues, at which point becoming a criminal hacker began to look like an attractive career move.

"You're practically begging me to learn your true identity," she said. "This your way of making me trust you?" He grunted as he typed. "So why are you here?"

"Because I didn't like watching what happened to you." He slid the glasses down his nose to give her a look. "All right, so maybe I ain't no black knight. Maybe I just love a challenge. Messing with Vik beats shuffleboard or whatever it is the over-fifty set gets up to these days."

So this is about you, she thought, uneasily observing this wild card in Fuad's deck. Recklessness might be the one thing she could trust about him.

"And here we are," he said. His laptop showed a page from Banque Rothorn. "Our friend Mister Gubinov is quite wealthy—too wealthy for a mid-level gangbanger. He's squirreled plenty of cheddar out of Russia, trading in his rubles for dollars. It's likely, though, that he's a conduit for buddies back in Moscow, you know, minding the store."

"Who is this Viktor?"

"Kind of a Fuad-type bro for the Russian mob. Him and Ingerholz go back a couple of years. You aren't the first lady they've assaulted."

"Did Fuad see it? The video?"

"You know he did."

She felt a pang of depression. The room seemed to turn a bluer hue. "I don't really feel comfortable talking to you about that."

"Then don't. Save it for your shrink or your girlfriends. I'm not here for a good cry, Penelope. I'm here to help you get payback. Where you want the cheddar to go?"

"What do you mean, go?"

"His money, stupid. He's got twenty-three million big ones in there and if it goes poof, it's not like he'll go complaining to the police. That's a career's worth of blood money that I've hacked. And if it's not all his, and it goes walking, Vik's gonna have a helluva time trying to explain it to the Moscow dons. So tell me, where you want your share?"

"My share?"

"Sure. Fifty-fifty."

She stared at the screen. "I don't know, Stack, this is all kinda fast. If this guy's Russian mafia, he's not going to react by calling a lawyer. I mean, is this really someone we want to piss off?"

"Yes."

"I know, but...Did Chuck Wisner ever figure out what happened to your colleagues' money?"

Stack grinned. "You ask good questions, Penny."

"Does Fuad know what you're up to?"

"That question, on the other hand, was dumb. You know what the consequences would be if he did. For both of us."

Something about going behind Fuad's back felt...right. Like she wanted to see where that might lead. Like she was back in Sante Fe finding new ways to push her father to the brink.

Penny looked at his computer screen. "How did you learn about Viktor?"

"Took a while. That phone of his was a burner, not much to go on, but enough, especially with the video of him in the Ritz. It rang a few bells on some black-market facial-recognition databases. Once I got his name, it was just a matter of time before I could get his aliases, financial statements and travel records, especially once I could correlate it with Ingy's movements. I think Viktor is actually playing Manfred just like Fuad was."

She tried to understand what that meant. "So this creep is a mobster who was pretending to be Ingerholz's colleague? Why?"

"Whoever Vik works for, they be blackmailing Ingy too. But instead of taking Ingy's money, I think Vik is making him share all of those hookers. Maybe they actually bonded over the rape thing, I don't know, but what I do know is, they been doing it for almost a year. I wish I had known before you got sent in."

"Yeah," she said quietly. "A real bromance." She frowned at his open laptop. "Stack..."

"Yes?"

"What's Ingerzholz's role in all of this? Why is everyone able to blackmail him?"

"Well, he is a prominent member of society with a side interest in fancy hoes. Since Vik got his fangs in him, though, Ingy's portfolio's taken on some interesting positions. Way short some stocks."

"Oh yeah?"

"Like he thinks a certain Franco-German oil company might just fail to meet earnings expectations. Schuman Corporation. And I've seen the bank statements: Viktor's bank account is providing the margin. He's financing Ingy's shorts."

"Let me guess," she said. "Schuman Corp is Fuad's client on this job?"

Stack smiled. "Who knows? What I do know is, take away Vik's deposit money, and when there comes a margin call on his trade, Ingy can't pay. Then it's time for the lawyers. It'll make for delicious watching. What do you say, Penny? Twelve large we're talking here. Kill two birds with one hack because you rollin' with Stack."

Penny fidgeted. "The Russian mafia would come after us."

Stack said, "I've set up a series of dummy accounts, untraceable connections and fake companies in six offshore centers. The only way Vik can ever figure out where his money went is if he hires me to find it."

Penny chuckled at his bravado. "Okay, whatever, Grandpa. I don't want the money."

He raised an eyebrow over the rim of his glasses. "You sure?"

"Yeah, I'm sure."

"Never met an evil maid who didn't want the money." He picked up Aeschylus. "What you underlined here? 'And I, I revel.'"

"I appreciate what you're trying to do, Stack. I really do. And yeah, I hate this guy. I don't know if I can do another job now because of him. Every time I go outside I think I see him. And I'm mad, man; I'm so mad I could slice off his balls and laugh. But this…"

"It's safe, Penny. He'll never know it was us."

Part of her wondered what Stack was fishing for. He'd

given her a clue about himself. Getting her bank details for transferring money would open her own identity. Mutually assured identification. But her skepticism wasn't what gave her pause.

She looked at the book. Every act of revenge in it seemed to stoke more violence. The Greeks didn't have a law to put a stop to things and levy blame. But what was the law to someone like her? She'd been asking for it, the lawman would tell her: she'd deserved what she got, because she was a free woman, too free. No judge would defend her, no priest would absolve her—not even if she faced an enemy of utter cruelty. "On the one hand I don't want the Russian mob after me. But doing it this way...I don't need to get back at the mafia. I need to get back at Viktor."

"And Ingerholz."

"If you empty his bank account, Stack, Viktor wouldn't know it was me. For all he knows I'm just some nobody stripper from Canada." Hatred bloomed in her heart. "When I get mine back, I'm going to make sure he knows who did it."

Stack pursed his lips, nodding as he digested it. Then he solemnly clapped his hands. "Your call, Pen. Respect."

She didn't trust him, but she admired his skills. And just maybe was willing to give him a little credit for coming here. He had actually put her in a better mood. She gave him a peck on the cheek. "But thanks."

He finished his vodka orange. "Well, then, I guess I'll be off."

"You can stay if you want. We can hang out, watch some TV or go get lunch."

"Nah."

At once, the loneliness of the past few weeks crushed her.

That old familiar blade of grief made a stab, and she had the idea that her father was in the living room at that moment. Loving her, no questions asked. The fact that he wasn't there, that he hadn't been in her life for ten years, made her incredibly sad.

It made her want to change her mind.

"Wait," she said.

He halted by her door, laptop in the crook of his arm.

A new urgency had muscled its way into her thoughts.

"Someone else should get the money."

"Who?"

"My sister."

"Penny Lee has a sister?"

"Believe it or not. Before I was Penny Lee."

"Go on."

"Her name is Vivian Tang. Unless she got married."

"I'm listening."

Penny said, "But she can't just wake up one day and find twelve million dollars in her bank account."

He sat back down. "What's her occupation?"

"I don't know. I dropped all contact a long time ago."

"Prudent."

"How about she wins the lottery?"

"Does she play the lottery?"

"Beats me. Can we make one up and, uh, mail her a ticket or something?"

"This is getting complicated. More Fuad's line of work."

"Come on, geezer, I thought you wanted a challenge. You're the computer genius, think of something. It couldn't be a real lottery anyway. We have to invent one."

"Where she at now?"

118

"Last I heard, Santa Fe, New Mexico."

"You know her social security number, anything like that?"

"No."

"You got some remorse you wanna clear up with your *hermana*?"

"No," Penny said. "I haven't thought of her much, ever. She was a loser when we were kids and she's probably still a boring nobody. If you think it's funny to rip off Viktor and his bosses, then it's even funnier if she's the one who gets his money. Besides, there's no connection between us; she thinks I'm dead. Fuad made sure of that a long time ago. So nobody gets hurt."

Stack thought about it for a minute before letting himself out.

She spent the next month alone and quiet, not answering emails or texts, just going for long bike rides along the Corniche or doing aikido solo practices: forward and backward rolls on her tatami mats, wrist locks, *jo* staff patterns, *shikko* knee walking.

One day she returned to find a piece of paper slipped under her door. It was a note with three words: "News from home."

She burned the paper in an ashtray and Googled her sister's name. Sure enough, she found a clip of Santa Fe TV news from two days ago. An ecstatic Vivian Tang was holding up a giant replica of a check from an organization called the Christian Children's Salvation Mission. The TV reporter rambled on about the big reward for being a charitable neighbor.

It was strange seeing her sister on the computer screen. They had never been close. They were four years apart, so Vivian was still a girl when Penny—Melody—went to boarding school as a rambunctious, boy-crazy teenager.

Penny scarcely recognized Vivian now: they had never looked alike, but adulthood had forged them into different identities. She felt detached from this stranger with the chubby cheeks and the more obviously Asian features. Their German mother had delivered them both, but Mom's chromosomes had lost out the second time around.

Looks aside, Penny's sibling appeared to be enjoying her life of quiet desperation in American suburbia. The reporter asked, "So what are you going to do with the money, Vivian?"

This is really happening.

"Well, I never expected anything like this from the baking raffle at church. So I'm giving most of it away, back to charities in our community."

Penny winced. *I should have taken the cash.*

"You're not going to keep even a little of it for yourself?" asked the reporter.

"Well, my boyfriend—I guess it's official now, I should call him my fiancé—Steve and I are planning to get married next year. We've always dreamed of visiting Italy, so we're going to Tuscany and we're going to have a blowout wedding!"

12

Five-gram shot

Penny told Fuad about how she and Stack had robbed Viktor Gubinov. Lines of angst revealed themselves across his brow. His left eye developed a tick that she hadn't noticed before. And then his expression—at first serene as a mountainside—crumbled under the gathering force of an avalanche.

She finished and tucked her bare feet beneath her legs, because she couldn't stand the cold of the floor any longer. The study felt like the cave it had once been.

"Fuad..."

"Shut up." His eyes darted around. He was trying to think but was too stunned to focus. He stood up, clenched and unclenched his fists, and paced. "Don't say a word. You have no right to even breathe the same air as me."

"I get why you're upset—"

"Upset is when Max pisses on the carpet. This is...beyond. Well beyond."

"Viktor found out who we are, Fuad. He knew how to reach me and Stack when we were exposed. He pinpointed our positions. He smuggled his men and guns into the Burj al

Arab. He's sent a man to my apartment here...he knows my name. He called me Penelope, not Veronique or Julie. He raped me and now he's trying to kill me."

"How did he know where to find you?"

"Funny, I had the same question for you."

"Shut up!" he raged. "Your little game has exposed my entire network! And you dare accuse me..."

That ground was too treacherous, even for her. "Then the only answer is Stack made a mistake when he hacked Viktor's account. Left a trail and Viktor's friends were able to—"

"Not friends, Penny...the bloody Russian mafia. *Ya lahwy!*"

She had no answer to that.

Fuad stepped away to regain his composure. He regarded the wall of black and white photographs. "You know who this is?"

She joined him. An official in a medaled military uniform and a fez was pictured shaking hands with a regal-looking man in a suit and fedora. She had seen these photos many times. "Your great-grandfather."

"Yes," Fuad said. "As Christians, our family could not serve the Turks formally, but my great-grandfather was a trusted advisor and courier for the mufti in charge of the Levant."

"He was a spy."

"The Chamouns have been an important family in this country for centuries. Never openly, because if you raise your head too high above the parapet, you invite a bullet. But we have always been here, helping our masters maintain stability and peace."

"Is that what you do, Fuad? Maintain stability and peace?"

"What *we* do, Penny. We live in age when the muftis and mullahs don't amount to a hill of beans. Today the giant corporations are the true sultans."

She shook her head. "That's pathetic."

"What?"

"I work for cash, Fuad. Lots of cash, so that I can live the rest of my life the way I please. Just the way you taught me. So let's not pretend that we're all patriots working for the greater good, okay?"

"I work for my family," he said coldly. "The Chamouns have lived in this compound for six hundred years. We are survivors, Penny, thanks be to Christ and to our wiles. We carry the weight of history and tradition, something that you Americans will never appreciate."

"Don't patronize me. I've lived here for ten years."

"It is not in your blood."

"You want bloodlines? I'm half Chinese. Five thousand years of culture."

"None of which seems to have rubbed off on you."

"Tell me this, Fuad. What if Viktor knew about the Dubai operation from some source other than Stack?"

"Impossible."

"That's what Stack said about Viktor knowing who cleaned out his bank account."

Fuad placed his face in his hands. The lion looked old. "After everything I've done for you, Penny..."

"Who was the client for Dubai? What was on Timur's laptop that they wanted so badly?"

Fuad stared at the photographs of his ancestors. Penny began to collect her things.

"You will stay for dinner," Fuad said.

"I'm starving. I'll stay for lunch if you let Etienne back in."

"And then where will you go?"

123

"I don't know. I can't go back to my apartment. Ever." The pile of spare clothes, phones and chargers, passports and cash, was now all that she owned. Maybe the house in Japan was still safe. Most of her life savings were trapped in the Beirut apartment, though, and she wasn't sure how she could ever sell it.

Penny Lee was little more now than a handful of forged identities and contents that fit inside one red backpack.

Fuad, still entranced by his family photographs, said, "This Viktor Gubinov knows too much. This won't end until one of you is dead." Then he left and she heard the click of a turning lock.

She wondered as he left whether he might be tempted to hand her over to the Russians. Fuad had mentored her for ten years. Sometimes she liked to think that counted for something human; that she was something to him more than just an asset.

But he had just made it clear that he didn't consider her family. And if she wasn't family, then she was disposable.

She shouldn't be surprised. She had no family. Just a long-forgotten sister...who was about to have a big wedding...with money taken from...

Maybe that's how Viktor had figured it out. Instead of wondering who had taken the money, the Russian mafia used an algorithm to find out who around the world might be enjoying sudden windfalls, no matter how seemingly unrelated to Penny and Stack. From there it might have been possible for him to connect Melody Tang to Penny Lee.

It still didn't explain how Viktor had traced them to Dubai, though.

Etienne came in with the tray of food. "You must be

famished," he said.

"It's good to see you, Etienne." She meant it.

He blushed. "It's always good to see you, Penny."

She should share her insight with Fuad, but right now her stomach was in charge. "So what have you brought me?"

He lifted the lid to reveal a plate of mezze. Hunger seized her and she greedily scooped baba ghanoush with a slice of pita. She sensed motion behind her as she stuffed it in her mouth but was too slow to react. Something stung her neck and cold, hard mercury shuddered down her spine.

Etienne squawked. Penny spun around and reached for her throat, not to eject the hypodermic needle but because her muscles were freezing up and she couldn't breathe. Fog closed in, obscuring Fuad's stern mien.

* * *

For the second time that day she came to on the bed in the cave-turned-study. But day had surrendered to night. The room was cold. The only light came from the window looking into the front of the compound.

She moved to touch her aching neck. There was a metallic rattle and the handcuffs made themselves known. She could sit up but her wrists were chained to the steel flanks of the hospital bed.

Her feet touched something metal and cold. She nudged it and it moved. Leaning forward she realized someone, probably Etienne, had left the tray of mezze at the foot of the bed.

She tested the handcuffs with some aikido wrist techniques, but the cuffs were too tight. Eating without her hands was going to be a challenge, but hunger trumped all. She embraced the tray with her legs and used her heels to push it into her lap. She pushed the lid off and it banged to the floor. Not that it mattered if the Chamouns knew she was awake. Leaning forward and using her feet and toes to manipulate pieces of food, she began to eat. Penny didn't know if the food was left as a kindness or to be degrading, as she buried her face into the platter, getting eggplant and hummus all over her nose and chin. She wolfed it down with a convict's haste.

Someone approached outside. The door opened and Fuad came in. The compound lights outside framed him in a silver halo and she could see his breath mist in the clean night air. He moved to the table and switched on a lamp.

Fuad pulled a chair beside her and sat down. He had regained his composure, but the deep facial lines remained, as though he had aged ten years in the space of a few hours. He steepled his fingers, reviewing what he was going to say.

"I mean it when I say you have been like a daughter to me."

Penny didn't respond.

He looked pained. "The Buribaev operation was some of the finest intelligence work I've ever seen. You caught him and put him exactly where we needed him. The data download was a success. But what impresses me is not just the technical excellence. What impresses me is your total commitment. The focus you brought to bear over many difficult weeks is commendable. And in light of the psychological implications of the London operation, your ability to set your personal fears aside to take on Buribaev is truly remarkable. You are the best field agent I have ever worked with."

Penny smudged the gook off her face with her shoulder.

"Which makes your personal lapses with Gubinov all the more frustrating and...and...regrettable. Unprofessional."

He looked at her directly.

"Unforgivable."

Penny looked down at her messy lap. *So this is it.* She wasn't frightened yet. Just angry.

"I explained as much of this as I could to the client. I didn't mention your name and they didn't want to know. All they asked was whether it was a member of my family, a Chamoun."

She waited.

"I said no, it was not a Chamoun, it was a field agent. They have requested your termination."

Nothing personal, right Fuad? You're just serving the greater good.

So you see, Penny," Fuad said, "I have no choice. You have brought this upon yourself. And it makes me very, very sad."

Penny said nothing.

"I suppose you deserve to know the name of your executioner. Michel L'Orancourt."

She hid her surprise. The client was the chief operating officer of Schuman, a state-linked oil major. The client could just as well have been the CEO of a pharmaceuticals company or a chemicals maker or a nuclear power operator, anyone who needed something done that was hard and dark.

But she waited. Fuad, who never revealed anything about his business, now couldn't stop himself from talking.

"Timur's laptop contained data concerning oil fields and refineries in Iraq and Syria, and which militia or government controls what. All of the factions in the war rely on oil for finance, so it still gets pumped and refined and taken around the country in little batches by truck. KazPetro thought it had the relationships and access to pipelines to become a bulk buyer and on-sell it to the Chinese, who are desperate for

127

energy supplies. Thanks to you, Schuman will try to corner the business instead."

No matter who was getting blown up on the ground, the money games continued. That's what paid her bills.

Fuad stood up. "I injected you with a gram of sodium thiopental. I can give you another injection of five grams, which should induce a coma within ten seconds. If you would prefer another way to die, now is the time for your request."

He was ready to throw her out with the trash. Fuad reached inside his blazer and withdrew a syringe.

"I have information you need," she said.

"I doubt that, Penny."

"Manfred Ingerholz was financing trades shorting Schuman stock."

The needle's tip touched her flesh. She didn't flinch.

"He is a trader. He shorts many stocks."

"Not with money posted by an account at Banque Rothorn owned by Viktor Gubninov."

That stopped him. "What?"

The door opened. Etienne, grasping the scene, stammered in French, "Brother, there is trouble outside."

"Not now, Etienne."

"A family of Syrian refugees is approaching."

"So? Send the beggars on their way."

"I think they are being used. As human shields."

"I don't care! Get—"

The outside flashed yellow and something, some great force, shook the cave. The humans inside rattled around like dice in a cup. The noise was an all-consuming roar, blotting out the Chamoun brothers' cries.

Penny looked out the window and saw a tower of flame. She

couldn't hold back a little wry smile. "Hello, Viktor."

Fuad ran for the door, Etienne on his heels. They collided clownishly at the exit. Fuad cursed in Arabic and pushed Etienne out of his way.

"Etienne," she called.

He turned.

"Be careful."

Etienne nodded gravely and followed his brother.

Penny raised her legs into a shoulder stand, then dropped her feet backward and jumped to the floor behind the bed. With her feet on the ground and her hands cuffed to the sides, she was bent forward, but at least she was upright. She pushed the bed before her so she could get a look out the window.

The dogs' barking filled the interlude and then she listened to the fugue: the quadrille of machine guns, followed by a bagatelle of return fire from the Chamouns. Something ablaze, presumably a car, blocked the main exit. Shadows flit about the hellishly lit compound; shooting and then a bullet whammed the wall outside her window.

She pushed the bed toward the room's sole table lamp, maneuvering her hand beside the chain. She clicked it off before anyone else could take a shot at her silhouette.

Now the cuffs. She closed her eyes and tried to relax every sinew in her arms and wrists. She had tried this before to no avail.

She had a hand half-twisted through a cuff when the scraping led to bleeding. She bit her lip and groaned and kept pulling, loosening, pulling some more.

The door opened. She could only see the outline of a man.

"Penny?"

"Etienne," she said.

"What are you doing?" he asked in French.

"Trying to get the hell out of here."

"Fuad...they've shot Fuad!"

Another explosion as loud as the first shook the compound. Viktor had loaded another car with explosives and sent it careening at the walled entrance. Etienne's form shuddered.

"Etienne, can you unlock these handcuffs?"

"My brother!"

"Etienne, come with me. We'll leave here together, okay? Just you and me."

He wavered as another round of gunfire filled the compound.

"Etienne, if Fuad's dead then we're both alone now."

"Just...stop," he pleaded.

"That's why you came in here, Etienne, instead of fighting. You don't have to hide your feelings for me from your family any longer."

She heard the jangle of keys. He unlocked one wrist. "You're bleeding."

"I'll be okay."

He undid the other cuff and Penny embraced him. He put his arms around her awkwardly.

"Penny, I..."

"Don't say it," she said, kissing his cheek. He lunged to kiss her on the mouth, but she dodged his face. "Later."

The firefight was getting closer. Bullets screamed across the compound. Penny threw off the frock, exposing her nudity that Etienne could half-see in the shifting light of spreading fires. He stood mesmerized as she put on her clothes. The warmth of socks and shoes was a blessing. She grabbed her backpack, doing a quick check of the contents. Everything was there but the Beretta. She slid her arms through the straps.

"How do we get out of here?" she asked.

"Passageway out the back: leads through a tunnel and takes you out at Arsoun."

"Out the back where?"

"You have to climb over the terrace wall."

"Then let's go."

She followed Etienne out of the cavern into the compound. She saw one of the cousins, Jamal, sprawled on the cobble-stones, half of his bald head spread behind him in a cone of bloody meat. A Rottweiler's corpse lay further on, toward where the Chamouns kept their cars. The Ducati bikes were aflame.

Shame about the Ducatis.

The house sat nestled within a curve of mountainside, up a path that led over the three doors leading to various caverns, the ancient Chamoun hideout. Etienne started up this way. She glanced back. People were still shooting, but she saw a figure climb onto the outer parapet. The flames illuminated Viktor Gubinov's broad features, the harelip a dark slash. He fired a machine gun wildly, heedless of a shotgun blast that came from Isa, crouching behind the trunk of the compound's cedar.

Etienne ran for the house.

Two more figures joined Viktor on the wall.

Penny followed Etienne and pulled up short.

"Traitor!"

Fuad was shot but he wasn't dead. He stood between his brother and the house, a sawed-off shotgun in one hand and his other thrust in what looked like a hastily made sling, stained by blood. He must have taken the bullet and retreated to the house for a quick mend, leaving Jamal and Isa to defend the walls. Now he was making his return.

He raised the shotgun at her. Etienne slapped it aside as it roared flame. The shot pellets whooshed past her cheek. Penny leapt on Fuad and together they crashed to the ground.

"Brother," Etienne stammered.

She grabbed Fuad's wrist and slammed it on the cobblestones, forcing him to release the shotgun, but she didn't sense the headbutt. She just felt it. Not just felt it, experienced it as a ripple of sheer blinding pain in her forehead. It was a glancing blow that missed crushing her nose, but it was strong enough to send her rolling on the ground, moaning in confusion.

A shuffling, a "No!"

She got to her knees, her head swimming. Her fingers found something sleek and plasticine. A cell phone.

Fuad raised his good hand in a grotesque triumph.

The syringe.

She caught his chop with both hands and traded stares with the tip of the needle. Fuad had the leverage, pushing down with all of his weight. She tried *kotegaeshi*, reversed wrist, but he was too strong for that.

Knee walking, *shikko*, was a basic form of aikido training. She moved her knees toward Fuad and relaxed her grip on his wrist, giving it a subtle shake. The combined effect sent a wave rippling through his arm and the needle thrust forward past her ear. He lost his balance and Penny raised herself onto her feet. She guided his wrist around, up and over her head. They danced to the music of gunfire, as close as lovers, face to face.

"Let go," she told him, meaning the syringe.

His face clenched into a grimace and he resisted her lead. Bullets defaced the walls around them. He broke free of her grip and with a backhanded swipe sent Penny to the ground.

Fuad roared. Then he looked down in amazement at the syringe buried in his chest.

"Penny," he said, "what have you done?" He collapsed.

"Brother!" Etienne cried, cradling Fuad's quivering body.

Viktor was crossing the compound, still exchanging fire with Isa. Penny called Etienne's name but didn't wait to see if he'd follow. She pocketed Fuad's cell phone, the one he had lost in the confusion.

He wouldn't need it.

III

TUSCANY

13

A ward of spies

Penny had used the Thérèse Nulty passport to fly to Paris on the first flight out of Beirut.

For a day and a night she contemplated doing nothing but this: bathe in her five-star hotel room with its view of the Eiffel Tower, drinking straight from the bottle of Krug. It cost plenty of Shokay Kasym's cash but she didn't mind, not a whit. She could swallow a bottle of pills right here, go out in luxury.

But that would mean Viktor would win. And while she wasn't interested in a match-up of egos, letting him get away with this was one thing no Fury would allow.

She needed answers. She didn't think Manfred Ingerholz would have many, but he only needed to have one.

Early the next morning she rented a Porsche two-seater and reached Geneva that afternoon. She could tell she was in the right place because she had parked by a big lake across from a square bland office building named for Geneva Partners Capital Management.

The city's lakefront boasted a high fountain jet that plumed like a sail made of money. She had arrived with certainty of

137

mission but glancing at the jet reminded her of all the times she had gazed at it from a different point of view.

How many times had she looked down at the city from those high green mountains? Before Penelope Lee had been created... her final days, although she hadn't known it, of being Melody Tang...

Melody took her seat in the principal's office, screwed on her best mask of defiance and tick-tocked her leg, because what's the worst they could say about her—that she liked boys?

The principal, Madame Roussel, expressed her displeasure by lowering her glasses a finger's width down her nose. Melody stilled her roving limb, but only to get this over with. Behind the principal's desk, bay windows revealed green mountains, sunlight playing on the flat belly of the lake and sparkling in the water jet within the curve of the distant city. The vista promised a bigger and less boring world.

"Do you know why you are here?" Roussel asked.

Melody had broken curfew last night and come back stinking of basement-bar smoke. She had finally made it with that guitar player and had hoped the acrid stink would cover up other, more loamy smells. She still tingled, a feeling that was worth whatever lame punishment the principal was about to dish out.

"Yes, madame."

"I don't think you do." There was of course expulsion. That would be the one thing she could never shrug off to her father. But...well, it was a stupid school anyway. She gave Roussel a little more chin.

"You have visitors."

Which mean...Daddy was here? Ready to take her home? Maybe she was in for a yelling, but the prospect of getting out of there was all too appealing.

But Roussel had said visitors—plural. So that didn't mean her father, unless he had brought her sister along, or suddenly acquired a girlfriend. Neither felt right.

"You are wondering who, I suppose?"

Mel nodded.

"So am I." Roussel pushed her glasses back up. "I am also wondering what people will think of the Institut, if we are training young women to be so ill-mannered."

Melody was like so whatever.

"What do you have to say for yourself, young lady?"

"I don't...nothing."

"'Nothing.' Miss Melody, I'm curious. When your father sent you here, were you excited or dismayed?"

"I was, um..."

"Um is not a word in any language."

"Sorry, madame. I was excited."

"As I had also believed. Etiquette is at the heart of Institut Château-Montclaire's education. And what is etiquette, Miss Melody?"

"Polite behavior in society."

"A code of polite behavior in society," Roussel corrected, and Melody thought, Here it comes. "And a code is a set of social rules and standards. Curfews for women under the age of eighteen are an important part of the learning of etiquette at ICM."

"Yes, madame."

"I believe one reason your father placed you here was in response to your lapses in discipline at...what was it...Española Valley High School. You have great potential, Miss Melody. You have a fine mind, an excellent memory. You show great aptitude for multiculturalism and absorbing protocol. And your training in... ballet, isn't it, yes?" The principal lowered her reading glasses to look at her. "Yes, you are a natural athlete who has taken well to all of the social sports. You have the raw material to make for an exemplary graduate of the Institut. And yet here we are, you and I, in my office, when you should be taking your exam on European table manners."

She could picture Dad's face when they would next meet, if not now, then at the Santa Fe airport. He'd be wearing that look of disappointment, the one that over the past few years had etched itself into a state of permanence. She'd once told him it made him look like a coolie, you know, the kind of Chinese slaving away in America cowboy towns, laying down steel rails. Insulting his heritage was always a reliable button-pusher. And Melody knew what he'd say, too, the sad sack. He'd apologize and blame himself for Melody's screw-ups: "I don't know what to do with you, Mel; I'd be a better dad if your mother was still alive."

If your mother *were* still alive, the ICM-trained student corrected him. But no image of her mom came to Melody. Her mother, Frieda Schalk, had come from Germany before moving to the United States, and this golden Valkyrie had married the China-born Jonas. West meets East, an all-American story, rah rah rah. Frau Tang had borne Jonas two Eurasian daughters in the United States but spoiled the happy-ever-after by dying when Mel had turned eight and her sister four.

"I promise I won't break curfew again," Melody told the principal.

"You can be sure your truancy will be reported."

"Yeah, I'm sure my dad'll really care." A bluff, but, whatever.

"It's not your father who has come."

That curve ball sent Melody's mind spinning. "I thought according to your code, madame, that visitors were prohibited to us young ladies without written authorization from our parents."

"You are quite right." The glasses went back to the bridge of Roussel's nose. Her matronly fingers raised a piece of paper from Melody's file and passed it to her. "Here it is."

The document said in English and French that the Chamoun family was appointed to be Melody's guardian in the event of Jonas Tang's absence, incapacitation, or death, and that they were to be given rights and access to Melody on a status equating to parenthood.

Signed, Jonas Tang.

"What the..." She had to force herself to silence the curse word. She handed the form back. "I don't know what this is all about. I never heard of any Chamoun family. This is such a forgery. Obviously."

"A lawyer from Geneva notarized this document here, in this very office," Roussel said, tapping a stamp on the paper.

"You're lying, you're making this up. Who the hell are the Chamouns?"

"Language, young lady." But from the reddening of the principal's cheeks, she too looked ready to let out a few choice words. "They are here. If you have questions, you can ask them directly. Wait."

The principal backed out of her desk and crossed her office. She opened the door and Melody stood. The moment had the quality of a dream, unreal but compelling. In walked two people, a man and a woman, both tall and trim, with olive complexions. They dressed elegantly. He wore a brown wool suit and tie and boasted a movie star's head of hair that was turning to silver. She equaled his height and wore a business suit with pinstripes that was tailored for her hips and curves—although these seemed in short supply, Melody observed.

"Monsieur Chamoun, Madame Chamoun," said Roussel, shak-

ing their hands.

"Mizz," the woman corrected.

A spinster, *Melody thought, taking renewed pride in last night's assignation.* I could have guessed.

"This is Melody Tang," Roussel said.

"A pleasure," the man said, extending his hand. Melody shook it, having no clue what to say. She offered her palm to the spinster Chamoun, and unlike the smiling man's hand, hers was as soft and warm as a glacier.

Melody protested to Roussel, "Madame, I don't know these people. They're no friends of my father's. I've never seen them in my life."

"It is true, we have not met before," Mr. Chamoun said. He had an accent, but she didn't know what kind. "I realize this must feel very strange. But I assure you, your father and I were once very good friends."

Were once?

"What are you doing here?" Melody asked. "Is it because of my..." Truancy? *She looked to the principal for succor. "Did you call them?"*

"No," Roussel said, "they have simply arrived."

"They're not here because I've been in trouble?" The terror of what that implied churned her insides, but Melody fought it down, because there was no way she could imagine being truly abandoned.

"Trouble, eh?" Mr. Chamoun said.

"A matter of disrespecting curfew," Roussel declared.

Mizz Chamoun narrowed her eyes. *"So, you've been a naughty girl."* Melody *sensed an amusement in the woman's demeanor. Like a cat licking its lips in anticipation.*

Roussel, perhaps aware that her clean-lined office had fallen into invisible disarray, opened her mouth to say something.

Tell them to leave, Melody wanted to urge the principal. She was sure the spinster was sizing her up, noting her breasts and hips. She's jealous. *But Melody had never seen a cat look jealous, and this one didn't now either.*

The man spoke first. "Principal Roussel, at the risk of abusing your hospitality, could my sister and I have a moment in privacy with Melody?"

"Of course," *Roussel said.* "Please, make yourselves comfortable. I'll be back in ten minutes."

"Thank you," *the man said and the principal left, looking relieved to be out of the discussion, and closed the door.* Mr. Chamoun said, "Let's all have a seat, shall we?"

They gathered around the sofas at the other end of the office, Melody alone facing the siblings across the coffee table.

"I don't know who you think you're fooling, but I know a pair of liars when I see one," *Mel snapped.* "My father would have told me about this...this...stupid thing. That stupid document. It's a load of..."

"Melody," *the sister said,* "we have news."

"That's right," *the brother added.* "Tragic news."

The temperature in the room skidded down an icy slope.

"Like, whatever," *Melody muttered.*

"Daliyah," *the man addressed his sister,* "perhaps we should emphasize the positive first. Don't worry about losing your place here, Melody."

"Yes," *the sister purred,* "we want you to complete your lessons."

"What is it?" *Melody blurted.* "What do you want with me?"

Good question. She knew the what but not the why—why her. The Chamouns had worked hard to distract her from ever really asking. She had been stupid enough to go along because

143

the alternative would mean too much grief, too much hurt.

Entering Geneva Partners Capital Management's lobby involved metal detectors flanked by security men. She passed through and walked to the reception desk. "I'm here for Manfred Ingerholz," she said in French. "Tell him it's Viktor Gubinov."

The receptionist murmured on a phone. After a few minutes, the lady came back to her. "He'll see you. Please register here and I'll need your ID, please."

She signed the registrar in Viktor's name but said, "I don't have ID."

"I'm sorry but—"

"Manfred will vouch for me."

The receptionist called back and there was a hushed to and fro and she resentfully handed Penny a visitor's lanyard. Penny walked through the turnstiles to the elevators, where a young woman waited for her, wearing a navy blazer, slacks, sensible shoes, and an office ID hung around her neck. The attendant escorted Penny to the fifth floor and into an empty, windowless meeting room. "He'll be with you in a mom—" Penny squeezed her unconscious and laid her in a chair, binding her hands behind its back with the cords from the table's conference phone.

A few minutes later, she strode through the office wearing the woman's ID, which as she guessed had an electronic passkey that opened the door at the end of the hall. She crossed through what she supposed was a trading floor, a cavernous room filled with row after row of people staring intently at towers of screens with lots of charts and graphs. No one paid her any mind until she reached the far end where she could see Manfred Ingerholz in his corner office, the door open.

Ingerholz froze when he spotted her. He blinked with disbelief. Then he reached for the phone on his desk.

"Hang up, Manny, or I tell everyone about our date at the Ritz."

He looked out at the floor. She was betting he would do anything to avoid a scene. He hung up. "There's a room..."

"Not good enough."

"The roof is just two flights up."

It was empty up there, just a few potted plants and ashtrays. Traders normally didn't have time for cigarette breaks. The view of the lake and the staid buildings of civilization oozed old, old money. He folded his arms, still searching for what to say.

"Viktor makes me buy girls in public places," he said. "You're not a normal girl, though, are you?"

"Why?"

"It's blackmail, to keep me making trades in the market. He wants these trades to be from me, not him."

"Trades like shorting Schuman stock?"

"What are you, CIA?"

She didn't know much about finance or stocks, but she knew that if a big hedge fund was taking bets against Schuman, it was like a form of warfare. "You do this more and more, for Viktor? Make these trades?"

"Yes. My risk officer just quit on me. We're breaching all our mandates." His façade was cracking. "My wife doesn't know a thing about this."

"We can keep it our little secret, Manny," she said, "and you can keep your charity board seats and keep your three little kids in their prep schools, if you realize that I will have no hesitation in hurting you."

He regarded Geneva. "You can threaten me all you like, Julie, or whatever your name is. But you will never scare me like Viktor can. Nobody's that sociopathic, not you, not whoever you work for."

"Where's he now?"

"Viktor? Why do you want to know?" He saw the look in her eyes. "It's your funeral, then. He's told me to meet him this weekend in Tuscany."

"Italy?" That rang a bell...

"He makes me join him on his...activities. He's paranoid about the money and the accounts so he keeps me close. Shows me things I never want to see again."

"We've always dreamed of visiting Italy, so we're going Tuscany. We're going to have a blowout wedding!"

She had to go. Right. Now.

"Do yourself a favor, Manny, and tell Viktor you're feeling sick this weekend."

Penny raced to her waiting Porsche and careened out of there like a NASCAR desperado.

14

The devil's prayer

She reached the medieval hill town of San Gimignano around 9 p.m. She didn't stop to eat or find accommodation. She followed her GPS to where the villa should be, a further ten minute's drive. The roads were good but narrow, the hilly curves treacherous. She slowed down finally, creeping along until she got close. She'd need to keep the Porsche out of sight. There was a nearby village, the sort of place that by day had a little piazza where tourists would enjoy lunches, but now was dark and quiet. She parked. From here the walk back to the villa would take an hour.

She followed the route memorized from the car's GPS until she reached a gravelly turnoff. The manor was down there, at the end, hidden among sunflowers and bare persimmon trees, a quaint building of uneven windows and narrow doors, one end connected to a Romanesque chapel. That's how it was described on the wedding's online announcement, anyway.

Heart-shaped balloons, silver and pink, hovered over a birdbath, their synthetic colors catching the moon's light.

She walked to the windows, inviting with their soft yellow

glow. Laughter. Glimpses of kids inside, adults chatting. She didn't recognize anyone.

Vivian's getting married tomorrow. The getting married part was too banal to matter, but the idea of a sister...now that was something.

One of Penny's earliest memories was of her mother returning from the hospital with a bundle that was Vivian. The scene was just an image, and who knew if it was even real. Her father had told her this was the baby—this thing that had been in mommy's tummy, this was her sister.

She had been four. Years later, in a moment of exasperation, her father had told her that for the next few weeks, Melody would leave any room if her mom came in with the baby. She had no memory of this protest movement, but hearing it from her father hadn't surprised her. It felt about right.

Four years old. Formative. First memories, impressions wedded to gut feelings. True or false, it's what she had decided had happened, if she ever thought about it. Penny's inaugural, bona fide memory, was of ostracizing her sister.

Four years old—that was Vivian's age when their mother disappeared. What kind of formative experience was that?

As a teenager, Penny's main obsession turned to boys, weed and skipping school. The only pursuit she had maintained that pleased her father was ballet. She had enjoyed the physical challenge and the sense that she was maintaining some kind of control over a body that was otherwise completely unpredictable—menstruation, breasts, hips, all of these developments out of her hands, with no mother to explain it, a father too clueless to help. Penny quickly realized the effect these changes had on the boys, though, and even the other girls, and lost no time exploiting them. Ballet became her training ground. She might not know what the next change her body might bring, but she sure could put it to use.

Eventually she learned to create the effect she wanted, and only later realized she was manipulating other people in a sad, confused bid to get her father's attention. Jonas Tang was a composed man with an important job, but his girls befuddled him. He never ceased to dote on them, no matter what torment Melody put him through. Leaving a tampon in the sink, a cigarette lighter on the kitchen table, a crumpled beer can on the counter...a condom on her nightstand.

The idea of having Vivian trailing her had horrified teenage Melody.

It might have turned out differently if Vivian had inherited a luckier combination of Mom's Teutonic cheekbones and golden hair, and dad's slender Chinese frame. Vivian received her genetic gifts backwards. She was more obviously Asian, unlike Penny's seamless blend, and had been endowed with Mom's fleshiness and Dad's receding chin. Had Viv had been a beauty, Penny might have taken her under her wing and taught her a thing or two.

Lucky for you I didn't, Sis.

When the Chamouns told Melody that her dad had died, she spent weeks crying and hissing at the instructors at her Swiss finishing school. Even now, approaching the manor, Penny had no desire to revisit those terrible vigils over the loss of Jonas Tang. But, she only realized now, there had been no mourning with Vivian. No thoughts of Sis. If Jonas Tang was dead, then the whole idea of family was, too. They were both orphans—one stuck in a foreign country at an institute trying to brainwash her into acting ladylike, the other transferred into the hands of a cousin of Jonas's who lived in the insular mountains of New Mexico. They were orphaned from each other.

No, that wasn't quite right. There had been a moment, in the wake of Jonas's death, when she had wanted nothing more than to embrace her only kin, to be with the only person who could possibly understand. Why weren't they allowed to see each other? The Chamouns wouldn't even let her send a postcard. Penny was convinced that her sister was living some cosseted life among aunts and uncles. It was as though Jonas's death had delivered Judgment Day upon his daughters instead of himself, with goody-two-shoes Viv rewarded with the embrace of family, and bad-girl Mel sent to fulfill her destiny as a whore under the thumb of the Chamouns.

Soon enough, she decided that if she was going to be the bad girl, then she ought to get the most out of it. To hell with her prissy sister.

When did I decide that?

Penny had used that resentment to allow the Chamouns to shape her into a tool—a worldly, disciplined honey trap. At first she hated what they had done to her. She didn't believe their stories about Fuad going way back with Jonas or how a drunken driver had killed her dad. And the things they exposed her initially shocked and repelled her. It had been Daliyah, not Fuad, who had finally unlocked Penny's secrets—secrets about herself, and her body, that even Penny hadn't been quite aware of.

She came to hate Daliyah so intensely the woman's presence could make Penny physically sick. But the money rolled in, and with it the Chamouns' cocaine that turned Mediterranean nights neon. It was Fuad's turn to save her, sending her to Shimura's dojo—a new kind of hell, an austere bondage she thought would kill her. But gradually it reminded her of those ballet lessons of long ago, and the empowerment they had given her. Of course, that power had to be put to some sort of use. She spent her days either training in Japan or partying in Europe, accelerating from one extreme to the next, always with herself, alone, at the center of it all. Melody Tang was dead, and good riddance.

That is, until a few months ago when she and Stack had decided to rob a rapist working for the Russian mob. Sending money to her clueless sister had not been an act of sibling love. It had been a tasteless joke, never funny, and now nobody was laughing.

Her sister was in there, somewhere in that house. *Viv, you should have stayed put in New Mexico. You're in my world now.*

Penny checked out the cars parked out front and their license plates. They were all rentals. She looked at the windows, catching glimpses of people inside enjoying themselves: talking over a glass of wine, raising a young boy onto a lap.

She walked around to the far side of the house. Back here was a pool, set amid a plateau of stone slabs that formed a patio. The ground sloped away from here toward more rows of grapevines: some of Tuscany's finest Vernaccia was produced here. Above the hills twinkled the lights of San Gimignano.

A trellis covered the façade of the house's garden side, vines infiltrating its crosses like a legion of black serpents. Penny's eyes followed the latticework up to a bedroom window. The interior light was on, but the white shades were drawn and she couldn't see inside. *Viv?* She felt like it must be, as though the prospect of reunion was dictating fate.

This is going to be harder than I thought.

From here she had a fine view of the kitchen, thanks to its

large windows overlooking the pool. A trio of adults, two men and a woman, flitted among the counters.

Wash dishes. Open a bottle of Amaretto. Slice cheese on the board. Chatter happily.

Most of the gathering looked Caucasian—the groom's extended family; the woman in the kitchen was Chinese, but she wasn't Vivian.

The wedding was to take place at the manor tomorrow. The two families were staying here. But who was Vivian's family?

The night sky was clear, the house and its details in precise if dark relief. Penny shivered in the gathering cold.

Hi, Sis, remember me, Melody? Ten years, can you believe it? Me, where have I been? Honey, you wouldn't have a clue, not you, little Miss Suburban Churchgoer. Marrying Steve who is an actuary at an insurance company based in Phoenix. Woo hoo! Yeah, I looked you up on the Internet. Congratulations, by the way. At least one of us is going to get married. Me, what about me? I've had more guys than there are grapes on this stupid vine, but then I always was the hot one. Oh, you mean what's my job? You know what a honey trap is, Sis? It's like a spy. Industrial espionage. James Bond stuff, way out of your league.

Why am I here, Sis?

Penny shook her head. Coming here had been a mistake. Waste of time.

Well now that you ask, remember that twelve million bucks you won in a church lottery? Well, there's no church and there's no lottery. The money was mine. I gave it to you. Call it a wedding present.

You're welcome.

Just one thing, though, before you tie the knot in this beautiful setting with your extremely exciting actuary fiancé. I got the money by ripping off this Russian mafia guy. He deserved it—let's not get into the boring details, all right? —but, well, he's on a mission. No, not a mission to get the money back. Maybe he wants it back, I don't know. But he's on a mission to murder me and anyone associated with me or his stolen money.

Which leads us to...you, dear Sis.

Cones of light appeared behind her: headlights on the little road above. The car pulled onto the winding dirt lane headed for the house. More guests in the wedding party, returning from a long day of sightseeing. Maybe Vivian was among them.

The car turned onto the dirt road, and the headlights switched off.

The car approached in the dark.

What?

Penny ran to the silent hills, catching only a glimpse of the car crawling darkly toward the manor. The blackened sedan reached the edge of the manor's drive and halted. Penny made a long loop, getting close enough to observe the car from behind the nearest row of vines. No one got out. Its engine purred quietly. After a long pause, the driver put it into reverse.

She darted to the shelter of a cypress near the manor's front door. The car backed into obscurity. She chased it carefully, but the driver found room to turn around. It accelerated away and she lost sight of it. The driver didn't turn his headlights back on until the car was already over the next hill.

* * *

Penelope Lee had been her invention. She had chosen the surname Lee because it seemed as ambiguous as she was. It could be a standard American name, like General Robert E.

Lee—you couldn't ask for a more traditional white-guy name than that. Or it could be Asian, Chinese or Korean, if Penny needed to turn that way. Fuad had beamed with approval at her selection.

"And the first name?" he had asked.

"Penelope."

"Why Penelope?"

"Because it sounds posh. The kind of name that rich girls have."

"Very good," Fuad had said. "You must believe you are a posh young lady, for sure."

But within a few days Penelope had shortened to Penny. She had never figured out how it happened; it just was, and the more she had resisted, the more entrenched the nickname had become.

The conversation came to her now as she greeted the Italian morning. Fuad, she realized, had told her to *believe* she was a posh young lady. For all her Swiss training, he didn't think she actually was one.

Why not let Penelope Lee go, too? Viktor had figured it out so maybe Penny was tainted forever.

I've been Penny ever since Dad died. Maybe even before that, in a way that she didn't realize at the time. All the boy-chasing and pot parties and blowing off school—that was Penny. And the ballet and the delight of exacting rigor over her body, honing it into a tool—that was Penny, too. *She's been me the whole time.*

And there was one thing she wasn't going to do, ever: go back to being Melody Tang.

She had slept hard beneath the oak tree, too afraid to let the manor out of sight. Now rays of sun turned the hills yellow and gold. The sky was unblemished. A perfect October day in Tuscany for a wedding. She stretched out the kinks and headed back to the villa, walking around to the back, with the pool and the barn and the windows open to the ground floor kitchen. More silver and white balloons fluttered silently from pink strings tied to the outdoor chairs and tables, and from the bare branches of the persimmon trees.

Penny walked to the trellis. The black serpents now revealed themselves in the sunlight as merry green vines that crept all the way to the roof. She gave the trellis a shake. She wasn't heavy, just a little over 120 pounds, about 55 kilos. It should hold. Penny began to climb.

She reached the bedroom window. It was ajar, letting in a chilly breeze that rustled the white lace curtain. Penny pulled the curtain aside. The room was broad and simple, with glazed terracotta floor tiles covered with an assortment of throw rugs. More silver and white balloons. And there, in the master bed, lay a lone person with a woman's hips.

Penny hesitated. Should she awaken her? Was it really Viv?

The squeal of a child's laughter penetrated from behind the closed door. The groom's family was waking up.

The woman in bed didn't budge and the child fell quiet.

Penny clung to the side of the house for a long while, ignoring the stress in her muscles and the ever-present throb of her gunshot wound. Something clicked beneath her. She looked down. A white man in shorts and a sweatshirt emerged from the house's back door, holding a cup of coffee. He had curly hair that was starting to thin on top. He paused right below her to admire the morning view and breathe in the country air.

Penny was going to get caught if she stayed on the trellis.

But he was too close.

The man ambled toward the pool, scratching his head and sipping his coffee. If he turned around from there, he would definitely see her.

Penny hustled up alongside the window and quietly twisted herself inside. The lump in bed didn't stir. Penny dared to move the lace curtain aside to check on the man down below. He was still admiring the view.

The sleeping woman breathed quietly, face behind shoulder-length black hair. The room was furnished with chests and mirrors, and an explosion of socks and underwear draped around an open suitcase. Behind this stood a wardrobe brimming with hangars and clothes.

Including a bright white wedding dress.

"Vivian."

The person in bed stirred but only a little.

"Vivian, wake up," Penny said. A little pathetically, she added, "It's me, your sister. Melody." She spoke the ghost's name through gritted teeth.

A snuffle, the modest sounds of awakening. The woman's hand fidgeted, as though to swat away the intrusive sounds. She turned slightly and the shock of recognition hit Penny. The last time they had been together, Viv had not yet reached puberty. Before her now lay a young woman, a veritable stranger. But whatever made that core essence of that person was still there in the unlined face, the chubby cheeks, the narrow eyes. No doubt about it.

"Vivian, it's me. Wake up."

Penny lifted one of the wooden chairs and walked to the bedroom door. She tilted the chair so the front legs were raised and jammed the back beneath the doorknob.

The sound of the chair's legs against the door finally got through her sister's sleepiness and the woman sat up. "Wha... ?" Then she bolted upright, hands flying to her mouth. "Who are you!?"

"Shh."

"What are you doing in my bedroom!?"

"Vivian, keep your voice down."

The woman looked at her with alarm, but her confusion was such that she didn't emit a scream.

"I'm not going to hurt you," Penny said. "I'm here to save your life."

"Who...who are you? What do you want?"

"Don't you recognize me?"

"No, why should I recognize a stranger...how did you get in here?"

"I climbed through the window. Vivian, it's me."

Maybe it was lingering cobwebs of sleep, or the shock of confronting an intruder. Or maybe she really didn't recognize Penny. She had been too young, it had been too long ago, and she had been told that her sister was dead.

Penny must look terrible, too, caked in dirt and twigs, and probably smelling like a farm animal.

Penny ran her hands through her hair, pulling it back so there was no mistake. "It's me, Mel, your sister."

Viv shook her head, but her eyes were wide, processing information that made no sense. "No, you're not. My sister's dead."

"I'm not a ghost." She took a step toward the bed. "It's really me, Melody."

"Stay back!" Vivian shrank against the headboard.

Penny raised her hands in supplication. "Please, Viv, don't

shout, okay? Keep your voice down."

"Where's Steve? What have you done with him?"

"Nothing. Steve's fine. Everybody's fine."

"Then why...how did you get in here?"

"I climbed in through the window," she repeated.

This admission only raised more alarms. "You did what? You're scaring me."

"We need to talk, alone, before you go out this morning and get married. Okay?"

"No, this is not okay. This is totally...not okay!"

"Lower your voice, all right?"

"Why should I? I should scream."

"In which case I'll run away, and then you'll get married, and then you'll die. So shut up and listen."

"Lady, you're really scaring me."

"I'm not 'lady', I'm your sister."

"You're lying. I don't know who you are, or why you're here, but my sister's dead."

"Boat accident on Lake Geneva, right?"

"That...that's right."

"The explosion was faked. The body belonged to a teenage prostitute from Serbia who had overdosed." Fuad's work, naturally.

Vivian looked at her as though seeing her for the first time. "You're crazy, you know that?"

"Look, it's me, Melody. Don't you recognize your own sister?"

Vivian was on the verge of tears. "Oh my God," she rasped.

"I know this is a surprise..."

Vivian threw aside the bed covers. Her body was chunky beneath its nightgown. She ran to Penny.

"...but it's important that...what are you doing?"

Vivian clutched Penny. She was stronger than Penny would have guessed. "Praise Jesus. The Lord really does answer our prayers."

"Uh, okay..."

Vivian parted just enough to look at Penny with shining eyes. "I can't believe it, but it really is you, Mel! My big sis is here, and on my wedding day!" She embraced Penny again.

Penny felt awkward. This was exactly what she had feared— this getting messy thing. But she had no choice but to put her arms around her sister, and surrender to the jitters creeping through her heart.

"It's good to see you, Viv."

Vivian was crying. "My own sister! I never thought—the Lord..."

"Works in mysterious ways? Yeah, no kidding."

"I'm not alone. I have a family! Not just Steve, but you, my own flesh and blood. This is a miracle. This is just..." She let out a shriek of sheer happiness. Penny clasped her hands over Viv's mouth.

"Shh! What'd I tell you about making noise?"

"But...but you're here. Why shouldn't we make noise? This is amazing! Let's make so much noise our parents hear us up in Heaven!"

If that's where they went. "Take it easy, Viv. Here, sit down." Penny guided her sister to the corner of the bed while she pulled up the other chair. "I've got some bad news."

"I don't understand." Viv's eyes returned to the chair blocking the door. "Why didn't you just...tell me you were alive? That you've been alive all these years?"

"Because I've taken a different kind of path, Sis. I'm in, uh,

I'm in espionage."

"You're a spy?"

"Sort of."

Vivian nodded furiously, as if this explained everything—as if it were perfectly normal. "Yes, but spies still have families, don't they? They work for the CIA and they go home at night to their families."

"I don't work for the CIA. I don't work for the government, not for any government. Do you understand, Viv? I'm not into ties, okay? I'm a...a citizen of the world." *Did I really just say that?* "I work for an outfit that works for big companies."

"Big companies."

"Yes, very big corporations that pay a lot of money for any kind of competitive advantage. Sometimes they have use of our services—me and the people I work for. The ones who trained me. The ones who faked my death."

"You're a spy for companies. You faked your death for these people."

"That's right, Viv."

Some revelation crossed Vivian's face. For a second her eyes shone with understanding, and then her expression turned morose. "The lottery money."

"Yes. The lottery money."

"It's yours and...and you want it back?"

"No."

"You stole it?"

"No. Well, yes, but not in the way you think."

"But you just told me you're a spy working for big corporations. So that money comes from them. If you can fake your death, you can fake a lottery prize."

"It's true that the lottery is a fake. I did that because I wanted to do something nice for you, Viv." *Almost the truth.* "So I made sure the money went to you."

Vivian looked around in troubled confusion. "You...you gave me stolen money? Is it blood money, Mel? Is that it?"

"Not exactly. I didn't steal it from a company. The money wasn't meant to be part of my job."

"I'm so confused," Viv said, starting to cry. "I need Steve. Get Steve."

"Steve needs to wait. We'll get him, but hang on until we've talked things through, all right?" Penny took her sister's hands. "We need to postpone the wedding."

"What are you talking about?" There was a mean edge in the question.

"I stole that money from a man, a very bad, violent man. He's with the Russian mafia. And I think he's figured out what I did and where the money went."

"He can't have it back. The money's gone to the church. I only kept a little, enough so Steve and me could have a beautiful wedding and a honeymoon, a nice house for when we have children..."

"I know you did, Viv. You're a good person. Unselfish. I know that." Penny took her sister's hands and guided her to sit together on the bed. "But this man, Viktor, isn't interested in the money. He wants revenge. For him, that means killing me. And it might mean killing you, too."

"Wh-why would anyone want to kill me?"

"Because it will hurt me. He'll let everybody know about it, too, because he's lost a lot of face because of what I did."

"This is...I don't..."

"Yeah. Um, sorry."

"Sorry?" Vivian pulled away and walked toward the door.

Penny wanted to leap up, to prevent her sister from removing the chair, but she forced herself to stay calm.

"Why were you involved with such a man in the first place?"

"This man, Viktor, raped me. I stole the money with the help of a friend who's good with computers. To hurt him back. I never thought Viktor would figure it out, but he did and now he's killed my friend, he's killed my boss, and he's nearly killed me. And he's here, Vivian. He drove here last night to check out the place. The fact that he didn't kill you then tells me he's waiting to do it today, probably at your wedding. To make it into a big statement."

Viv's eyes had the deer-in-the-headlights glaze. "What?" was all she could manage to say.

"This is no dream, Sis. And I'm sorry, but your prayers haven't been answered. You might want to ask for something else."

"Don't you mock my faith!"

"I'm not," Penny said as sympathetically as she could. "I'm just saying...I'm not worth a single one of your prayers."

"You're my sister."

"I get paid a lot of money to sleep with rich and powerful men so they can be blackmailed or manipulated. I'm good at it. I don't owe anybody anything. Except for you, Viv. I got you into a jam and I'm here to make sure nobody gets hurt. Do you understand?"

Vivian's wet eyes drilled Penny with an unexpected vehemence. "You haven't changed."

"Why should I?"

Viv pointed to the window. "Get out."

Penny slowly approached her sister with beseeching palms. "Listen, Viv, think whatever you want of me, I probably deserve

162

it. But you have to call off the wedding. Just postpone it for a few weeks, until I have time to take care of this thing with Viktor."

Vivian slapped her, hard.

"Ow, what was that for?"

"You stupid, selfish bitch," Vivian seethed. "I wish you really had died."

"Okay."

"You have three seconds to climb back out that window, before I scream for Steve."

"Listen to me, Sis..."

"One."

"You have to call it off!"

"Two."

"Please, I'm begging you!"

Vivian opened her mouth and screamed Steve's name.

15

Bullets for the bride

Penny dropped the last few feet off the trellis. The man with the coffee cup stared at her in amazement.

"Who the..."

Penny ran past him and into the vineyard. She had to swipe at the tears confounding her vision. After a few minutes of hard running nowhere, the ground rose and she turned. No one was following her. She couldn't see the rear of the house but the morning seemed undisturbed. The sun was gently frying the nighttime chill. The crisp rows of vines, the golden hills, the stone town, the silver balloons. Everything seemed in place except for her. She breathed hard and her brain seemed unable to understand what had just happened. Catching her breath, she suddenly felt thirsty. Hungry, too, but the thirst was bad, and she was out of water.

It was seven-thirty in the morning. The wedding party was scheduled to file into the church at eleven. Feeling helpless and stupid, she made the long walk back to where she had parked the car. She was desperate for water, for food. The village was awake, the locals getting ready for the day, opening stalls in the piazza for a weekend market. She found a bar that was open, old men gossiping over cappuccinos and cigarettes. She ordered espresso, pastries, and a glass of water, and wondered if she should simply melt away and leave Vivian to her Lord.

There was no Plan B. When Viktor showed up, there was nothing Penny could do.

This time she drove to the villa. The house was alive now. People were walking back and forth out front, making their way to the chapel abutting the stone end of the house. She saw a van pull into the drive, and she followed and parked behind it. Musicians, a string quartet judging by their instrument cases, dressed in formal black, stepped out of the van and headed around back.

Now or never.

She froze, trying to work out the words.

Some seductress you are.

Penny swallowed her doubts and knocked on the front door. It was opened by an older white woman with a broom of graying hair and too much lipstick. "Can I help you?"

"I'm looking for Steve."

The woman seemed puzzled. "Do I know you?"

"I'm a friend of theirs. My name's Penny."

"There's no Penny on the guest list." The woman figured it out. "You were the one who came here this morning, aren't you?"

"Yes."

"You need to leave this instant."

"I need to speak with Steve."

"You've got some nerve, disturbing my son and Vivian on their wedding day."

"It's important."

"Get the hell out of this house."

"Mom, what is it?" It was the man she had seen earlier, the one starting to lose his curly hair. He was in his mid-twenties, just a few years younger than Penny, and wore wire-rimmed glasses. He hadn't changed clothes yet, as he was still wearing shorts and a sweatshirt.

"It's that woman, the invader."

"I'm not an invader," Penny said. "Steve, can we talk outside?"

"You're a nutball psycho," Steve told her, "just like all of the others."

Penny didn't know what that meant.

"Please, Steve, five minutes." Penny pointed to the stone steps gathered around the door's exterior. "Just right there."

"Don't go with her," the mother snarled. "She's a money-grubbing trespasser."

"I'm not what you think I am," Penny insisted.

"Of course not, dear," the mother sneered. "You're a good Christian with the most needy charity in the world."

"Ever since we won the lottery, we've had a lot of visitors," Steve explained. "People begging for money, or telling us some line about their work for the dispossessed, or selling investments...and yeah, we already had a couple of Vivian's long-lost relatives show up, too."

Penny hadn't thought of this. Her stupid joke, ricocheting back in spades. "How can I prove I'm Melody?"

Steve folded his arms. "What's Viv's favorite flavor of ice cream?"

"How should I know? I haven't seen her since she was eight years old."

"Wow," Steve said, "you didn't even try."

"This nutjob broke and entered," the mother said. "Call the police."

"You're all in danger," Penny said. "I'm only trying to avert a disaster."

"See?" the mother said. "She's crazier than your Aunt Tina."

Uncertainty clouded Steve's face. "I don't want you scaring Vivian anymore, okay, miss?"

"I'm afraid I have to scare all of you. A man is going to come here today. He's going to come with guns and he's not here to rob or steal. He's here to kill Vivian and anybody else who gets in his way."

"And why on earth is that?" the mother demanded.

"I'm Vivian's sister. The man wants to hurt me."

"So throw yourself at him and leave us alone," the mother said. "If you caused some problem, let him kill you."

"Mom, we must listen first—remember Luke 24."

"Steve, this woman's either insane or a criminal."

Steve asked, "If I talk to you for five minutes, will you go away and leave us in peace?"

"Deal." Penny walked through the door and turned, waiting.

"Steve, don't."

"It's okay, Mom." He shuffled out beside her. The sunlight didn't add any layer of handsomeness to him. He was a nerd, skinny by accident. "Okay, miss, say what you came to say."

She tried to speak rationally, calmly, better than she had managed with Vivian. She drew him the contour of the situation. She pleaded with him to call off the wedding. He listened to her impassively. Another car drove up, a just-washed white Alfa Romeo, and from the backseat emerged a tall, silver-haired man in a suit with a red sash across his chest.

"Hold on a sec," Steve interrupted her. "Mr. Mayor?"

"*Si, si, sono il sindaco*," the man said.

"Welcome, sir, come right this way." In the sunshine on that serene ground, the distant conversation of bumblebees amid the sunflowers, and the breeze rustling the mayor's hair, carried away the sense of threat like incense.

"Look, lady," Steve told her as he directed the mayor and his assistant toward the chapel, "I listened to what you had to say. I tried to listen to you just like Jesus listened to the Samaritan at the well. But now it's your turn to listen to me. I'm really busy with the most beautiful day of my life, and it's time for you to leave me and Vivian alone."

"But—"

"Deal's a deal, right?"

"Please, Steve, you've got to believe me."

"The mayor of San Gimignano is here to officiate for the Italian state. Our family pastor is on his way to bless our union in the eyes of God. I've got to get changed. You've already freaked out my family. I gave you your five minutes."

The look on his face was final. Penny turned around and walked down the gravel path. Maybe he really had given her the benefit of the doubt, but her story was just too much; even to her it had sounded bizarre, coming out of her mouth in that jumble. Was she a fool, a loser, a crazy woman? She wasn't certain anymore. Who was Penny Lee, anyway?

No good Samaritan, that was for sure.

She sulked against a distant oak tree.

To hell with them. To hell with them. To hell with them.

More guests arrived. The family pastor was a curly-haired fat man who carried a giant Bible and joyfully embraced everyone. The driveway filled with cars. People hugged and cried and laughed and walked in twos and threes toward the chapel. The string quartet's music reached her, faintly and buffeted by the breeze. Steve, wearing a tuxedo, and his mother, dressed in a sunny yellow dress, emerged from the house and followed the other guests.

The front yard fell quiet and the noise of the gathering muted as everyone filled the ancient chapel. The front door opened and an old Chinese man emerged, also in black tie. This must be one of Penny's distant relatives, perhaps the cousin of her father who had raised Vivian. The bride clung to the crook of his arm, a little rotund in her creamy dress, holding a bouquet of roses. She was crying and the old man kissed her on the forehead. Viv paused at the chapel's door and looked around... for what? *For me?* Then Vivian was inside, gone.

Penny stood up by the tree. A dark Peugeot sedan came to rest at the back of the queue of cars. Her heart skipped. For a long moment, no one got out of the sedan. Then three doors opened. The men wore camouflage outfits and black balaclavas, the leader pulling his mask down as he got out of the car. He was of medium build, economic with his movements, with a tease of blond hair peeking from beneath his mask. He carried a sawed-off shotgun. The other two were physically bigger, broad-shouldered and thick-necked. One carried an AK-47, familiar from its curving magazine, and the other what looked like a machine pistol.

This isn't happening.

But clearly, it was.

She could have screamed, but no one would have heard her. Her stomach tightened and her head exploded with *No no no no no no no.*

169

Viktor and his gunmen walked toward the chapel with casual ease.

Think of something. Do something. No no no.

The men turned the corner toward the chapel, whose doors were behind her view of the manor.

I should give myself up. Take me, it's done. Leave them alone. Don't kill anyone. Just kill me. You win, okay?

But she didn't move.

This is all my fault. I can't just let them—

The first shot echoed over the hills. It was the boom of a sawed-off shotgun.

She crumpled to her knees. All her fault. All. Her. Fault.

The screams were bottled up inside that stone chapel. But they still reached her ears.

IV

PARIS

16

Render unto Caesar

The rain sent the hobos scurrying out of view from her window overlooking Gare du Nord. The balmy autumn had turned suddenly bitter; the season of cruelties had begun.

She rolled a blunt in the darkening hotel room. The chamber was big enough for the bed she sat on, a small table, and a doorless wardrobe. She could peer through the window over the wheezing radiator. The only accent of color besides the cracks in the wall and the mold growing between the floor tiles was her red backpack.

The weed, bought off the hotel's Algerian receptionist, was terrible, but the tobacco paper's sweetness masked the poor quality of the cannabis as well as the grotty smell leaking out of the walls.

The six passports were spread on the bed. Thérèse Nulty. Julie Belroix. Miko Tarazuka. Tamara Camden-Pryce. Zhou Daiyu. Penelope Lee.

In her bag, the other iPhones were tucked in their Faraday sleeves, and were only a risk when turned on. The Faradays, gloves of conductive mesh coated in nylon and polyurethane, blocked the phones from connecting to cellular networks, Bluetooth, or wifi, shielding her from snoops and hacks. She'd learned to stick with encrypted tools—Tor browsers, Telegram chatrooms, Signal messaging—and to keep her mouth shut. One digital crumb might be harmless, but two made a line and three, a trail.

Viktor's people knew how to collect crumbs.

Sprinkling some data, the right kind of information, could confuse her enemies. The personas invented for five of her passports all had some kind of online history—Facebook posts, invented friends, credit statements, Instagram pics of make-believe holidays or parties, LinkedIn profiles. Fuad and Etienne had been careful about the photos, keeping them all just a little fuzzy, to thwart algorithms that could match one of her faces to another.

The only persona without an invented history—well, not completely made up—was Penny. She had no social media or online presence other than the unavoidable financial statements. This identity wasn't like her other fictional lives. It was the one she inhabited fully, the one that never did jobs.

When Viktor Gubinov died, it was going to be Penelope Lee who made it happen.

The iPhones remained tucked away, except the one belonging to Thérèse, plus something else: a cheap LG model, the one she had pocketed while fleeing Fuad's compound. It had been one of his burners, and he had been conducting business on it when Viktor burned his home down.

Only a single day in the life of Fuad had been on that LG cell, but it had been a productive one. The log showed two separate conversations on his encrypted Signal line, both to Paris.

Michel L'Orancourt, he had said. The Paris-based COO of

Schuman Corporation, his client, had ordered her termination. Schuman Corporation, whose stock Manfred Ingerholz's firm had been frantically selling short, under the instructions of Viktor Gubinov.

The hit from the blunt made up for quality with quantity. She leaned back and let the weed do its work. She knew that getting high was not going to help her track down Viktor or get her life back. But it was good for not thinking about Vivian, or Fuad, or the blood on Penny's slender, manicured hands.

Being high was better than lying awake at night hearing the gunshots in the chapel, hearing those muffled screams, like out of a coffin. Being high was better than catching yet another garish headline on her phone or on the street: Red Wedding in Tuscany, Americans' Dream Wedding Turns Into Bloodbath, Police Baffled by Italy Wedding Massacre, What Kind of World is it When Good Samaritans Get Gunned Down?

My world, bitch.

The iPhone vibrated on her bed. Her message on Signal had been returned.

From: XMDM0498924. In French, *How did you get this number?*

Thérèse: A mutual friend in Beirut.

XMDM0498924: *I don't play games. Au revoir.*

Thérèse: Our mutual friend is dead.

She waited for ten minutes, but the person on the other end wasn't responding. Penny typed in a final message from Thérèse: La Chinoiserie, Tuesday, 1pm.

She didn't need a reply. She had two days to get ready. Her period had started; two days might not be enough, but Penny didn't expect her menstruation to get in the way. In the meantime, she'd need to buy clothes and get dolled up.

Two days to do nothing but shop in Paris. Under other circumstances, it would have been a holiday. But holidays were about escape, and right now the only distraction that interested Penny was to roll another blunt.

* * *

She wore a Burberry trench coat short, just enough to cover her rear, with the belt knotted in front and the sleeves rolled partway up her arms. She left her black hair free to spill over her shoulders from beneath a matching beige Saint Laurent wide-brimmed hat. A bright Hermès scarf was tucked inside the coat's wide collar. Beneath the trench, a Chanel black cocktail dress with a low neckline and a hemline that ended just under the coat. Butterfly-shaped Louis Vuitton sunglasses completed the look of mystery.

But the pièce de résistance was the leopard-print Manolo Blahniks, their stiletto heels gifting her an extra four inches. Because she wasn't afraid to look like an expensive whore. That was the point.

Penny sauntered out of Madeleine station with a new bag slung over one shoulder, a Hermès sport-chic calfskin with a print of peacock colors. A fancier home for all the possessions in her shrunken world. The red backpack was more practical but right now she would leave it in the hotel room.

The rain had abated, giving Paris a final taste of late October sun. She strolled past Fauchon, its tables filled with people enjoying an outdoor coffee, oblivious to any unpleasantness to come. Men and women stared at her as she crossed the street toward the church. Had she cared to look back, she knew she'd spot them still fixated on her departing derrière.

She mounted the stairs, ignoring the tourists and the beggars, and entered the Madeleine. Penny wasn't religious, and she was too cynical to indulge even the most harmless horoscope. But a church of the Belle Epoque, built in the name of the world's most famous prostitute—now that meant something. She walked through the massive interior toward the main altar with its statue of Mary Magdalene, ascending from a dais of winged angels, her face marbled in serene ecstasy.

The ecstasy of prayer. That's what they said. *No other kind?* The Madeleine seemed to be rising towards the fresco in the half-dome above the altar, filled with a mélange of figures from history, all men draped in courtly or church attire. In the far distance was Jesus, his head illuminated from behind, raising a welcoming palm. But before reaching her savior, the Madeline was going to have to get past Napoleon, who had commissioned the fresco. He was down front and center, his back turned but his roving eye catching her over his shoulder.

You see the power you wield? Daliyah Chamoun had once whispered into her ear. *This is your church. That is your patron saint.*

Penny now knew that was a lie. Sure, Mary Magdalene got to have her name on this fancy church. But it was the Napoleons who got to possess her while the getting was good. Render unto Caesar the things that are Caesar's, and unto God the things that are God's. Well, the Madeleines and the Pennys definitely would be rendered unto Caesar.

But Penny's Caesar? He was going to pay for it. Pay in ways he never imagined.

Vivian would be kneeling, crossing her chest, adoring Madeleine. She'd never see the Napoleons coming. Or the

Daliyahs.

There was no sign of Daliyah now. Penny regarded her teacher's shrine. *You don't own me anymore.*

She had said what she had come to say.

Penny had work to do, hunters to hunt.

She exited the monument and headed up Boulevard Malesherbes, a busy commercial street overwhelmed by honks and busy walkers. The confidence she had conjured in the Madelaine, puffing her chest, soured. The acid of fear nibbled away, and she considered returning to the decrepit hotel and burning one. But she had arrived at her destination, and grim determination regained her commanding heights.

La Chinoiserie was part of the Grand Hyatt, quiet and spacious, its tables hogging sunlight beneath a canopy of glass and wrought iron. The lunchtime crowd hummed with the well-heeled who had come from the fashion houses around Place Vendôme or the trading floor of the Paris bourse. Men in dark suits crouched over slabs of beef, plotting their next business deal, while women gossiped over the ridges of their lipstick-stained teacups. By the bar, a satisfied-looking couple negotiated over a menu.

In the center of the room sat a lone woman in a dark pinstripe suit that did nothing to hide her generous curves. She had glorious blonde hair tied up in a bun and pouty rouged lips. She noticed Penny at once. The woman didn't move or send a signal of any kind, but it was obvious that she had been waiting for this moment.

Penny walked over. The woman watched passively, not even twitching any of the fingers holding her menu. Before her was a glass of water, nothing else. Not bothering to remove her hat or sunglasses, Penny took the seat opposite.

"So you are Thérèse," the woman said in French.

Penny plucked the menu out of the woman's hand. The woman was startled; she had let Penny make all of the moves. The whole thing stank.

"And you're just a whore," Penny snarled. "Tell your boss over there I don't play games either." She nodded toward the man and woman at the bar. If Penny had any doubts, they were laid to rest when the blonde turned her head all the way around to look at them.

"Go on," Penny told her. "Beat it."

The blonde froze. She wasn't trained for this sort of thing and hadn't expected to be made out so quickly. By now the man and woman at the bar were watching. The woman gave the faintest nod and the blonde got up. She exited the restaurant with a sad grace.

The woman from the bar took her place. She wore a Chanel black-and-white-checked business suit and carried an expensive little blue purse that matched her sapphire brooch and her eyes—the blue of ice. She had thin, humorless lips and a helmet of long, dark hair with straight bangs.

"You have the manners of a pig," the woman said.

"Your girl has the brain of one." Penny noticed the man had remained by the bar, watching them discretely. The casual eye might mistake his girth for just fat.

The madam gazed after the departed blonde. "She is my top earner this year. But you're right—she is made for admiring and for screwing, not for thinking."

"What does she bring in now?"

"I'm not at liberty to discuss private business affairs. Especially not to a rude cow."

"I can double it."

179

The madam arched an eyebrow. "Oh yes?"

A waiter approached and asked if they'd like to order.

"Just a café for me," the madam said. "We won't be staying for lunch."

"And for me," Penny said.

The waiter heaved off.

"I'm the best," Penny said.

"Hiding behind that outfit, I'm not confident."

Penny removed the hat and the sunglasses and gave her hair an ostentatious shake.

"I have lots of pretty girls."

"I'm not a pretty girl," Penny said. "I'm a beautiful woman."

"Some men prefer the former. Most of them, I'd say."

"I specialize in the more discerning customer," Penny said.

"You'll have to excuse me, but I am not comfortable with this open dialogue. How do I know you're not recording this?"

"You can search me. You might enjoy that."

"Watch your mouth. I am a respectable woman."

Penny jabbed her chin toward the man at the bar. "Respectable women hang out with that thug?"

"I don't see what we possibly have to discuss." The waiter returned and laid down their coffees along with a plate of petit-fours. The madam popped one into her mouth.

"Fuad Chamoun is dead," Penny said.

The woman's jaw paused then resumed chewing.

"Never heard of him."

"Cut the crap," Penny said in English.

The madam took a careful sip of coffee. "You worked for him?"

"I was his best field agent," Penny said, returning to French.

"I'm not a cop. I know about you because I've done work for you, through Fuad."

"Tell me what you think you know about me."

"I know that Fuad pays you to get access to some of your customers. You did it once out of greed, now you do it out of fear. If word leaked out about you, it would be very bad for your business. Fatal, I'd say."

The madam leaned back in the plush chair. "You're bluffing."

Penny reached into her sport-chic bag and pulled out a USB stick, which she slid across the table. "Ciao, then." She stood up. "Thanks for the coffee."

"Sit down," the madam snapped, raising her voice for the first time. A few heads turned. Her fingers, nails painted a bold red, took the USB. Penny had recorded a copy of Fuad's phone history on it, bona fides for the madam.

Penny remained standing. "I only take orders from people who pay me."

The women glared at each other. The madam relented, gesturing for her to sit. "Please, Ms. Nulty."

"Thank you." Penny sat. "I believe we can work to mutual benefit."

"Your patron is dead so now you come running to me. I have never been one to ask questions of certain people. Mr. Chamoun, for example. He was a known quantity to me. But you understand... of you, I have many questions that I must ask."

"Of course."

"You contacted me on a very secure channel."

"On Fuad's phone. We worked very closely."

"But why is he dead? Did you kill him?"

181

Penny smiled. "What gives you that idea?"

"I don't know," the madam said, leaning forward. "I don't know why I have that idea, but I do, Thérèse, I do."

"The Russian mafia assaulted his compound in Beirut. I'm not sure who else made it out, but I was there and saw Fuad die. You will have to make your own inquiries, naturally."

"And why was the Russian mafia so upset with Fuad?"

"They think he stole from them. It all stems from an operation he did involving one of your clients. Manfred Ingerholz."

The madam raised a hand. "I would prefer we keep such names out of this. Everyone has their reputation, no?"

"You're right, it doesn't matter. What matters is that I am now available to work for the right operation. I am looking for a network that values quality, discretion and the highest level of service."

"It may be that such networks are not currently looking to expand their labor force."

"Yours is. It always is."

The madam shrugged. "Such networks value trust and loyalty. That requires a certain familiarity with one another. A familiarity that you and I lack, Thérèse."

"Then perhaps you would consider me for a trial assignment."

"Unlikely but go on."

"I have a particular customer in mind."

"Then I'm afraid we are finished here, my dear Thérèse, because this is absolutely not how I work. The service provider does not choose her customer. It goes the other way."

"This case is exceptional."

"You are not the sort of asset for my books, mademoiselle.

You have learned to do what you do under the Chamouns, and I agree that can be a useful education. But I am not interested in spies, even ones that spy while lying on their backs."

"I didn't come here to ask," Penny said. "I came here, madame, to threaten."

The madam's eyes turned a paler shade of crystal.

"I have a job I need you to book for me," Penny said. "One job, I'll pay you Fuad's rate, and then I leave you alone."

"Fuad did always have a penchant for blackmail," the madam said.

"Yes, he did."

"The problem with blackmail is that even if the victim agrees, she has no guarantee that it will end. Perhaps it is better in such a case to let whatever slander be aired and deal with it then. Perhaps the source of the slander can be neutralized." She turned and waved her fingers at the bodyguard. He raised his fork, keeping his eyes on Penny, and tapped the prongs against his fleshy cheekbone, just beneath his eye.

The madam said, "Such countermeasures can be very messy, very painful."

Penny spat on the table. Again heads turned.

"*Crétine!*" the madam gasped.

Penny switched to English. "Listen, bitch," she growled, "you're going to give me this job or every aristocratic john in this town is going to know you rat them out to industrial spies. What part of that did you not get?"

The madam looked at the glob of spit on the table. "Tell me why. How much money is in this for you?"

"None."

"None? Then what on earth are we doing here?"

"I'll pay you, like I said, but it's personal."

183

"Personal? I thought you were a professional. There is no personal, it is forbidden. It is stupid. I should call your bluff, you are so pathetic."

"I don't care what you think."

"Personal, my God." The madam turned to English for the first time: "What are you, the hooker with a heart of gold?"

"Try black coal."

The madam threw her napkin over the offending globule. "Americans." She closed her eyes for a moment. In French, she sighed, "All right, Thérèse Nulty. Of course you are assuming whoever you have in mind is actually on my books. I'm not the only broker in Paris."

"I'm pretty sure he is," Penny said. "Michel L'Orancourt."

17

The pimp

The time had come to find a secure place for her stash. After the meeting with the madam, Penny walked toward Place de L'Opéra and entered the Credit Agricole branch, where Thérèse Nulty had her account. She showed her passport and requested a private box.

In it went the other passports, spare iPhones, credit cards, and the last of Kasym Shokay's cash—after flights, shopping and other expenses, Penny was down to about twenty-five thousand euros, plus another seven thousand euros on deposit under Thérèse's name. Penny's other identities had their own financial arrangements, but the fewer trails she left, the better. Thirty K, minus the fees she'd promised the madam, was pocket money. She couldn't get through a week partying in Ibizia on that, at least not without doing the Holly Golightly routine.

When Penny left the bank, her handbag felt light for the first time. She faced the grand opera across the busy street, a house for contrived drama . The madam's parting shot was starting to sink in. The bitch had been gloating.

Her stomach rumbled so Penny headed down a side street and sidled into the nearest café. She ordered a *croque monsieur* and a glass of white wine and thumbed her phone.

She had already done some research on L'Orancourt. Chief operating officer of Schuman S.A., a Franco-German oil field services company, with activities in over sixty countries, employing over fifty-thousand people. As big as they came. Its various divisions provided products and services for petroleum and natural gas exploration, as well as construction of refineries, oil fields, pipelines and chemical plants, mostly in the sort of countries where no one could scrutinize a big corporation: Iraq, Nigeria, Angola.

L'Orancourt himself had little in the way of a public profile. The firm's CEO, an affable German, was the face of the company. But L'Orancourt was the one who ran the business day-to-day. He was the spider at the center of the web, the magician behind the curtain, who made things happen.

And when things didn't happen the way he liked, he called Fuad.

His public information indicated Michel L'Orancourt was married with two daughters, both young adults—one an engineer in Britain and the other in the fashion industry in Milan. Born in 1950, he had graduated from L'École Nationale d'Administration, *the* university for France's public elites, and worked his way up state-owned energy companies as a member of the Socialist Party. Somewhere along the way, he acquired the nickname "Le Bouteur"—the Bulldozer.

In 1997 the left-wing prime minister appointed the Bulldozer as deputy minister for economics, finances and industry, a role that ended over corruption charges involving the national oil company. It didn't seem to stop the Bulldozer: today

L'Orancourt sat on boards of directors; was a professor at the Paris Institute of Political Studies; and advised the French President and the IMF.

She found only one video clip of him, giving a lecture to a group of students. She inserted her earbuds and pressed play. It was only about two minutes long. He was charismatic—now sixty-five, he still came across as vigorous, if a bit stout. He had the build of a *bouteur*, with a barrel chest, a full head of white hair and dramatic black eyebrows in the center of a square face. He strode across the stage in a dark suit, white shirt and conservative tie, the epitome of a powerful mandarin at the top of his game.

"You ask me what it is like to do this job," he said on the clip. "It is very stressful, I must tell you that. There is no rest, no peace. But that is the price we pay for the privilege of serving the country, of serving Europe—the modern world. It is companies such as ours that keep the lights on, that keep your homes warm in winter, that keep the trains running and the cars on the road. It is complex and the challenges we face in these countries...well, Iraq, you can imagine. So my phone is ringing twenty-one, twenty-two hours a day. I spend more time in an airplane than I do with my team, which is a regret. I sometimes go weeks without seeing my wife, and now, of course, my daughters are grown up and have careers of their own. So it is lonely. But it is a privilege and an honor, and it is a duty, an important duty, that requires absolute attention and focus. If we relax, if we abandon our post for even just one moment, then, well, what can I say? It would be like abandoning the world to chaos."

Telling an off-the-books spymaster to murder his field agent: L'Orancourt had forgotten to mention that part of the job.

"Fulfilling one's duty is its own reward. When President Hollande called me, just last week, he said, 'Michel, it's two in the morning and you still answer the phone.' I said, 'But of course, Mister President.' So, he asked, 'That is why they call you the Bulldozer?' I said, 'Well, they can call me what they like; they call me all sorts of things, but what does it matter?' And the President said to me, 'Michel, it is men like you who are the saviors of Western civilization.'"

Penny dropped the phone into her bag and finished her lunch. The savior of Western civilization, she knew, might have other reasons for not seeing his wife or daughters. He spent too much time with Fuad...and maybe, she thought, with Viktor Gubinov. The Russian had been acting against Schuman, but for a reason. They knew one another, even if Viktor was just filling in for someone higher up in Moscow. The financial attack on Schuman stock could be a way to get L'Orancourt's attention, to send a message...like...like...'back off'? Or: shall we hurt each other like this or shall we collaborate?

Using L'Orancourt to reach Viktor was not a wild shot, just a long one.

And, of course, getting back at the savior of the free world would be its own reward.

Her instruction from the madam was to see a Serb named Andrej Kovac in the eighteenth *arrondissement*, the Goutte d'Or neighborhood below the Sacre Coeur. He'd meet her at a bar off Boulevard de la Chapelle tonight around ten. It should be an easy walk from the flophouse she had been using by Gare du Nord. It wasn't the sort of place for wandering alone at night, so she decided to check it out first this afternoon and get her bearings.

She took the metro back to her hotel. The Algerian working the desk smiled the smile of a co-conspirator. Whatever. She walked up the three flights, not trusting the tiny lift. Wires hung out of the ceiling of the dim hallway. The desire to preserve her cash for things like new clothes had prompted her to take this place; it was a worse dump than she had imagined, but its decrepitude had fit her mood.

She unlocked her door. The strand of hair she had left balanced on the doorknob was missing. There was nothing in the dilapidated room to have taken. Her meager change of clothes lay neatly on the wardrobe's shelf. The spare set of panties had been folded carelessly.

Penny took off her new clothes and changed back into jeans. Before putting on a T-shirt, she went into the bathroom to check out her arm. It hurt if she raised it above her chest. The flesh around the surface wound was a swollen mass of yellow and brown bruises. She had gone to the hospital two days ago, shortly after arriving in the city, and a doctor had removed her stitches. She had given Penny some painkillers and a fresh dressing, and told her the wound should heal within another five or six days.

She stared morosely at the savaged arm. She had gotten away with the most superficial of gunshot wounds, a low-caliber burner that had taken a little bit of skin, a pinch of nerves, a tablespoon of capillaries... She wondered, if she ever faced a man with a gun again, if she'd charge him like she had done in the bathroom of the Burj al Arab.

At least the wound no longer smelled like pus.

She put on her shirt and zipped up the biker jacket, slipped on the Patagonia hiking shoes, stuck her shades over her forehead, and at the last minute took the Hermès scarf so she could wrap something around her throat. She trotted back down to the reception area. The Algerian guy grinned. Penny walked up to him and flexed her left hand. She chopped him on the neck, close enough to the windpipe to make him feel it but not so close as to do lasting damage. The man's eyes ballooned as he collapsed to his knees.

"Next time you beat off with my panties," she told him in French, "I break your neck. Got it?"

His eyes were a mixture of panic and anger. But he nodded feebly, still struggling to get his breath.

"Good." She lowered her sunglasses and strode out of the hotel.

Deciding she should at least make something of the weather, Penny took the metro to Montmartre and nosed around trinket shops, side-stepping the buskers and the touts. The Sacre Coeur loomed above the bohemia-turned-tourist trap like a holy spaceship of hardened cocaine. She made her way up to the cathedral and began the descent toward Goutte d'Or, where bohemia turned into a gritty migrant neighborhood. The street musicians pumping out French classics and jazz morphed into shops blaring Senegalese pop. The streets became dirtier and grimmer, the clothes brighter and the skins darker.

She found the street. A mosque filled one side, facing stores selling Congolese fruits, second-hand cell phones, Moroccan pastries, and bales of herbs and spices that filled the lane with mint and zataar. Although one corner boasted a hipster brasserie that brewed its own craft beers, the bar she was looking for was not so trendy. In the late afternoon its front was still blocked by a cage mesh.

She noted the location and headed back, stepping over empty bottles and hypodermic needles.

* * *

Night over the City of Lights: above in the clear early November sky, the Sacre Coeur was lit up, the ivory spaceship cleared for launch; below in the warren of streets, the only lights were neon.

She approached the bar, having changed back into her expensive whore clothes. Groups of African and Arab men huddled on street corners, calculating their odds of getting away with a pass at her. She entered the bar, its interior glowing beneath scarlet lights. It was a small place where all the punters looked like they knew one another. Knots of men hunched over the bar or the handful of standing tables. Some were already quite drunk, and the place stank of fermentation gone bad. The only two women in the place, one African and one white, looked as burly and humorless as the men.

Penny walked to the bar. "Excuse me," she said, indicating the two men should part to make way for her. They were Africans. One let out a guffaw. This was no place to start a fight, so Penny gave them a friendly smile. "The lady would like a drink."

"This ain't no place for a pretty lady to be coming in by herself," one of the men said. He was smiling, but it wasn't entirely friendly.

"I'm not by myself," she said. "I'm with Andrej."

"Well, there's nobody named Andrej here," said the other man, the one who had laughed at her. He puffed his chest. "But Gregoire can take care of you tonight."

"I don't know, boys, you don't look like you can afford it," she told them, still smiling and forcing her brain to keep from freaking out.

191

"You don't look like you'd give me what I like," said the other man.

"Now don't say that," Gregoire said, "look at her, man, she is prime *minet*. Baby, you don't want to be lonely tonight."

"I'm pretty sure you can't afford my *minet*," she said. "And besides, you're too clumsy to know how to make it happy."

That led to a round of laughter from around the bar, but a bass voice cut short the merriment. "I say who can afford it and who can't." She turned around to see Andrej Kovac. Baldness made his soul patch stand out, as dark as his two stony eyes. He wore a black leather jacket, black jeans and a blood-red shirt over a short but muscular body. In her Manolo Blahniks, Penny towered over him, but what he lacked in stature he compensated with a menace that caused the African men to shrink into themselves. Andrej added, "And nobody cares if your *minet* is happy or not."

She extended a hand. "Andrej? Thérèse. Charmed, I'm sure."

He ignored her hand. "Maude's girls are usually younger. They go on strike?"

By younger, she guessed he meant teenage. "I'd like to think Maude's upgrading."

"Pfff. You two scram already." Gregoire and his friend traded looks of resignation and slunk off with their beers. Andrej checked her out. "Okay, nice."

"Thank you."

"I'm throwing a party for a friend. I do this for him every now and then. You like to party?"

"Sure, I like to party."

"I bet you do. I can't tell you exactly what day, so give me your number. Two thousand euros."

"Five thousand."

"What? You think this is a negotiation or something?"

Penny didn't care but Thérèse was meant to be crème de la crème. "I'm worth it, believe me."

Andrej sized her up again. "Two and a half."

"Five. You're asking me to reserve all my time to wait around for your friend. I might as well be burning twenty-euro bills."

"Three, and you say another word and we're done."

"All right."

"Maude's got some explaining to do, sending me a girl with a big mouth."

"Doesn't your friend like girls with some initiative?"

Andrej thought it over, working his square jaw. "You shaved down there?"

"Sure."

"No shapes, no landing strip. Full Brazilian, got it?"

"I love Rio."

"You talk back a lot for a whore."

"It's called making conversation."

He pulled a phone out of his pocket. "Just shut up and tell me your number."

The message came two days later. Her period had ebbed away a few hours ago. She was in her room, smoking the last of the Algerian's dope. *Be at the bar in two hours.* That didn't leave her much time to wash up, do her hair, and change. She checked the wound. The swelling had receded and the bruising was fading. She removed the bandage and looked at the scar. It wasn't big but it stuck out. The sight of it brought back a dark sense of futility.

Snap out of it, Pen. It's showtime.

Over the wound she clasped a gold-colored arm brace she

had picked up in Montmartre. She looked at herself in the rusting bathroom mirror. The metal armband made her look like Wonder Woman and hid the scar. Not bad.

Buoyed by the sense that she could still be sexy, Penny changed into her set of fashionable clothes and headed out to meet Andrej. It was a bright, sunny and unseasonably warm beginning to November. She arrived at the bar a few minutes past two p.m.

"You're late," he said. Without waiting for her reply, he walked to a parked Renault hatchback. "Get in."

She slid into the passenger seat and reached for the seatbelt. The narrow confines pressed against the wide brim of her hat.

"Why don't you get rid of that stupid thing?"

"I like to keep it on," she said.

Andrej shook his head in amazed disgust.

"Don't worry," she added, "the rest comes off." She added a smile to her joke, but he just scowled and popped a CD into the car's player.

"So where're we going?"

Loud heavy metal assaulted the Renault's interior. He turned the volume up. *No chitchat: got it.* She decided it was a relief, even if the music was tuneless, just squealing guitars, unchanging drumming and a singer's screech—it could have been Serbian, it could have been English, either way she couldn't make out a single word.

It took a while for Andrej to navigate out of the medieval Parisian streets. They reached a ring road and turned north, through the drab *banlieus*, immigrant ghettos and the ugly wreckage of discarded factories. The music gave her a headache, and as they changed from one highway to the next and headed for the border with Belgium, she started to get nervous. This had been the only way she knew how to reach L'Orancourt and it was going to be touch and go. The memory of the madam's parting taunt played itself in her head again.

"You know," Maude had said as Penny was leaving their table at La Chinoiserie, "they call him 'the Bulldozer'. And now you're going to learn why."

18

The Bulldozer

The drive toward the Belgian border involved passing through flat, dispiriting towns that even the bright weather and late-autumnal colors couldn't cheer. Andrej's heavy-metal CD finished. When he moved to slip a third disc into the receiver, Penny stayed his hand.

"A little quiet, okay?"

He glanced at her fingertips on the back of his knuckles and made a fist. She thought he was going to punch her, but he relaxed and put the CD back into the glove compartment.

"Thank you."

"I have to make a stop. Stay in the car."

He turned off the A1 motorway at an exit for Arras. They avoided the city center. He drove into a faceless suburb of strip malls, gray apartment blocks and houses that had given up on anything fey. They stopped on a stretch of street fronted by squat, blandly square buildings. Above one rose a giant photograph of a woman in lingerie and stockings, sucking on a lollipop. A few doors down, the shop windows were filled with garish silhouettes of nude pole dancers. Club La Passione was its name.

Andrej was only gone five minutes, returning with the same agitated look.

"Business troubles?" she asked.

"This economy," he grumbled. "It's easier to get girls but harder to get customers."

"So why are we here?"

"You do good today, my friend likes you, and maybe you come work for me here." He eyed her legs. "A little dancing, pour drinks for the clients, and whatever you negotiate with them is your business. I take care of my employees; nobody dares to raise a hand against a Kovac girl."

She smiled. "I'll think about it."

"You want to see the inside? It's a classy place."

"Don't we have to meet your friend?"

"You should get warmed up first. In there."

"With you? Andrej, I don't do freebies, not even with my pimps."

He rubbed his soul patch. "Today's going to be quite a day." He got in the driver's seat. "Maybe when we're done, you take the train back."

"Fine with me."

He gunned the ignition. "You're right about the hat. Keep it on."

It was another thirty minutes before they turned off the A1 into Lille, France's biggest city north of Paris. The outskirts were the usual post-industrial dilapidation. They drove along a main drag, Rue Nationale, which culminated in a Grand Place. It was a typical great square of lowlands Europe, flanked by the baroque facades favored by medieval burghers.

They drove slowly through the Grand Place as pedestrians

crisscrossed around them. Locals filled little cafes, or sat by the fountain at the base of a statue's column, watching the world pass, and for a moment Penny envied them their boring lives in this dull city.

"Is this it?"

Andrej didn't reply but aimed the car into a subterranean channel full of parking signs. He found a space in the underground lot. He motioned for her to follow and took a set of concrete stairs back to the Grand Place. The hum of gentle conversation, the bubbling of fountain water, the surprise of a flock of pigeons suddenly taking flight. They left all this behind and walked to a nearby corner. The hotel was comfortable if a little worn in its French nineteenth-century style, a bland rest stop for Lille's business travelers.

She followed him to the reception desk. He gave them a name and the uniformed woman passed him a guest key. "Give me your phone," he said.

"What?"

He opened his palm. "It goes in the hotel safety box. No phones upstairs."

"I didn't bring one." She opened her peacock bag. "Check my pockets if you want."

"Nobody doesn't bring a phone," he said.

"I appreciate discretion," Penny said.

Andrej shifted around the contents of her bag. "Excuse me," he said, more for the receptionist than for her, as he patted down her trench coat pockets. Not quite satisfied, he said, "Okay, let's go," and he led her to the elevators.

The room was on the third floor and was marked Suite Coupole: the main fixture inside was a wooden spiral staircase that led up to the master bedroom wedged inside the building's fourth-story attic.

Andrej opened the door.

Three young women sat on the striped sofas ringing a coffee table. Naked. An Arabic looking woman with thick black hair, fleshy cheeks, and meaty thighs, a few rolls of belly, and generous breasts. A skinny blonde with angelic cheekbones, giggling as she reclined and wiped her nose, the arch in her back exaggerating her small chest. Leaning forward on hands and knees, her nose touching the white lines on the coffee table, a gorgeous black woman with a red-carpet body. She looked up at Penny as she was about to snort the line of coke, gave her a smile, and inhaled.

"Take off your clothes and join the party," Andrej told her. "My friend will be here any minute."

"Hi," Penny said to the women.

"Hi," the Arab said back.

"Come join us," said the black girl, licking white powder from her upper lip.

"Strip for us," giggled the white girl, her French thick with a Slavic accent.

"Where can I put my stuff?" Penny asked.

"Who cares?" Andrej said. "I have to wait in the lobby."

He left and Penny regarded the three prostitutes, trying to hide her apprehension. This was not the setup she had imagined. The point had been to get a one-on-one with L'Orancourt.

"Don't worry, honey, you new?" the black woman said.

Penny smiled. "Yes."

"Let's see what you've got," the white girl said, still giggling. She splayed her legs to reveal a bald mound.

"I like to do things with...a certain style," Penny said. She walked into a small kitchen and slid out of her trench coat. She then removed her sunglasses. Checking to make sure the other women couldn't see her, she lifted her hat and removed the iPhone from where it had been nestled in a headband. She shook her hair loose and turned on the iPhone's video recorder. She removed her dress, her bra and panties but kept the leopard-print heels on, and slid her arms into the trench again. The phone went into one pocket, the headband the other. She strode back to the sitting room and posed with a hand on a hip, the coat open, its belt dangling, showing everything. Total pornstar look.

"Bravo," the black girl purred. "Woman with attitude."

"Skanky showoff," muttered the white girl, helping herself to another sniff of powder.

Penny knelt on the floor beside the coffee table where there was a five-euro note. She rolled it and snorted a line. The hit was instantaneous. She hadn't done coke in a long time—it had been the fuel of her earliest days working for the Chamouns, but she had discarded the vice. Daliyah had been her first supplier of cocaine, reason enough to avoid it. But now the drug made her feel like getting up on that table in her high heels and dance.

The door opened and Andrej entered, gesturing obsequiously for his guest. Michel L'Orancourt wore a raincoat over a dark suit, a monochrome complement to his snowy hair and jet eyebrows. The sight of the four nymphs snorting cocaine prompted an unhurried smile.

"Bonjour," he said simply as he undid his tie.

Behind L'Orancourt came another man wearing a suit. Mid-forties, wire-frame glasses, a carefully maintained layer of stubble on his gaunt face.

"Allow me," Andrej said, removing the coat from L'Orancourt's shoulders. "Everyone, this is my friend. And..."

"And my friend, Pietro," L'Orancourt introduced his companion. To the women he said, "So you like to swing."

"We love to swing," the black girl said.

"Join us, *mes amis*!" called the Arab.

L'Orancourt removed his suit jacket and his tasseled loafers. He was shorter and older looking than he had appeared on the video. He knelt beside Penny, who handed him her euro note. He took it, but she didn't let go. He paused, a little startled, which was long enough for Penny to lunge and kiss him full on the mouth. L'Orancourt growled in pleasure as she let his tongue explore hers, his other hand reaching around her coat to press her breasts against him. She tasted flesh and sinew on him mixed with menthol; he had recently come from lunch and taken a breath mint.

"Now snort," she commanded, giving him a wink.

The other girls gathered around L'Orancourt and Pietro, giving Pietro the minimum of attention but knowing to focus their ministrations on the Bulldozer, touching him, pressing against him, running fingers through the last lines of coke and rubbing it on his gums.

"What beautiful creatures," he told them as they removed his clothes.

They had lost track of Andrej, who had gone upstairs and was now coming back down. He had changed out of his street clothes into a white terrycloth robe. So the pimp was going to enjoy his friend's party. This seemed to be a routine. L'Orancourt said, "Andrej, help me take these angels upstairs."

"Would you like a show first?" the pimp asked.

He weighed the suggestion with mock seriousness. "Pietro, what do you think?"

"I leave it to you, monsieur." The light in his eyes said enough about what Pietro might like to see.

"If you insist then... Girls, give us a show."

The other women seemed to have been through this before. Penny joined their lineup, she alone draped in her open coat. She was eager to remove it somewhere nearby where the action was going to take place, and jumpy at the prospect of the phone's being detected as she wedged herself between the Arab and the African. The four of them swayed as they embraced each other, trading tongues and gentle rubs, Penny twisting her body to keep the hard flatness of the iPhone from a press or a caress. Pietro watched spellbound but L'Orancourt leaned on his elbows, affecting nonchalance, even as his eyes missed no detail.

The four of them were arranged in a chain spilling over a sofa. "Good," he purred. "A good start."

"They could continue," Pietro suggested.

"Don't worry about that," L'Orancourt told him. "Let's go upstairs."

Andrej led the procession up the twisting stairs into the master bedroom, a spacious affair with a king-sized bed between roundel windows. Andrej or the women had prepared the room—the bed's giant mattress, plus a spare they must have requested from the hotel, lay side by side on the floor, creating a giant arena of white.

Penny held back as the three women tumbled onto the ocean of mattress with the sort of playful giggles she could tell were partly artificial but lightened by the drugs and the need to keep the buzz going. Andrej removed his robe, L'Orancourt and

Pietro the last of their clothes. Andrej was a potbelly with squat, muscular limbs, while Pietro sported weakling shoulders and a hollow chest. L'Orancourt looked to have been a strapping man in his youth but had by now decayed into thickness, his broad pectorals carpeted by the same white hair that adorned his head. The men were erect, no doubt with a little help from Viagra.

The trench coat slipped from her shoulders, revealing the last of her flesh except for the golden brace around her right forearm. She placed the coat around the back of a chair on the far side of the room, where there was a breakfast table by one of the windows, bristling with flowers. L'Orancourt was watching her even as tongues explored his belly and chest. She smiled and gave him a pose, even putting one high heel on the chair to maximize the effect. Then as the other women moved down on the men, she pulled the iPhone from the pocket and planted it amid the flower stems.

L'Orancourt gestured for her to join the squiggling mass of limbs on the floor. She obliged, letting the coke speed her way. No point in holding back—no exit from this until L'Orancourt tired out or had to go. No escaping from any of them. The mattresses held firm against hands and knees, against buttocks and feet. Her mouth joined another mouth, and then another, and another, and she had to stay in the moment, let her body respond just enough. She had to know when to act, when to quiver and when to release. The giving of pleasure was as indiscriminate as its taking, but all the time she was thinking of L'Orancourt, making him notice her and keep her in his focus even when it was another body in his heartless embrace.

L'Orancourt called a break for another "show", and amid the

chaos she pleaded the need to pee. She entered the bathroom and closed the door against the women's animal sounds. The sight in the mirror, hair mussed, limbs quivering, was like glimpsing a ghost in the corner of her eye.

This is why vampires don't have a reflection, she realized. *They couldn't bear the sight.*

But Penny was there for a reason, and time was running out.

She grabbed a few shampoos and returned to the arena. She grinned as she showed them she was going to steal these from the hotel, and crossed to her coat. She blocked the view with her body and returned the iPhone to its pocket.

A woman's voice turned from pleasurable moans to protest. "No, no, please, I don't like."

It was the skinny white girl. Andrej had retired from the scene, at least for a while, and wandered into the bathroom, and Pietro seemed to dissipate. But L'Orancourt was nowhere near finished. He had been taking the Slav from behind, but now he pushed her pelvis onto the mattress and straddled her.

"Is unnatural," she cried as he changed tactics.

"You like it," he replied, pushing into her.

The look on his face was brutal, the humorless ecstasy of a jihadist or a backwoods preacher. He was done with the white girl and moved onto the Arab. Not physically sated—for by now his penis was an empty, Viagra-infused husk—L'Orancourt lusted for another kind of power over them.

"At least use some jelly," she protested, but he struck her across the jaw with the back of his hand. "Shut up and take it," he barked as he seized her, too.

Penny and the black girl exchanged looks. The African seemed resigned. She got on her haunches and waited, her eyes going blank, the beauty in her face hardening into cement.

Penny knelt beside him and kissed him. "Do me instead. I like it like that."

"Ah oui?"

She wiggled her backside onto him. "I'll make you finish." His eyes lit up. His hands grabbed her waist and he pressed her body down. She clenched her jaw and dug her chin into the mattress, wanting to get this over with. But she remained aware as she gyrated softly against him, cooed for him, held back the tears and pretended it didn't hurt. *You think you're in control, but I'm using you, you bastard.* She had to talk herself through it. In the midst of his grunts she turned her head and smiled. "That's so good, baby, keep going."

This sparked a last bit of life in him and he climaxed with a little moan. He reclined on his elbows, breathing heavily, his face covered in sweat. He regarded her with a smirk, and she moved to fit inside the crook of his arm.

"What time is it?" he asked, turning away from her.

Andrej had watched the final act from the chair holding Penny's coat. "Sixteen hundred hours."

"I wish there was time for a rest," L'Orancourt said. "But that is my life: never any rest." He rolled over and walked into the bathroom.

"Get dressed," Andrej told the women. He crossed to the stairwell and descended.

Penny sat up. The other three women lay on their stomachs at random angles to one another, their backs covered in perspiration. They had surrendered every inch of their flesh, and the way they laid there made it look as though they would never move again. It was a slaughterhouse.

Pietro was the first to leave. He slipped downstairs and was gone before they knew it, not so much as a handshake for his pal.

L'Orancourt gave them just a cursory glance as he went downstairs, a little smile curling up his cheeks. He returned a minute later with his clothes draped over his arm, and entered the bathroom. She heard the water's hiss.

The other women waited for a turn to shower. Andrej handed them each a bundle of euros. Penny checked to make sure he had paid her what he had promised. L'Orancourt hustled out as the women counted notes. She slipped the trench coat on, this time wrapping it closed with the belt, and padded downstairs.

She caught L'Orancourt as he headed out the door.

"That was fun," she said.

He seemed surprised. "It was. Look, if you want a tip, ask Andrej. He handles that side of things."

"I don't want a tip," she said, palming the back of his head and kissing him.

He was delighted. "You are a very adventurous girl."

"You're an amazing lover," she replied. "Can I see you? Just the two of us? I've got a job on a cruise ship, so I only have a little time left."

His mouth moved, as though he were testing a sip of wine. "Do you have a number?"

"Of course." She had already written it down on the notepad by the telephone. She folded the paper and stuffed it inside his jacket pocket. "I'm Thérèse."

"I'll call you," he said. A moment of sense took hold as he adjusted his tie's knot. "Although you must understand, beautiful women throw themselves at me all the time. It is natural for a man of my position."

"Do beautiful women do this?" She placed his hand beneath the back of her coat, cupping her buttock. The fingers roamed but his urges were now spent.

"Perhaps."

"Those others aren't like me and you know it."

"I'd like to find out if that's true." He kissed her hard and pulled back. "What is that in your pocket?"

She masked her alarm and withdrew a shampoo from the other pocket.

"I'm taking everything I can."

19

Martini rouge

There was no stage for self-pity. If the acting sometimes got a little rough, there was no blaming the other players. They didn't know the field agent was performing her role. They were unaware of being a target; sometimes, they would live the rest of their many luxurious days never having known.

Even if Penny wanted a shoulder to cry on, she was short of friends. She went by herself to a women's clinic to make sure she hadn't picked up any diseases in Lille. She practiced aikido routines alone in the Luxembourg garden. Mealtimes were solo excursions, each one leaving her a little hungrier. Who knew for how long she'd have to stretch her cache of euros?

Maybe it was better that she was so alone. Friendship had never a priority. For someone who was so good at insinuating herself into a target's life, she knew she had a lousy record at making friends, particularly with women. She could recall only one girlfriend from her junior-high days: Cindy Bellamy, the white-trash girl who ran with the Latino lowrider crowd. Perhaps they had sensed a kindred tie in each other. Cindy had no idea how to make herself pretty, or how to flirt with the boys she liked. In turn for Penny's makeover, Cindy introduced her to LSD tabs and shoplifting.

Jonas Tang, she was pretty sure, had never caught on to her boosting clothes from the shops at Bealls. It was one vice Penny had decided not to advertise.

Cindy Bellamy. What had ever happened to her? Probably divorced with two brats and a mindless job packing crates, or maybe she had gone into the army. Those were the usual fates for people like that—for dead-enders who needed friendships to make their tawdry lives feel like home.

People complained about loneliness, but wasn't being alone the ultimate freedom? If there hadn't been any sister, no Vivian Tang squeezing her chubby haunches into a wedding dress, then there would have been no loss, no family for Viktor to murder. Penny could have gone dark, escaped to Shimura's dojo. She could have cleared her head until she figured out her new life.

Attachments had only complicated things for her, but at least now she really was alone. Truly, utterly alone, with only the clench of her stomach at night when the guilt made her want to retch. So, no, she didn't want to pour her heart out to some "friend" and listen to their drivel. She was now at liberty to remove any threats—anyone who knew her true identity—and, in the case of Viktor Gubinov, to ensure that he would know it was Penny who was going to kill him.

The text message came three days later: *I have time Friday evening.*

Do you want to see me? she messaged back.

Very much, he replied immediately.

Take me to dinner.

He made no immediate response, and she didn't send him

any more messages. Penny wasn't interested in another of the Bulldozer's parties. She had dangled the lure, and now the big fish had to bite.

Later that day, he sent her the address of a restaurant, Le Pré Catelan. She was to meet him there at 8 p.m. and ask for Monsieur Michel.

Penny Googled the restaurant: expensive even by Parisian standards, three Michelin stars, and out of the way in the Bois de Boulogne. L'Orancourt was trying to impress her while remaining discreet. She smiled as she confirmed the rendezvous.

The best part: the appointment was on November 13th. Friday the Thirteenth: L'Orancourt's unlucky day.

She took a taxi from the long queue at Gare du Nord. It was a warm evening for November and the people in line were impatient. They had come by train from London, from other parts of France, and it was the last mild Friday evening they were likely to enjoy until next summer.

Penny wasn't in any hurry.

When her cab wheeled around, she instructed him to take her to the restaurant in Bois de Boulogne. By the time they left the ring road for the park, the woods were dark. They cut through the heart of the *bois*on Allée de Longchamp until the driver turned onto a small road that at this time of night was almost devoid of traffic. They passed the occasional van parked along the road. She caught glimpses of the prostitutes inside, limbs dangling out the open doors, vamping for anyone passing by.

The restaurant sat on the grounds of a hotel in the middle of the woods. The taxi passed through the outer gates and drove over a bridge straddling a stream. Ahead on a straight path rose a sturdy chalet vaguely resembling a dwarfish White

House. A valet in a dark suit opened her door. She paid the driver and looked around. From the straight driveway to the gate there were a handful of private cars and another taxi in the mix, but she knew that getting out of here would be a matter of luck. If she needed to run for it, she'd have to take her chances with the woods.

"Would mademoiselle care to wait inside?"

"Thank you," she said to the valet and mounted the stairs to the entrance. The waiting room was lit for intimacy. A small group of Japanese and an older American couple were sipping drinks as they waited for their seats.

"I have a reservation with Monsieur Michel," she told the maître'd in French.

"Ah yes," he said. "There is no need to wait, Mademoiselle Thérèse, is it?"

"Yes."

"Would you like to leave your coat here?"

"No, I'll keep it on." It was part of a new wardrobe she had acquired yesterday, but she was more interested in quick exits than in coveting a new possession.

"Very good. My colleague will show you to your table. Bon appétit."

The manager's assistant, a young woman in a tuxedo, guided her down a side passage, away from the main corridor with its glass views of the woods. The route separated her from contact with any other diners. It turned a corner and the escort pointed out the lady's toilet. Then she came to a door and knocked.

"Enter."

The woman gave Penny a perfunctory smile and opened the door into the room. Michel L'Orancourt sat at the small chamber's only table, facing the door, his back to the large

211

windows with their generous view of the lamp-lit grounds. The walls were paneled white, the curtains were black, just as he wore a dark suit beneath his snowy avalanche of hair, juxtaposed by his thick, black eyebrows. He set down a reddish cocktail and rose from his chair. His sure movements belied his stoutness and his age.

"Thérèse," he cooed, circling the table. "I'm so delighted you came." He kissed her cheeks three times, the French formality, and she slid past before he could plant his lips fully on hers.

"I can't think of a single place I'd rather be this moment, Michel."

"Come, take off that coat. Take her coat, would you?" he snapped at the hotel staffer.

"But I'm still cold, Michel," she said.

"Then you must have an apéritif, no? Get her a martini rouge," he ordered, sending the hotel servant on her way. The door closed with a click. "It is so good to see you," he said, his voice turning wolfish. He kissed her hard and this time she responded, placing her hands behind his head.

"Don't eat too much," she teased him, "or you'll spoil your dessert."

His eyes sparkled at that. "Take off this monstrosity," he said, pushing her coat away from her shoulders. "Let me have a look at you."

Beneath the coat she wore a cranberry cocktail dress, sheathing her from below her collar bones to just above her knee, with a split that led up the middle. It was at once both conservative and suggestive, the sleeves covering her arms adding to the allure—and hiding her bruised wound. It was the sort of dress that would make a fool of most women, and flatter only a few.

"Beautiful," he said, genuinely awed.

"You like it?" She turned her body, revealing the naked back. Her legs ran down to the slender shoes that seemed to consist of little more than a string of faux diamonds and a four-inch stiletto. "It's Scala."

"You're like a dream."

"So is this place."

"You approve? It's completely private here. And the food is exquisite, you'll see."

"I love it."

After some more kissing they sat down at the table, lined by a thick coat of beige leather. The settings and the décor were elegant but understated, and L'Orancourt maintained a certain propriety while the servers came and went, keeping himself seated across the table from her. After their drinks came bread, the *traditionnel*, which filled the room with a mighty aroma, and an amuse-bouche.

"Your accent," he said as he picked a wine from the sommelier's list. "Where exactly in France are you from?"

"Why do you ask? You don't like my French?"

"No no, it's not that at all...I just can't place it."

"Guess."

"At first I thought perhaps the Basque area—they have that rough sound, but it's not quite the same."

"Guadeloupe," she ventured.

"Ah, an overseas department. I should have realized."

"It's obscure, I know."

"Something as exotic as you could not have come from any place ordinary."

The servers ushered in a pairing of an emulsion and caviar with citrus. The food was impressive and not too flashy.

L'Orancourt ordered a bottle of Meursault to begin with. The conversation was as light as the *crème légère*. She was happy to let him drink more than his fair share of the wine. By the time they moved on to the hare, served with gnocchi and truffle oil, he was quizzing the sommelier on red burgundies—just a glass each, for he was saving the Margaux for the *boeuf l'onglet à la poêlé*, giant shanks of bone served mainly for their marrow.

"I've always been attracted to bone marrow," L'Orancourt said, greedily spooning a blob of the stuff. "Something vital, the essence of life, on one's tongue."

"Something that you take for your own?"

"Of course," he said. "That is why we live, is it not? Not merely to consume, but to consume with style."

"I'm getting full."

"Darling, you must try the marrow. Even if it means bursting out of that dress of yours. Especially if it means that."

"Very well—but first I need the ladies'."

She excused herself, kissed him as he swirled his ruby wine, grabbed her little purse and opened the door. She let herself totter a bit on the high heels and tittered back at him. Let him think she was plastered.

Penny fingered her throat and vomited into the private bathroom's sink. The wine had, in fact, been getting to her and the food was going to induce sloth. She needed to be a sprite. Time was running out. She washed her mouth and swallowed a mint. Before leaving she opened her purse and palmed a couple of coins.

She returned as the servers were confirming L'Orancourt's pleasure with the beef. Penny thanked the waiters as they backed out of the room. She whispered, "And now could we have some privacy, please?" and the waiter nodded. She closed the door herself and wedged a one-euro coin into the thin crack between the door and the jamb. The coin would act like a keystone, channeling pressure in order to make it impossible for anyone to open it from the hallway.

"Mm, Thérèse, you must try this," he said, attacking the meat with his steak knife.

She took the knife from his hands and shoved his plate and service to one side. She sat on the edge of the table and swung one leg over his head, straddling him.

"Dessert already?" he said, trying to sound amused but obviously annoyed.

"No one will disturb us. Not for a little while."

He put his hands on her. "Then you won't mind if I make a tear in your beautiful dress."

"But it's expensive."

"I'll buy you a new one."

One hand was on the neckline, the other exploring the slice in her hem. She put that roving hand on the table. He looked up, again not sure if he should be irritated.

"Michel," she said.

"What?"

She stretched back and grabbed a clump of beef from his plate. "Eat from my hand."

Presented on her palm, the glistening flesh was appalling, and impossibly too big to fit a human mouth.

"You're being vulgar," he said. "Stop this nonsense."

"As you wish," she said, mashing the meat on his face, forcing him to bite down on it as her other hand raised his steak knife, flipped it in the air to catch it blade-down, and slammed it into the back of his hand flat on the table. His face burst into a galaxy of scarlet stars and he cried out, but she shoved the gravy-slopped side of beef further into his crevice, muffling the exclamation.

His free hand grasped her arm, the one pushing the beef into his face, but she said, "Michel, look at my heel." The pain and surprise was not so overwhelming as to obscure her command. He glanced down. The steel stiletto rested on top of his crotch. Her leg muscles were taut. One quick push, or even the relaxation of her thigh, and she'd squash his testicle.

"So you're going to be quiet, right?"

When he didn't respond she nudged the knife and pressed the meat and absorbed his scream. The pressure of his hand on her forearm was intense, but he was in no position to break anything.

"Right?" She relaxed her weight onto his balls. He nodded vigorously.

"Good boy," she said, withdrawing the mangled meat and leaving his face covered in brown gravy, as if he had dined at the trough. Which is what, actually, L'Orancourt had been doing for most of his career.

"My hand."

"Release me," Penny commanded.

He pulled his good hand away. He was holding back tears.

"Please, take the knife out."

Good. He had no idea how much worse that would hurt.

"No. Tell me where to find Viktor Gubinov."

This time his face clouded.

"Viktor Gubinov," she repeated. "The man who blackmailed Manfred Ingerholz into shorting Schuman stock. The man who disrupted Fuad Chamoun's operation in Dubai—but not before you downloaded everything from Timur Buribaev's laptop. You know Viktor."

216

"We are in negotiations," he said. "My information on KazPetro in return for a cessation of hostilities."

"It's so sweet to see you boys learn to share." She wiped her hand clean of gravy on the tablecloth.

"Who are you?"

"Viktor. Where do I find him?"

"London. He's in London."

"Where?"

"I don't know."

She thumbed the knife in his hand and he roared with pain. "They're going to come in here any minute."

"No they won't," she said. "Where in London?"

"He's at the house of Sergey Konstantin. The mansion in Highgate. They're holding him there."

"Holding him?"

"Viktor's finished. The Russians are going to kill him as soon as they're satisfied they've settled with me. They want their share of Daesh oil, and they want to make amends for what Viktor did to me—and to my operatives."

"Fuad Chamoun."

"How do you know that name?"

"Fuad's dead."

"What makes you say that?"

"I killed him."

His eyes widened. "Who are you?"

"Before I go, Michel, tell me—has it been worth it? Trying to get oil from the Islamic State and sell it to the Chinese?"

"You think I shouldn't deal with Islamic fundamentalists, is that it? What are you, CIA?"

"I don't work for any government. But I'm curious: the jihadists make strange partners for you."

"They make the facts on the ground. They control half of Syria, half of Iraq, and a lot of oil. So they're crazy, who cares? Let them do their suicide bombings in the Middle East. What can they do to me? This is France—this is the West. We have the power and the Chinese have the money. There's nothing more."

She let her leg relax downward and he screwed his face in pain. "Please don't."

"When I leave this place, you are going to count to twenty before you remove the knife."

"What makes you think you're getting three steps out of this place before dying?"

"Because if I disappear, then a certain video of us in Lille the other week is going to make the rounds."

"You're bluffing."

"Believe that if you wish. But remember when we left, you felt something in my pocket?"

"You're just a whore."

"Sure, that's all that I am." She lifted her leg up. If he was going to make a violent move, it would be now, but the pain and the terror kept the Bulldozer at bay. Penny swung her leg over his head and jumped lightly off the table. She removed her cell phone from her purse and took a photo of him, hand pinned to the table, its white cloth soaking up a widening pool of blood.

"You bitch," he seethed, "I'll kill you for this."

"You can try," she said.

Penny removed the coin from the door as he gingerly tried to extract the knife. The attempt left him whimpering.

"I'd have a doctor do that if I were you," she said before she closed the door. A pair of waiters was about to enter.

"We heard a call."

"Is everything all right, mademoiselle?"

"Everything is fine," she said. "Would you please mind giving Monsieur L'Orancourt a few minutes? He's making an important telephone call—shouting at whoever's on the line. I wouldn't interrupt him if I were you."

She picked her way through the Bois de Boulogne. She came to a van where the prostitutes waited. They were riveted to their cell phones. They barely acknowledged her, seeing Penny was too elegant to be one of them, but there was none of the usual primping and trash talk. Something was amiss.

"What's happening?" Penny asked, wondering if she had underestimated L'Orancourt.

"Shootings, attacks all over Paris," one of the women said. She wasn't crying, but she looked shaken. "It's the terrorists, Daesh."

V

LONDON

20

A walk on the heath

The mass murders in Paris buried Europe's unusually long autumn and ushered in a cold, wet winter. Even Penny couldn't ignore the somberness that suddenly overcame the everyday.

A hundred and eighty-two people had been killed across the city that night. The murderers were young fanatics, convinced that each innocent corpse amounted to a ticket to heaven and endless copulation with angelic, permanently virginal whores. Such was the promise of Daesh, the Islamic State—Michel L'Orancourt's would-be suppliers.

Until that moment, Penny had little time for other people's problems. She had spent her days in Paris working out how to find Viktor and hardening herself against the knowledge of her own evil. Every step had been toward a path of some kind of absolution, a cobblestoned pathway back to the footloose life of parties and no attachments she had thought was her gift.

Terrorism penetrated her fog and struck uncomfortably close. She had been with a man who had sought back-channel dealings with Daesh. This man had been her enemy; a man

223

who had casually ordered Fuad to kill her; a man who rented her flesh and who, in his arrogance, thought he had owned her loyalty. But now he could not be separated from the enormity of what had taken place, and nor, therefore, could she.

Every little thing reminded her of what she had fallen into, what she was, and what yet she might become. The muted defiance of Parisians repopulating their cafes. The closure of French borders and the military raids that disrupted the city's *banlieus*. The lines that deepened people's faces—the lady at Penny's local *boulangerie*, who now paid more attention to TV news than the change she counted; the way the Algerian at her hotel and the other Muslims seemed to shrink into themselves and avoid her gaze.

She had first been aware of losing her sense of control in Dubai, when she couldn't get Viktor out of her head. Now it seemed everything around her was turning lunatic, robbing her of the luxury of living for herself—robbing everyone.

The pallor over life, like the suddenly awful weather, extended across the Channel. She had always liked London, and even that terrible night with Ingerholz and Viktor hadn't ruined the city for her. Now, though, as November collapsed into the year's longest nights, the city evoked a gloom that she resented. Not you guys, too, she wanted to protest.

She arrived via the Eurostar once more carrying the entirety of her possessions. She had left very little in the safety box at Crédit Agricole. She was still traveling as Thérèse Nulty, but she could sense the thinning of the sands in that hourglass. Saint Pancras Station was far newer and smarter than Gare du Nord, but the people moved with the same dolor. The headlines on the tabloids were obsessed with the same depressing news.

She walked through the terminal at Saint Pancras to a

storage company. Satisfied that its security arrangements would suffice for the near term, she was ready to hand over the Pacsafe, a hi-tech bag she had bought at Printemps, which functioned as a portable safe for her passports, cash and credit cards and fit very nicely inside her red backpack. The Pacsafe's skin was made from the same polycarbonate that went into bulletproof glass and was drawn shut by a steel cable and padlocked. It would resist a knife and a low-caliber bullet.

She lifted it out of her backpack now and showed the storage attendant Tamara Camden-Pryce's British passport. She'd hold on to that, and to Thérèse Nulty's identity, but Penny didn't plan to use Tamara's iPhone, so she left it in with the other four lives. She would take Thérèse's and Tamara's items with her—one to use, the other, like now, to cover her tracks and as backup for when the moment came to kill Thérèse.

If someone didn't kill Penny first.

The Pacsafe was placed into a locked cabinet, under the eye of a twenty-four-hour manned desk and a CCTV. The attendant had the same morose posture that seemed to have overtaken everyone in Paris and London in the past few days; his sense of helplessness sapped her gait.

Snap out of it, people. She hadn't come to London to play the victim. The prey had become the hunter.

Time to get to work.

She used Thérèse's phone to check out short-term rentals on Airbnb. London was a big city and she didn't want to spread herself too thinly, so she concentrated on the north: Arsenal, Highbury Hill, Finsbury Park. Close to Highgate but with across-the-tracks rental prices. This was London, though: the exorbitant values of the homes bought by absentee tycoons in the city's toniest boroughs had turned the city into a financial charnel house for everyone else.

Penny met a few of the people looking to let their flats. She wanted an illegal arrangement, a renter ready to sub-let for ready cash, no questions asked. These proved easy to find. She swapped cash for keys with a fat twenty-three-year-old woman who swore the place was clean.

"If the landlord knocks, tell him you're Tracy's mate," the woman instructed.

"Okay, Tracy."

"The last girl in here left her period blood all over me mattress. And the one before that left behind some other stains. I don't mind going back to sleep on your sex blanket, love, but just wash up after yourself, all right?"

"Sure."

The landlord had turned a roomy apartment into a series of one-bedrooms. Tracy's was a kitchen on the second floor with a bed stuck inside. The bathroom was communal. Acrid cigarette smells oozed from the walls, and the person in the room next door had a serious thing for Adele, replaying "Hello" at full volume.

But nobody wanted to know Penny's name.

The building overlooked the train tracks at Finsbury Park station. Outside, the neighborhood was Muslim: men in shalwar kameezzes, their big beards dyed crimson, loitered around the tube station's entrance or on the steps of the terraced houses that lined the streets. A few blocks away, toward Arsenal stadium, the run-down streets turned whiter and working class. It was a rough part of town, but one that kept an uneasy peace. She ate in a chippy whose cook was liberal with the vinegar and the grease. The meal tasted like she felt.

She took the tube to East Finchley, one stop up from High-gate but closer to Sergey Konstantin's residence. As the crow flies, the tube station was a short distance from Finsbury Park, but they might as well have been in separate worlds, linked only by the Underground. It was dark by the time she emerged at East Finchley. It began to rain but the corner Boots was selling small umbrellas cheap.

The Bishops Avenue stretched from the station toward the northern end of Hampton Heath. It was a big, noisy road, impersonal and banal. Either side was lined with giant houses behind tall, locked gates and walls. The phosphorous lamps provided a yellow light that, in the rain, clung to the sidewalk like a putrid mist. She peered through the iron bars and through the breaks between gates. Most of the houses loomed in blackness, their sterile driveways and gigantic archways bleakly silent. Only a handful had the lights on, the occasional mansion lit up in a display of ostentatious size.

A quick online search had revealed that Sergey Konstantin owned one of these monstrosities. This was Billionaire's Avenue, a dumping ground for the vast, opaque wealth of foreign oligarchs, Saudi princes, friends of Putin, and the odd footballer. Few of these luminaries lived here, and even in the shadows of the rainy night she could tell that several mansions had gone derelict. Tens of millions, or even hundreds of millions of pounds, all to claim an address on this ugly street, to own a rotting dump next to other criminals' rotting dumps. She walked through the heart of the global crony-capitalist order, a street paved not with gold but with crumbling cement.

But as she approached the end of the avenue, where it formed in a T-cross with a highway encircling Hampstead Heath, she found an unusual buzz of activity. White spotlights wreathed

227

the last mansion in a harsh, bright glare. Workers in orange day-glo uniforms, arms full of equipment and furnishings, crossed between the mansion's entrance and a trio of delivery lorries. A cement truck's abdomen rotated while a backhoe awaited its next orders.

The orders of Viktor's uncle and protector, Sergey Konstantin.

She marveled that the construction crew was allowed to continue in this residential neighborhood despite the obvious noise and inconvenience they were causing. But the mansion next door was dark behind its wall, as was the one across the street, so perhaps no one was around to complain.

This is why Konstantin had been easy to find. He had made the news. The mansion he had bought three years ago from a Kuwaiti prince was undergoing a massive refurbishment, adding a vast double layer of basements that had caught some attention. An intrepid reporter at the *Daily Mail* had penetrated the layers of British Virgin Island and Isle of Man paperwork, picked up some clues from unhappy neighbors, and made a crafty guess. If Sergey Konstantin wasn't the owner, then the *Daily Mail* had made it clear it welcomed his defamation lawsuit.

The house, she had read, was in the Queen Anne style. She saw now that it was tall, fashioned of brick, with a series of floor-to-ceiling windows in tidy, conservative rows, their edges painted red. The mansion rose three high stories, with a triangular frieze over the central section and a quartet of stout gray chimneys boldly capping the roof. It was a most respectable and bland façade, as though the owner was happy to let the neighborhood location rather than the exterior proclaim his obscene wealth.

She shivered. The rain was a sheet of cold pellets, and the umbrella was too small to offer much protection. She was bedraggled and catching the sniffles.

But that wasn't what made her shiver.

Penny returned the next day, from a different direction. Strangely enough, the construction activity during the daytime was muted. The trucks were there but not in use, and there was no sign of the work crew—at least not on the outside. They were burrowing down, she guessed, adding to the mansion's square footage one layer at a time.

She studied the security cameras perched around the perimeter of the house. Some of the cameras pointed down at the streets, at the heath, at the surrounding houses. Some pointed within the mansion's own grounds. Spying on the spies.

Taking paranoia to a new level.

She knew she'd get noticed if she crossed this way too many times. The traffic on the street was forced to a crawl as it navigated the construction equipment at the junction of the two roads. There were no other pedestrians here; on a summer's day, there might be more people coming in and out of the park, but not now.

She kept her distance on the third visit, aware that the heath's edge was under surveillance. The day was cold and cloudy. Her fingers were raw as she maneuvered the binocular lenses from a park bench. She didn't need details, just a sense of the workers' movements. She sat until she was stiff with chill and then went for a walk. She returned a little later wearing a hat, to try to look different, and found a spot by a clump of trees that provided a view of the street corner.

Workmen came and went, but there was no sense of shifts. A shuttle bus made the rounds, disgorging workmen or scooping them up. But she couldn't tell if it kept steady hours. No other cars entered or exited the compound. Her next step would be to rent a car and tail the shuttle. She would need to get herself a uniform and whatever passes the men used to gain entrance.

Penny had hoped she could catch some workers walking away from the site, to grab lunch or enjoy a cigarette. Any clue to how she could infiltrate the mansion. But she saw no sign of that being permitted. She could trace the workers to a source, but even with a uniform and a hard hat, how could she remain unnoticed on their shuttle bus?

Day four it rained again. The weather was blunt and un-apologetic. She hunched over in a hooded raincoat, crossing the edge of the heath, the damp penetrating her jeans, the mud sucking at her Patagonia hiking shoes. Work seemed to have paused. The chimneys loomed over the park like a ghostly version of a steamship docked in the fog.

A figure emerged on the heath. A short man in a long gray raincoat, striding beneath a golf umbrella that hid his face. She had encountered a few wanderers in the park over the past few days but none today, probably because the weather was so miserable. The man wasn't really heading for her, and he moved with purpose. She envied him his destination.

She kept an eye on the man as he vectored down the path that lay behind her. When she glanced back toward the house, she realized there was someone else approaching from the other side—another man, taller, skinnier, also wearing a gray raincoat, umbrella just obscuring his face. He was going to cross in front of her, and he walked with a strange jaunt, waving a cane in front of him as if he were blind.

Two gentlemen dandies.

Crossing as they reached her, one behind, the other in front.

The cane. Dubai.

She bolted to the right, but the mud clung to her ankles. The cane shot out unencumbered and snared her arm. The mud conspired with him. He had discharged his umbrella to wield his cane with both hands, extending it like a sword, and with a quick twist he sent her sprawling onto the heath's mire. The sloppy earth was cold against her body. Penny rose to her hands and knees. The shorter man behind her grappled her from behind, pinning his closed umbrella over her chest.

"Let's don't brawl in the mud," he said.

"Let go of me."

"I apologize for the unpleasantness," said the taller man with the cane. "But we'd rather you didn't run away."

"Yes, we'd rather you didn't, Miss Lee," echoed the man holding her tight with his umbrella. Both of them wore bowlers that protected them from the rain; the tall man's eyes loomed large behind his square secretary glasses. They looked like a pair of old bankers transported from their wood-and-leather City offices. But the speed with which they had trapped her left her stunned. She didn't rate her odds of fighting them off.

"Why don't you join us for a nice cup of tea?"

"Just the thing for this beastly weather, a cup of tea."

Penny relaxed beneath the man's grip.

"All right," she said. "But only if you have biscuits."

21

Invitation to kill

Instead of walking her to the front door—around the heavy trucks, through the gate—they paused by the roadside. A Range Rover Sport emerged from the rain and rolled to a stop by the curb. The car's masculine lines were a dark electric blue, flashing like the scales of a watery predator.

The dandy with the cane opened the rear door and she felt the shorter one nudge her from behind. Penny got in, the two operatives flanking her inside the back seat. The driver was dressed as a construction worker, minus the hardhat. He had a bland face, straw hair and a flat nose, all belied by sharp eyes. Without awaiting instructions, he pulled the Range Rover into traffic and made the first left off Hampstead Lane. Another boulevard of rich people's houses beckoned, but this immediate corner was parkland.

The car slowed and turned left again, onto an oak-lined biking trail dividing the plot of grass and trees. They halted before a lowered beam and the driver clicked a remote control. The beam lifted and they drove around a bend into a paved lane that immediately descended into the earth. The driver used his remote to open the underground entrance of steel teeth.

They drove into a tunnel that circled downwards until they emerged in a low, long parking garage. Penny guessed this was the lowest basement of Konstantin's mansion. The space was mostly empty, but to one end were several luxury cars: sedans, roadsters and a bronze Maserati that, even tamely asleep between its white lines, looked ready to pounce. Workers had left a bulldozer parked further away, as though not to embarrass the owner's classier rides.

The driver halted the Range Rover a few spaces away from the cluster of luxury cars. "They've got the lifts working now," he told the others, sliding the car keys above the sun visor. His English was almost good enough to mask his Slavic accent. "No need to take the stairs."

"A few ground rules, Miss Lee," said the shorter of her captors. "No running about unaccompanied, please."

"It's not that we doubt your manners," the other said.

"It's just that we'd rather not have to disable you."

"And cause a mess."

"That's reassuring to hear," Penny said.

"Right, then." The shorter dandy opened his passenger door.

She scooted out of the back seat, trying to get a sense of direction, but the circular descent had interrupted her orientation. On the far side of the garage, opposite the ramp leading up to the meadow, was an industrial-sized elevator, its doors closed; it was a car lift that would take vehicles up to the front gate, but her captors had opted to bring her through the tunnel for discretion, or to simply avoid the confusion of construction outside.

The dandies escorted her in a lateral direction, toward an elevator designed for people.

"One moment please," the shorter man said, frisking her from behind.

"Terribly sorry," the other said.

"I do hope you understand." The man held up Thérèse's iPhone and the binoculars. "She's clean."

"I want to speak to Konstantin," she said as the taller man punched B1. They were currently on B3. "I have something for him."

"I regret to inform you that Mr. Konstantin is not home."

"He'll want to speak with me. I have something that he wants."

"And what is that?" asked the shorter man.

"Leverage over Michel L'Orancourt." The video, edited to remove any clear shots of Penny's face, was on the phone that the shorter man had pocketed.

The lift doors opened on B1. "We'll be sure to pass that along. Now, we promised you a spot of tea."

They walked down a tall corridor of paneled cherry wood. Each door was decorated with a brass plate inscribed with Cyrillic letters. One was open and she saw a barber's chair and a countertop cluttered with scissors and sprays.

"This way, please."

The two men ushered her to a T-intersection and into what she guessed was a guest apartment. The suite was decorated like a contemporary hotel, with clean lines of beiges, whites and browns, and included a small kitchen, a sitting room with a television and a game console, and a pair of bedrooms. There were no windows, but there was a wall lined with books.

"Have a seat, Miss Lee," said the tall man, heading for the

kitchen. "Charles, has this been stocked?"

"Yes, Chester," said the shorter man. She saw this one, Charles, was gray, gray-skinned and gray-eyed, with a large chin that tucked into his barrel chest as he contemplated a vape pen.

Chester scanned the cabinets, lithe as a balding cat, eyes big behind his lenses, and put a kettle on.

Penny sneezed. Getting the sniffles was the least of her fears.

"I'll fetch the tissue box," Charles said, ducking into a bathroom.

Chester said from the kitchen, "I find Darjeeling particularly effective against an inclement chill."

She sat down on the sofa. The clipped accents, stuffy suits and overwrought manners didn't fool her. These two were killers.

Chester brought out a trio of porcelain teacups on a platter, along with a sugar bowl and creamer, all held with one hand; the other gripped his cane, which he only released to pour each of them a cup through a strainer. "You poor dear, you sound like you're catching a cold."

"As you say, Chester, it's not nice out there." Penny tried to hide her gratitude for the first sip.

"Your snooping skills are rudimentary," Charles told her as he passed her the tissue box. "You should have saved yourself the bother and simply knocked on the door."

"You would have let me in?"

"Well," Charles said, "we do admit we were surprised to see you."

"Quite surprised," Chester added.

"Chester, where are our manners?" Charles exclaimed. "My dear, please accept our condolences for the loss of your sister."

"Yes," Chester said, "that was a terrible business."

"Which your man committed," Penny said. "Viktor Gubinov. He was working for you."

"Well, not quite," Charles said.

"He doesn't report to us," Chester added.

"And you two?" Penny asked. "You work for Konstantin, don't you?"

"Yes," they said together.

"And you helped Viktor in Dubai. You helped him murder Stack and Lev, and you helped him try to murder me."

"It was more of a performance review," Charles said.

"We provided an opinion," said Chester, as though agreeing that the weather was indeed inclement.

She took another sip of the tea. It was starting to warm her insides. "You want me dead."

"Our interest in you is tangential," Chester said. "When you and Mr. Stack robbed Mr. Gubinov, you were taking more than just *his* money. You see, Mr. Gubinov is not a man of means. He lives a comfortable life on the graces of his patrons."

"Meaning Konstantin," Penny said.

"Among others," Charles said. "Mr. Konstantin's relation-ships in his home country are extensive."

"Many mutual interests."

"Overlapping objectives."

"Konstantin oversees Russia's energy sector," Penny said. "Enimash is his company. He's got ties to Gazprom, Rosneft, coal."

"Don't believe the media," Charles objected.

"It's a gross caricature," Chester chimed in.

"A crude misunderstanding. No pun intended."

"And the Russian mob," Penny snapped. "Not that there's

a difference now."

"You really deploy the most unsophisticated language," Charles sighed.

Penny said, "You probably think Stack took twenty-three million dollars out of Viktor's bank account out of greed. But that wasn't the reason." Well, not the only reason.

"We suspected something along those lines," Charles said.

She brushed aside a cautionary stab of shame. Penny had no time for bearing the sins of others. "He did it for me. Viktor raped me, here in London, a year ago, and Stack had to watch it happen. Yeah, we took your boss's money. Don't expect an apology."

"A heart-wrenching tale, but a greater principle was at stake," Chester said. "Our employer and his business associates in Moscow...they are really quite strict regarding these matters."

"Rigid, even," Charles said.

"How did you find us?" Penny asked. "How did you know we'd be working on a job in Dubai?"

"The important thing," Chester said, ignoring her question, "is that Mr. Konstantin held Mr. Gubinov responsible for the breach in his finances."

"But Mr. Gubinov had hitherto been a loyal operative," Charles said.

"He and Mr. Konstantin have a familial bond."

"Therefore Mr. Konstantin agreed to give Mr. Gubinov the chance to make amends," Charles said.

"By killing us," Penny said. "In Dubai."

"Yes. We were along merely to observe. Mr. Konstantin wanted a clear response—"

"Very clear."

"But one that would not involve the Emirati authorities."

"Or one that would jeopardize his affairs in the Middle East."

"Or embarrass him in any way."

"Which meant—"

Penny said: "I had to die in Timur's suite, out of sight."

"Having the spectacle move into the public sphere caused us some complications," Chester said.

"Quite a few challenges," Charles said.

"And I didn't die," Penny said. "I got away. Why didn't you two kill me when you had the chance?"

"That simply wouldn't have done," Chester protested.

"Not at all appropriate!"

"So this was Viktor's job and he blew it," Penny said. "Flunked Konstantin's test. I didn't see you two at Fuad Chamoun's compound. Did Konstantin order the assault?"

"No," Chester said.

"We had other plans for the Chamoun operation," Charles said.

Penny finished her tea. "Viktor was becoming a liability for you. Maybe he was trying to make up for everything going wrong in Dubai, get back in your graces by killing me in Lebanon. And then that didn't work, so he murdered my sister at her wedding."

"A string of errors," Charles said, "of which we had no foreknowledge."

"It has put our employer in an awkward position."

"I'll bet it has," Penny mused. "I helped Schuman steal KazPetro's data. That data proved Russia was using Timur's company to secretly broker a deal for Russia to get its hands on oil under the control of Isis and sell it to China. Sergey Konstantin had been assigned the job of trying to negotiate with L'Orancourt, come up with a deal to save everybody's face, maybe split the proceeds from the oil deal. Which the French might say yes to, because they don't care about a bunch of jihadis running around Syria and Iraq—that's America's problem. But Konstantin's operative, Viktor, because he's a goddamn psycho, got in the way by trying to murder me in Dubai—pissing off L'Orancourt and the Europeans, who now don't want to deal with the Russians, and might turn to America for help instead. Especially now that your friends in Isis have gone around murdering hundreds of people in Paris, an operation financed by the money they're getting from foreign oil companies."

"Coordination among so many moving parts," Chester lamented.

"Quite the challenge," Charles agreed.

"But you still haven't told me how you knew I'd be in Dubai."

Penny leaned back on the sofa. "Clown school. I'd have expected better from the Cheka." She copied an old habit of Fuad's, using the original name of the Russian intelligence service from its Leninist days. Cheka, KGB, SVR...the names had changed but the clique of despotic espionage services hadn't.

"Chester, she thinks we're Russian intelligence."

"How droll, Charles. No, Penelope, we are merely Englishmen with a certain disaffection for our present system of so-called liberal democracy."

"And Mr. Konstantin is a generous employer."

"Why am I still alive?" Penny asked.

"We have been impressed by your ability to survive," Charles said.

"And the fact that you work for various free enterprises."

"For generous pay, rather than the siren's call of patriotism."

Penny folded her arms and looked up at the two dandies. "You guys have one bizarre recruitment pitch. Do you know why I'm here?"

"You think you want to kill Mr. Gubinov," Charles said.

"A wish we might be disposed to grant," Chester added.

"You have useful skills."

"And a valuable family background."

That last one threw her. "Fuad?"

Chester and Charles exchanged an uncertain look.

"Viktor murdered whatever family I had left."

"We can offer you a new one," Charles said.

"Sorry," Penny said. "I'm not looking to take on new obligations. I have dirt on L'Orancourt I can trade for Viktor; Schuman Corporation doesn't have to be a threat to your oil interests anymore."

"Charles, what do you think?"

"Well, Chester, our employer might consider a trade."

"Provided, of course, he trusts the counterparty."

The eyes behind the big square glasses revealed the soul of a praying mantis. "There are ways to determine trust."

"Is Viktor alive?" Penny asked.

The two men exchanged a look. "Come with us," they said together.

Charles led the way, vaping an e-cigarette—his boss forbade actual smoking inside, he said—and Chester loomed behind her, his cane's taps harmonizing with the clacking of their leather shoes and the occasional squeak from her rubber soles.

The upper basement was dedicated to leisure. In addition to the hair salon, she saw the entrance to a cinema, a bowling alley, and a room full of game tables—air hockey, foosball, table tennis. The entire place seemed empty, although she heard a muffled thumping and metallic scraping sounds, which suggested work going on below, on the floor between her and the garage.

"What's down there?" she asked.

"The swimming pool and the ice rink," Charles said.

The hallway meandered and most of the doors, identified in Russian script, were closed. Charles led them to a halt. She heard a ruffle and saw Chester remove a wallet from his breast pocket.

"And upstairs?"

"The manor house proper," Chester said.

"The usual trappings," Charles added.

Chester's long fingers plucked a plain white plastic card from the folds of his wallet. "Here we are."

Charles reached behind his back and removed something tucked into his belt. He handed it to her: a knife. She was surprised how well it had been concealed beneath his jacket, because it was a thick, six-inch blade with a sturdy but small handle, perfect for her size, with just a little jibbing in the middle and a crescent hook opposite for different kinds of grips.

Penny took a step back. "Whoa," she said, keeping her hands at her sides but prepared to fight. She knew how to disarm an opponent, but she didn't know how fast Charles might be— and it was a meaty blade.

Charles offered her the knife with both of his hands. "Take it."

"I'm not touching that thing until I know what's going on."

Chester touched the card to the brass plaque by the door. She heard an electronic beep and the door gently swung inward. Heat poured into the hallway from within.

Chester said, "Viktor is inside. Kill him."

22

The cobra watches

Penny pushed the door open, her right hand clutching the knife near her breast, as though it might calm her heartbeat. She faced a changing room: two rows of spacious, wood-paneled lockers, flanking a cushioned bench and ending in another door. A layer of humidity shined on the floor's dark mosaic tiles. The banality worsened her terror.

She didn't need to turn around to sense Charles looking up at her back and Chester gazing down, like a pair of vultures mismatched in size but not in appetite. Penny had to do this. She looked inside the locker room again, felt the solidity of the weapon clenched in her fist, and tried to clear her mind. The fear couldn't be dismissed, but it could be boxed up and set aside. She stepped into the locker room, and the door quietly closed.

She did look back, then, at the bland black face of the door and a new kind of fear slithered through her mind. *I'm not an assassin.* Another thought surprised her: *Daddy didn't want this for me.*

What a time to think of her father, to plow the fields of grief. She couldn't allow such indulgences. But the question lingered. What had she come here for? What was the price of exit?

Her movements squeaked against the tiles, so she knelt to untie the laces and removed her shoes. She pulled off her socks and stuffed them inside the sneakers. The tiles were warm against her feet.

She advanced, then thought again and looked for a low-level locker to stow her shoes in, as though this was a perfectly normal visit. She didn't bother taking the key, but she noticed that two of the lockers were missing theirs. Two.

Viktor wasn't alone.

Keeping the knife high, Penny opened the opposite door. It swung inward and she entered a bathroom. Shower stalls lined one side, a mirror and sinks the other. No one was there. She crept through the bathroom, pausing to nudge aside the door leading to the toilet. Empty. She caught a glimpse of herself in the mirrors. Perhaps it was the size of the knife, six inches of broad black blade, as dark and wide as her eyes, that made her look so small.

She adjusted the knife, moving it back and low. The weapon with its small grip was comfortable in her hand, but its balance was centered further down the body of the blade, not where it met the handle, making the knife want to thrust forward. It was an eager weapon.

It would get its chance soon enough.

The shower stalls ended at an intersection, left or right. She paused and heard nothing. She turned left and entered a green-tiled chamber with a trio of plunge pools. The furthest one gave off a whisper of steam.

She turned from this dead end and walked the other way.

The stubby corridor concluded at a door made of light-colored wood, with a narrow window slit: a sauna.

Procrastinating, she tried a few different knife holds. *I've never stabbed anyone before.* Aikido had taught her how to disarm an opponent coming at her with a blade or a gun. Not how to stab someone. *This is crazy.*

She looked at the sauna door. Go in violently, do a roll and spring to her feet, the blade at Viktor's throat? Burst in with a blood-curdling battle cry? Scream *This is for my sister* and start slashing?

Penny unzipped her hoodie and let it hush down to the floor. Wearing just her T-shirt and blue jeans, she pressed the door and walked inside.

A cloud of steam enveloped her. The temperature was choking hot. She was not in the sauna proper, but a wood-paneled vestibule with a low shelf. On it were a wooden bucket, a pair of felt gloves and a bundle of green birch leaves.

That's when she heard it: *thwack.* And again: *thwack.*

She peered around the corner. The sauna was roomy, striped by planks of pale wood. Steam hovered over fist-sized rocks piled in the center atop a heater.

Thwack.

The standing man, naked, was crafted of ruddy muscle. A brown felt helmet covered his head, obscuring his features, but she could tell he was golden-haired—it covered his body, and even through the mist she could see the down gilding his broad back, clinging to his rock-like shins. He raised a fistful of branches, their leaves an incongruous bright green, and brought it down again on the other man.

Thwack.

Viktor lay on the bench, also naked, whiter, shorter, skinnier than the man flagellating him with the broom. Red lines crossed his back and his upward-facing thighs. His hair, also blond, had been shorn to a buzz, making him look almost bald, but she recognized him at once. In the heat of the sauna, his harelip pulsed a shade of pink.

Viktor opened his eyes. Those hadn't changed—the dull, casually cruel brown orbs of indifference. He looked right at her.

The man in the felt hat stopped his blow in mid-air.

Penny stepped into the sauna. She kept the knife low because she didn't want them to see it shaking in her hand.

The man in the felt hat had golden pubic hair. His penis was limp and tick-tocked harmlessly. His Chinese eyes, though, blazed from below the rim of his hat, and seeing her sent blood into his sex. He stepped to one side as Viktor propped himself up on his elbows, raising his head with a cobra's displeasure.

Aikido lesson number one: never look your opponent in the face. Number two: keep your hands low. And number three: never wait for your opponent to strike.

The knife was becoming too hot to hold. The man with Chinese eyes and the growing erection stepped around the rocks, brandishing his broom. This prompted her to raise her knife. She saw murder written in his face. She froze.

Slash slash—she grunted with the movements, a childish attempt to ward him off. Everything was wrong. His birch branches deflected her thrust and *bam* he punched her. She heard the crunch, felt every solid knuckle knock her face— everything was *wrong*—sensed the blood flying in the air might be hers, and then she slipped on the wet flooring and collapsed.

Her training kicked in and she turned the fall into a roll,

avoiding the axe blow of the man's heel. She found her knees, but the moisture in the air weighed her clothes down, making them heavy. She tried to breathe, but the acrid air denied her a satisfactory inhalation and her heart began to scream. The man closed in as she straightened up. She blocked his branches with one arm and flicked the blade toward him, letting its natural weight do the work. She missed but was on her feet now and her thrust forced him back.

Viktor didn't move. The cobra watched.

The man with Chinese eyes chopped her left arm with the side of his hand. He might as well have been the one with the knife: the karate blow sent a cold shudder through her arm, and she cried out. Her legs were pressed to an empty bench, her back to nothing at all. The knife burned in her hand. All she wanted to do was release it.

Her attacker paused to make a snide joke in Russian. Viktor's men had this habit of treating her like a plaything.

That's when she appeared at his side, inside his punching arc, and slashed the blade, aiming for his throat. He bent backwards in time, but she etched a dangerous line across his inflated torso. It was a scratch, but her knife was incapable of anything dainty. He looked down at his fleshy pecs with disbelief. Then he attacked her, everything swinging, and it was all she could do to fend him off. He was enraged and her left arm was turning numb. All she had was the knife, but it was like stabbing someone on angel dust or LSD: the man didn't seem to care. He took her slashes and kept coming, smashing his fist at her, on her, into her. With a blaze of stars, one of her eyes sealed.

His hands got a double grip on her—elbow in her throat, the other hand's fingers grasping her lips, ripping her face off if he couldn't first snap her neck. They groaned at each other, eyeball to eyeball, swapping spit and sauna air.

Viktor, the idea of Viktor, saved her: he didn't know it, but she wasn't going to die like this, not with him spectating. No way.

But there was nothing she could do except struggle against the blond man's slow squeezing of her life. She lost track of the knife, her two hands staving off the rupturing of her jaw. She hissed out her breath and struggled to inhale a new one.

He fell against her and the break didn't come. Something hot and gushing pelted her belly. The man's weight was fully against her, the hands were still groping her face, trying to complete the kill.

He stumbled sideways and looked down. The black blade was buried in his ravaged abdomen. With both hands he gripped the hilt and extracted it with a long groan, in the process unzipping a mouth. Out peeked blue eels. He dropped the knife and tried to scoop up his intestines. She thought her heart would explode as sulfur filled her mouth and lungs. The man with Chinese eyes, her fellow Eurasian, looked at her with cloudy fear and toppled onto the rocks. Their sizzle was audible over his scream and sent up a new, pink-tinged cloud.

She keeled over, ready to puke.

Viktor hadn't moved. He regarded her with serpentine cool.

Penny swallowed the bile. She could only see out of one eye, which seemed to cast the sauna in a shifting shadow. She scooped the knife from the floor, the act rushing blood into her head and making her woozy. The weapon was too hot, so she passed it from one hand to the other. She faced the man she had come to kill.

Viktor remained propped on his palms, elbows tucked into

his elongated torso, looking bemused.

She stepped around the dead man and raised the knife. Its black steel was completely covered in blood. So, she realized, was she. Her feet left tracks of it.

Penny took a step closer. She was within striking range, and the forward weight in the blade begged her to stab. This was it. This was what she had come for.

And I, I revel.

Viktor didn't smile. He didn't question her. He waited.

Letting L'Orancourt abuse her in every way. Submitting herself. Lying, bribing, fighting her way across a continent. Transforming herself from prey into the hunter, to rid the world of this tormentor.

Viktor grabbed her knife wrist.

Her focus snapped back.

He extended his neck in that cobra position and drew her knife toward his throat. He didn't look crazy, or suicidal, or sad. He looked patient.

His grip was strong and she was weak. The room spun. She couldn't breathe. Her vision clouded. He squeezed her wrist, demanding her answer as he maneuvered her blade against his jugular. Her fogging eye focused on the dead Eurasian's blood seeping from the blade down Viktor's throat.

Do it.

Do it, he said. сделай это!

Not like this.

She didn't know where the thought came from. But she couldn't ignore it. Resistance overwhelmed her. *Not like this.*

Because this is not your revenge. This was doing a service for Charles and Chester. This act was not going to bring release; it was going to make her their servant. Slashing Viktor's throat was as good as signing a contract in blood.

She loosened her grip on the knife. She didn't want Viktor to kill her, but she was so tired, her heart was so angry, and her lungs were so desperate, that maybe she would accept that. Maybe, staring into her enemy's eyes, that was what she deserved.

He pushed her away. She was too weak to do anything but fall on her ass. He got up, her rapist's penis showing no sign of interest. He walked out of the sauna.

Penny tried to get up, but she couldn't. The dead man's blood was pooling across the floor. It was in the air. Some of it was hers, too. She had to crawl. That was the best she could do. She crawled on her elbows and knees away from the corpse cooking on the rocks, slipping on his blood, avoiding the long blue rope connecting to his guts, and made it to the vestibule.

Viktor was gone.

She pushed the door open and collapsed in the hallway, gasping.

She pulled her legs out of the sauna and the door closed behind her. Penny lay on the floor panting, trying to stop the spinning in her head.

Black wing tips, brightly polished, beneath gray pinstriped pant legs. Two pairs. Charles and Chester each grabbed her by the armpit and dragged her toward the showers. They didn't bother with her clothes. They dropped her inside an open stall. The water was a frigid surprise and she choked on it, squirming beneath the torrent. They shut it off and grabbed her again. She might have been saying something like *No no no*, but anything coming from her mouth was just a ragged moan.

I should have killed him.

The thought crystallized as Charles and Chester manhandled her body through the locker room.

The pain, the injuries, the futility of her situation—none of it mattered. She had blown it. Viktor was alive.

"Disappointing," Charles said, as though reading her thoughts.

"We had expected better," Chester said as they dragged her into the outer corridor.

They dropped her without ceremony in front of the apartment door. Chester pressed the electronic keycard to the lock.

"What now?" she mumbled. It came out thick through her lips, but it was two clear words.

"Now we consult," Charles said.

"And you wait," Chester added.

"Although I suspect we know the outcome."

"Mr. Konstantin is consistent in such matters."

She had a question, but when she opened her mouth, out came a whoosh and she was crying. She couldn't believe the force of it. It was profoundly embarrassing, but she couldn't help it: grief possessed her. Vivian...Fuad.

She had betrayed them all.

"Pathetic," Charles said as they picked her up. She wanted to enter the living quarters on her own steam but felt utterly defeated.

"Yes, you might have seen your father again." They dumped her in front of the sofa.

Penny said, "He's dead." It seemed pointless to correct them; the response was merely automatic.

"Perhaps not," Charles said.

"Not after all," Chester said.

"Wait," Penny said. "What?"

"Mr. Konstantin might shed some light," Charles said.

"He's privy to all sorts of information."

She hoisted herself to a sitting position against the sofa. Time for a full sentence. "My father died in a car accident ten years ago."

The two men shrugged simultaneously, like a pair of vaudeville players.

"Wait," she rasped, but they had already shut the door.

23

The gift of a Glock

Revulsion wouldn't leave her be. It was the same sensation Penny had experienced in the wake of the massacre in Tuscany. It was a deep-in-the-gut howl. Cooped up in that underground, windowless apartment, the insatiable, blind static was the only thing in her mind that kept her from finding a way to kill herself. That... and the enigmatic shrug of the two vaudeville clowns. The comedians with the knives and the canes had cast her a lifeline. They had done it with purpose. She had failed their test—or maybe she hadn't.

Jonas Tang alive. Could it be true?

Thinking about him helped when she looked at the bathroom mirror. Her nose was swollen and red. Bruises ringed her eyes like obscene sunglasses. Any distraction helped, although when the construction workers began their drilling, sending the room into booming shivers, the pain grew nearly unbearable.

That was not the only thing hard to endure. The idea that he might be alive was no unalloyed blessing.

She had adored her father. She had wept for him more times than she cared to admit. Had she failed him by not getting to the bottom of his death? Or, worse...had he betrayed her?

She thought about these things as she lay on the sofa with a bag of frozen peas from the kitchen fridge pressed against her nose. She kept her head propped up on pillows to counter the swelling, wishing for an aspirin or something stronger. Even a can of beer would have helped dull the pain.

She had no sense of time: the construction work was too sporadic, fifteen or twenty minutes of intense noisemaking, punctured by long silences or the occasional hammer's staccato.

The coldest comfort was that, most likely, Charles and Chester were clever liars who knew how to manipulate her. They were playing her, teasing her along to complete their mastery over her. They wanted to convert Penny to their side, so they had served her a sham sandwich with extra rubbish.

Which would mean Jonas really was dead. Some happy ending.

They left her with plenty of time to think things through, to refreeze the bag of peas and to tend to a possibly broken nose, to endure the intermittent drilling. The bookshelves were lined with freshly printed classics in hardback, and she found Aeschylus again, hoping to finish the Orestes, but it hurt too much to read. Time stretched and she slept, awoke, slept again. Maybe a day or a day and a half? The fridge and the kitchen cabinets were stocked with basics: granola and cereal, oranges to peel, bread she could toast, pre-sliced cheese and salami, tea to brew. No knives though, or forks, just some dull spoons for the sugar.

Penny had spent the first years as Fuad's ward obsessing

over his relationship with her father. Fuad's story never really stacked up: how in the US he had saved Jonas's life in the wake of an accident, how he had introduced him to the beautiful woman from Germany studying on a Fulbright scholarship, how Jonas seemed to owe so much to Fuad that he made him the godfather to his daughters, only for Fuad to break off contact long ago.

She had probed Fuad and Daliyah and even Etienne about these things during those first, difficult years in Beirut. Fuad kept to the same line, and gradually she came to recognize it as a cover story: his recollection was always too precise, too consistent, to be true. But by the time Penny had recognized the obfuscation, she had become invested in the lifestyle. Shimura's dojo became her refuge in times of doubt; she began to enjoy the work and grew addicted to its benefits. She had grown out of her teenage anger and blossomed into someone of surprising confidence and competence. At some point she decided she didn't care anymore. Melody Tang was gone: she was now Penelope Lee, and the past could go to hell.

Always a loner—yet she had never felt more isolated than in Sergey Konstantin's prison. Penelope Lee had been a fabrication that she decided had become real. But if Jonas Tang were alive... then who was she? What was she?

The only answer she had: *I'm not theirs.* Such a reaction made no sense, of course. With Fuad dead she had no employer. She had no income, no work. Why not switch to Charles and Chester's operation? What did it matter who they worked for, if they were prepared to be generous employers? As they had said, she didn't work for a government or a cause. She had always worked for herself —for cash, lots of cash that she burned through as quickly as she could make it. She had embraced industrial espionage with no strings attached.

So why not work for Konstantin?

Maybe it had been the Daesh killing spree in Paris. Or perhaps something deeper was going on, something she couldn't pinpoint. Maybe this charade about her father was part of the problem. But she knew in her gut—a feeling almost as strong as the revulsion that now sickened her—that she couldn't work for these people. The Chamouns and their corporate clients were far from noble, but there had been an underlying contract, perhaps never voiced, that stipulated for her a degree of independence and dignity. Fuad had thought she had betrayed him. She'd give him that much credit.

On Konstantin's side, no matter how shiny the diamonds, they were baubles worn by slaves.

And the one thing she didn't regret was sparing Viktor. She wasn't going to let him die that easily, or on someone else's terms.

Penny had worked that much out, when the door opened.

She couldn't believe who had just come in.

He entered with no warning. She was dozing on the sofa when she heard the soft electronic beep of the door's lock. Penny roused herself as the door opened. Alarm sped her awake, because only predators prowled on the other side of that door. But she knew when she saw him that he hadn't come to murder her.

At least, that's what she hoped.

He slipped inside with a furtive motion that suited his slender frame. Kasym Shokay closed the door with a quick backward glance. He looked wary and worn. The cheesy mustache quivered, and he had lines of stress around his black eyes that she hadn't noticed before. He wore a dark suit, no tie.

The bulge beneath his jacket was obvious as he leaned against the door. His eyes darted around the room, returning to her over and over. He looked as though he was already regretting having come here.

Penny stood up but remained by the sofa, her hands loose at her sides.

"This is a surprise," she opened.

"Yes, it is."

They remained standing apart.

Penny gestured to the coffee table with its empty mug and a plate of orange peels. "Would you like something to eat? Or some tea?"

"No, thank you."

"I don't have any alcohol here."

"I don't drink," he said. And that was right. She couldn't remember ever seeing Kasym participate in one of Timur's binges. "I am a true Muslim."

"Of course," she said. "Well, then, would you like a seat?" She gestured to one of the two chairs facing the sofa.

"No."

"All right," she said. "Then we'll stand."

"In here, you are alone?"

"Yes." As he peered into the bedroom, she asked, "How's Timur?"

"Chairman Buribaev is fine, no thanks to you." He seemed to be working up a sort of courage. "Don't waste my time asking these things. We both know you don't care."

"So why are you here, Kasym?"

He paused. He shouldn't be there. The next words would be his Rubicon.

"I'm the...how do you say...the diplomat, between Sergey

257

Konstantin and Michel L'Orancourt."

Penny conjectured, "You've been back and forth between here and Paris. Trying to get a ceasefire."

"Here, Paris, Astana, Moscow."

"Will there be peace?"

"*Inshallah*, there will be peace."

"You know, Kasym, I believe that is the first time I ever heard you use that expression. Or refer to yourself as a Muslim."

"Of course I'm Muslim. Kazakhs are Muslim."

"Some are more Muslim than others, from what I saw."

"I didn't come here for listening insults."

She raised her palms. "Sorry. Just an observation."

"You have caused us great harm. Why do I come here, to listen to an ignorant kafir?"

Penny said, "I'm going into the kitchen to get a glass of water. Would you like one?"

"No, stay where you are."

"Okay."

He wasn't reaching for what looked like the gun beneath his jacket, and Penny didn't sense he was a physical threat, at least not yet. Kasym was wrestling with his decision to visit her, and she wanted to understand what was going on. "So," she said, "you've been spending a lot of time in this house. Want to tell me about it?"

"Why did you attack us?" he demanded.

"L'Orancourt paid us to steal Timur's plans about creating a pipeline of Iraqi and Syrian oil. You know this."

"Do you know how the oil would get to Kazakhstan?"

She hadn't thought about that. "Turkey?"

"Don't be stupid. Across Syria by truck to Tartus—Tartus where there is a Russian military base, where the Russians launch attacks against the anti-Assad rebels. From there by ship, across the Black Sea to refinery at Novorossiisk, then by pipeline through the Caucasus to the Caspian Sea, to Astrakhan, where finally it comes into our hands. And then we export to China."

Penny wasn't sure where this was headed. "It sounds complicated," she said.

Kasym said, "It is simple. The hardest part is for having the jihadists to get the oil into Russian hands. Neither side wants to be seen dealing with the other. That's where they need us."

"Fellow Muslims?"

"Yes. We tell Isis that they are selling to us. They knew where their oil will go, of course, but we put a warehouse in Tartus with a Kazakh flag and we pay the highest price, so they don't care. This arrangement would have doubled, tripled their revenues."

"And Schuman? The Europeans?"

"They thought they could make similar deal, taking the oil via Turkey. They convinced themselves this lets them to maintain stable supply from the Levant once the war ends and Isis is destroyed."

"If word got out about that, after the Paris terrorist attacks, Schuman would be destroyed."

"I understand you have provided Konstantin with the means to keep L'Orancourt silent. Forever."

Penny didn't respond to that. "So you win."

"No," Kasym said. "I don't win. Our company doesn't win. Our country doesn't win. We are losing."

"I don't understand," she confessed.

"Didn't you follow the course the oil will take? The Russians are handling everything, from their base in Syria to the Kazakh border. It's all part of Putin's turn toward China. We are simply a...a conduit. It's our name on the contract, but it's the Russians who get paid, the Russians who win friends in Beijing."

"Aren't you on the same side?"

His eyes flashed with anger. For the first time he moved away from the door, and she kept an eye on that bulge beneath his jacket. "You were with the Chairman for how long? A month? Six weeks?"

"About that."

"And you learned nothing about us?"

"You don't love the Russians," Penny ventured.

"Do you know what it has taken for our people to secure independence? Do you know of what we endured under Soviet occupation? The deportation of Kazakhs to Siberia under Stalin, the terror of the Cheka, the famine, the destruction of our pastureland so that Khrushchev and Brezhnev could grow more wheat to feed Russian mouths?"

She had nothing to say to this. Kasym was shaking with anger, far worse than any pique he had directed her way when they sparred for Timur's favor.

"And today we are still under their shadow. We must praise our brotherhood and promise economic cooperation. We must accept Cheka spies to serve as our security detachments. The Russian invasion of Ukraine has left us no doubt about what we must do just to maintain illusion of independence. So when we are sent to deal with Islamic terrorists on the one hand, and the hungry Chinese on the other hand, do you think this was our idea?"

"Maybe you should be glad that L'Orancourt tried to disrupt the deal."

"Glad? The pressure we are under, it is unbearable. And now it is worse. The Russians suspect we may have been aware of the whole thing. They're looking for excuses to keep us under their thumb. You have put KazPetro, our country, in danger."

"Me? I haven't exactly benefited from any of this. Viktor Gubinov came after me because...we have a bad history, him and me. It was personal. What happened in Dubai, it wasn't about Timur."

"You are wrong. The attack in Dubai was not just about you. It was also to make sure we could not act independently. The Russian nightmare is encirclement. Schuman and KazPetro, perhaps working together—Moscow will do anything to prevent something like that from ever happening."

"I didn't get the impression L'Orancourt was trying to be your friend."

"Putin is our enemy. The West is Putin's enemy. Who is a friend?"

Penny shrugged. "Kasym, this is interesting. But it's beyond me. What do you want?"

"I heard Konstantin is trying to recruit you. That you are saying no."

"So?"

"You aren't going to work for the man who also employs Viktor, are you?"

"No, I'm not."

"They will try one more time to turn you."

"And then?"

Kasym's mustache undulated like a worm as he chewed on his lip. "We want Konstantin off our back. We want to distance ourselves from this terrorist oil business."

"So distance yourselves."

"I've told you, is not that simple. We can't be seen to be opposing our big brother."

Penny took a guess: "You've learned about the L'Orancourt sex video."

"Konstantin plans to blackmail Schuman with it and make the governments in Paris and Berlin go silent. They will accept Russia's oil deal with Isis. But if that video is in the public... then Konstantin loses all leverage. He can't blackmail L'Orancourt because he'll already have been humiliated, destroyed. The Isis deal will collapse."

Penny had planned on giving Konstantin the video in exchange for getting the drop on Viktor. She had played into the Russian's hands, though: Konstantin would have given her Viktor anyway. She hadn't realized the video's impact would stretch back to Timur. Funny, a few weeks ago she would have loved to have seen Kasym Shokay quivering before her, but now it just made her feel small.

"The video is on my cell phone," she said. "Bring it to me."

"I can't. Charles has it. I'm not supposed to be here."

"You're already caught, Kasym. That keycard of yours, it'll leave a record of you coming here."

"It belongs to one of the security men. Their office is on this level, at far end. I need to return it to his desk before someone realizes it's missing."

"I always knew you were a sneak," she said. "Get the phone—you can do it."

"Charles keeps the phone on his person. I can't get it. Most important, I can't be seen trying to get it."

"What makes you think I can?"

"They'll be coming for you soon, him and Chester."

"So?"

Kasym opened his jacket. The gun was hanging out of his inner pocket. It was a .45-caliber handgun. A serious weapon.

"I thought you were a Beretta man," Penny said nervously.

He put the gun on the floor. "I wish I had shot you in Dubai."

"That's a Glock, right? You get this from the security guard's desk, too?"

"I'm giving you this chance to escape. Get your phone back. Expose L'Orancourt. Take away Russian leverage. That will end the oil deal, and keep KazPetro out of it."

"And you?"

"I'm flying to Almaty in three hours." He slid the gun across the floor. "I don't know how many bullets are in there."

She knelt and picked up the weapon. It was a Glock 17. She released the firing pin safety and released the single-stack, 10-round magazine, and a bullet in the chamber. "Enough," she said, slamming the mag back inside the grip.

Kasym put his hand on the doorknob. "You owe Timur this."

She didn't reply, thinking she didn't owe Timur a damn thing. "Hey, Kasym."

"What?"

"How did Viktor know how to find me in Dubai? How did he know exactly how to do that?"

"You ask interesting question." She wasn't sure if he knew; he didn't look eager to tell. He opened the door and checked the hallway.

Penny said, "You're a snaky son of a bitch, you know that?"

"That's why I'm on the outside, and you're stuck in here."

She blurted, "I'll do it. I'll expose L'Orancourt."

He paused, acknowledging her words. "If you get the chance, you might check swimming pool on the level below."

"Why?"

He gave her a final look over his shoulder. "They really did something on your face. You're finally ugly." He smiled. "Is more honest."

24

Dreadful Penny

When they came for her, they came politely. One of them knocked on the door before the other key-carded the lock.

"Come in," she said, playing along.

Penny sat upright with her legs extended the length of the sofa, bare feet pressed against the cushion, arms spread wide along the spine and the armrest. Empty, harmless hands. She had showered and pulled her hair into a ponytail, the facial swelling had ebbed, and she now wore the same outfit: T-shirt, jeans. The raincoat lay draped over the coffee table, beside the bag of frozen peas.

Charles entered carrying her shoes and her hoodie folded neatly on top. Behind him loomed Chester, tapping his cane. They wore matching double-breasted suits of brown wool with a thin square pattern in orange, white dress shirts offset by silk white hankies, and royal blue ties held by matching silver clips. Chester's eyeglasses were thick, horn-rimmed squares.

"Good evening," Charles said, moving toward her feet.

"Good evening," Chester echoed, stepping into the space

between the living room furniture and the kitchen.

"I feel under-dressed," Penny replied.

"Your belongings," Charles said.

"Thank you," she said, gesturing toward the coffee table. Charles put the shoes on the floor, the hoodie on top of her coat.

"You're looking better," Chester offered.

"More like your old self," Charles said.

"My nose is broken and I've got two shiners," Penny said.

Charles moved his hand to his jacket and Penny felt a sudden surge of panic, which she managed to swallow. He withdrew the iPhone belonging to Thérèse Nulty.

"We appreciate the information you brought us," Charles said.

"Thank you so much," Chester added.

Penny said, "That's in exchange for Viktor."

"But we gave you Viktor," Chester said, leaning over his cane.

"You had a blade against his throat," Charles said.

"You weren't giving him to me," Penny retorted. "You were trying to buy me. I came to trade, not to sell myself."

"But isn't selling yourself rather your forte?" Chester asked.

She gave them a thin smile. "That's not how I see it."

Charles returned the iPhone to his inside jacket, switched hands and removed a big Samsung Galaxy from the other. "You'll excuse us if we fail to spot the nuances," he said.

"Not to say we don't respect your abilities," Chester hastened to add.

"We value them highly," Charles said. "As does Mr. Konstantin."

They were forming a pincer, Charles nudging toward the

back of the sofa, Chester drifting toward her open side. The greater the divide between the men, the longer the odds against survival. But she needed one last piece of information.

"So where is Viktor, anyway?" she asked.

"On the premises," Charles said, dialing a number on the Galaxy.

"You don't want to see him," Chester said.

"He's in a beastly mood," Charles mumbled. He waited for a connection.

"What's he doing?" Penny asked.

"Asking for permission to come in here," Chester said. "With his comrade, a pair of pliers, and a hacksaw."

"We've told him no," Charles said, "for now." The Galaxy chimed. "Can you hear us all right, sir?"

"Yes, yes," came a voice.

Charles held the device's face up so she could see. A window opened to a video screen. She recognized Konstantin from his Wikipedia page: a bland, middle-aged face with a brown mustache and rectangular wire-frame glasses, the sort of look favored by computer engineers from the 1980s. He appeared to be in the cabin of a private jet.

His English was heavily accented. "Thank you for video recording," he said.

"It's in exchange for Viktor," she replied. "An even trade."

"You are in my house, one of my houses," Konstantin said. "You see what man of means I am. I am generous man. You will see."

"I'm not here to interview for a job," Penny said.

"I am generous, yes, but I can get angry, fast. Very angry. This you do not want to see."

"That's a threat," Penny said. "I don't work for people who

threaten me. Do we do a trade or not?"

"I have sex video already," Konstantin said. "What trade do you propose now?" He squinted at her. "Your face is very bad. What is such big deal about this girl?"

Chester told her, "I'm afraid you're running short of options."

"And time," Charles added.

Penny said, "Viktor's embarrassed you. Why is he still alive?"

Konstantin sighed. "He is nephew."

Of course. What else could explain why a vicious bumbler like Viktor was still alive? Cronyism. Ties that bind, the kind she had wanted to sever. "You were ready to sacrifice him," Penny said. "I don't think you'll miss him."

"Work for me," Konstantin said, "and I tell you where you find father."

She said, "My father is dead."

"We both know is lie."

"I know," she said, "that I don't believe a word you say."

"Stubborn, stupid," Konstantin said. "Enough."

Charles turned the screen away and looked down at his boss. "Sorry, Mr. Konstantin."

"Dreadful woman, this Penny Lee," she heard Konstantin say. "Kill her."

They moved fast. Charles fluidly lowered the Galaxy while his other hand darted up the back of his jacket. Chester blurred to the corner of her eye. The Glock had been nestled beneath a side cushion; now it was in her two hands. The recoil was modest for such a loud bang. Her shot hurled Charles up and back against the door, arms open, surprise splashed across his face. He dropped both the Samsung and the black six-inch knife before his knees folded and he slid down, his throat disintegrated into gore.

The cane snarled her wrists, and with a quick turn Chester forced her to release the gun. It clattered to the floor. Penny rolled off the sofa, avoiding the cane's next blow. She came up and raised an arm to deflect the swinging stick.

"What have you done to Charles?" he screamed.

She spun away from the next blow, head swimming. She tried to get to her feet, but the dizziness caused her to stumble. She fell against bookshelves, with their hardbound Victorian classics. Chester swung the cane against her shoulder blades and she *oof*ed against the shelving. Another thumping like that and bones would start to break.

Penny's hand found *Paradise Lost* and flung it behind her. It was enough to buy her the inch she needed to avoid Chester's karate chop. She rolled toward the kitchen as his hand snapped the bookshelf in two, and this time she bounced onto the balls of her feet.

Chester's gangly reach found her, the cane knocking her on the chin, spinning her. Her hands found the ceramic countertop. She hurled the kettle at him. Chester dodged the attack as water splashed across the floor. She hurled oranges, the sugar bowl, anything to fend him off. But the cane bit her again.

Jo, the staff; *tori*, blending with the attacker's energy. The cane came like a punch at her face, *ganmen-tsuki*, so she slid offline, hand touching the weapon. She had a hold of it just above the curving head, but Chester knew how to react: instead of resisting her, he went around and projected force, causing her to stumble. She sensed the cane being used to pin her down and she rolled free before he could immobilize her.

They faced each other with wary respect, Chester holding the cane forward like a kendo sword. They met in a ballet of sudden tensions and releases, hands trying to win control over the cane—the object one moment in her power, the next lost to Chester, as they pirouetted around the room, stepping onto the coffee table, leaping onto the spine of the sofa, tumbling back toward the bedroom, the cane gathering speed in this kinetic dance, smashing dents in the walls.

They fought back toward the door. She jumped over Charles's body—his feet were still quivering and he made a gurgling sound as his fingers tried to hold together what used to be his larynx. He was oblivious to the battle, or unable to do anything but experience the draining away of his life. She rolled away from a strike and came up with Charles's knife in her hands. She hurled it at Chester, but he improbably lunged forward on one knee, turning the cane vertically to deflect the flying blade.

"Lucky," she said.

He allowed a humorless grin. "I batted three wickets for Cambridge against Oxford in Nineteen Eighty-Two."

She turned away from his next strike, but he surprised her by withdrawing the cane before she could touch it and he struck the back of her hands with painful speed. Chester was too fast, his reach too long. He could always hurt her, grind her down, so long as she failed to penetrate his inner space. He could match her when sparring over the cane. Penny had to change the game.

She rolled and attacked on her knees as the cane hissed overhead. He recalibrated for the attack from below. Penny crossed her arms to parry the blow and then she reached for his knees—bring him down to the ground and maybe she'd have a passing chance.

Even this failed. Instead of resisting her forward energy, Chester stepped lightly backward, accepting the direction of her lunge. He too rolled backward into a somersault that brought him up to his knees, now holding the cane by its curved end and pointing it at her. Penny recovered her poise with a roll of her own, but as she straightened, she saw for the first time the cane's hollow core. The barrel swung toward her as Chester gave the head a little twist. *Click.* His forefinger wrapped around a newly released trigger.

She lurched to the inside of the cane as the barrel made a wooden *phtoot* and spat a pellet. Chester's face tightened, the eyes behind his thick glasses red with determination, but she was advancing on her knees, *shikko*, and pulling the cane along her waist, *jotori*. He had fumbled his surprise. She arced the weapon, bringing it around to her other side, as her elbow and forearm pushed at his face. Lift and project: but instead of the usual move to break him away from the weapon, she leapt inside his circle of space and smashed her elbow against his face.

Not a move taught in aikido.

As he collapsed, his hand grazed her injured nose and that brought them to their knees, each blinded by their own kind of pain, deaf to the other's groans. Now they were rolling on the floor, his hand on her throat, forgetting the cane, and she flailed against his superior length. His tie was akimbo, his glasses knocked to a strange angle, his hair disheveled, but he was on top, using his weight and his span to choke the life out of her. He was an animal in his hatred, bathing her in his snot and saliva.

Her fingers found the cane and banged it uselessly against

him. She saw stars and then nothing but a fade as both of his hands squeezed her to unconsciousness.

* * *

Penny opened her eyes and coughed. She inhaled, coughed again, and felt the soreness of her throat. She rose on an elbow and the pain in her forehead burst to life.

She was in the apartment, that much she knew, but it would take her a few minutes of focused breathing to be able to keep her eyes open and the aching at bay. The furniture was out of place, the floor slick with water, the kettle lying still in a corner, the knife blade lodged in a floorboard.

Chester sat across from her, long legs straight, his back against the wall. The barrel end of the cane had penetrated one of his lenses and was fixed inside his eye. The pellet she had fired had left most of his brains displayed in the panorama behind his skull. The other eye was still wide open. He had died in a state of astonishment.

Penny got up. She didn't know how long she had been out. Her nose and her face ached once again. She put on her shoes and socks as though she were moving through a vat of molasses. She zipped on the hoodie. She leaned over—whoa, head spinning—and tugged the knife free. A quick search of Chester's pockets secured his electronic passkey.

Charles's corpse soaked half the floor with blood. His ruptured throat stank, and his unmoored head was tipped at an unnaturally sharp angle. He had survived long enough to die in terror—that much was written on his frozen features. She didn't want to look at his mangled body or smell his bloody stench, and snaking her hand into his jacket made her woozy with disgust. She retrieved her iPhone but found herself on her hands and knees, retching.

Penny finally got up and stumbled to the kitchen, ran cold water, drank it, washed her bruise of a face as gently as she could. Then she scooped up the Glock from beneath the coffee table and let the door close behind her, leaving the carnage for some unlucky soul to discover.

The basement was vast, with many rooms. It could take her a long time to search it. Then there was the house above—how many stories? Three, four? Full of bedrooms and ballrooms, libraries and kitchens? And then two basement levels below?

There was another, faster way of finding Viktor.

Penny padded down the hallway, moving as much to keep her head clear and her balance sure as to ensure her rubber soles remained quiet. She advanced with the knife in her rear pocket and both hands holding the gun, her arms semi-relaxed in front of her.

Game room, quiet. Bowling alley. Hair salon.

After the elevator, she passed a cinema and then a gym populated by exercise machines, all of them still. She had a hard time imagining Konstantin passing the time down here.

She finally came to the end of the corridor. The final door was closed, its brass plaque inscribed with Cyrillic letters. She pressed Chester's card to the door handle and heard a click. She opened the door. Inside: a bank of screens, leading from a desk-sized console up to the ceiling, a conversation of shifting black and white closed-circuit camera images.

Penny closed the door and sat in the swivel chair. The left-most side of screens showed scenes from the exterior of the house—the grounds, the driveway, the street corner, the heath. The next column of screens monitored certain rooms

273

in the main house, which looked as opulent and oversized as she expected. The final column of screens showed interiors from the basement levels. Including one of her apartment cell, showing Chester seated on the floor, his head leaning into the cane in front of the painted wall.

She waited, noting the rooms as they paused on a screen, each visible for three seconds before being traded for a surveillance image from somewhere else.

Chester and Charles had been in charge of security, at least at this hour. Otherwise, someone would have seen the fight and come running. The low manpower explained the timing of Kasym's visit; the wily Kazakh had figured out when he could risk it.

She waited to be sure. The workmen had gone home for the day, and nothing disturbed the building's exterior. The image from level B2 was too strange to decipher. But she counted only three men in the mansion. The first was in a room on the ground floor: the sandy-haired man with the flat nose, who had driven the Range Rover Sport, reclined on a sofa to watch a soccer match. Another—Viktor—paced in a bedroom, mobile phone to his ear, gesticulating in anger. And the third man, wide and bald, had just entered her apartment at the opposite end of the corridor. He was processing the horror scene.

The image flitted to the empty sauna. She waited for it to return. It took about ten seconds for the screen to move between other locations before it returned to her apartment. Empty. The man was gone.

She saw the driver guy rousing himself from the match, phone glued to his ear, a gun in his other hand. Viktor was nowhere to be seen—already on the move. *Coming for me.*

25

The ancient song

The elevator bisected the basement corridor. Beside it was a recess leading to a stairwell, in case a fire or a power outage disabled the lift. This being Konstantin's mansion, the humble shaft was layered in luxury woods, with a chandelier lighting the landing where Penny waited, the Glock in her two hands.

The bald man who had stuck his head into the apartment, at the far end of the corridor, should have been more paranoid. He had seen the corpses of the manor's two gentlemen, still dressed in their Bond Street suits, one missing a throat, the other with a cane-cum-rifle shoved into his skull. The man should have crept along the hallway, checking every door. Maybe then he might have survived.

He ran towards the security office, rushing past her lurking in the stairwell, watching the corridor through a narrow window in the door. She burst out. He spun around, a fat spinning top, and Penny noticed the white bandages plastered over his bullet-shaped head, and the tattoos climbing up his neck. More eyebrows than face: the assassin from Dubai. The killer she had spared. He was right in front of her, three feet max, when she pulled the trigger, absorbed the recoil, shot again.

The first bullet punched him in the right shoulder. He twisted around and down to his knees. His hand still gripped his gun, but he couldn't raise it to shoot back. Where a moment before there had been connecting tissue, muscle and bone, there was now just the gaping hole of an artery spewing his blood.

Her second shot missed.

He grimaced, and from beneath those heavy brows she saw his eyes, alive with fury.

They faced each other, the man's left hand unclipping a phone from his belt. Despite his wound and her pointing a Glock at him, the assassin moved with a relaxed surety. She had lacked the stomach to finish him off once before, back at the Burj al Arab. Now he'd taken her best shot; he'd taken her measure. All he was going to do now was make this call, that's what his grin said, he was going to tell Viktor he'd found the foolish—

Penny exhaled and squeezed the trigger. She lost track of how many times she shot him. He would never come back from whatever hell she'd sent him.

She picked up his cell. It was connected to 'Виктор'. She put it to her ear and heard the man on the other end take a breath.

"Penelope," Viktor said.

She disconnected the line. Let them track its GPS coordinates and find their dead comrade. Or...

If they caught her in the corridor, she'd be trapped. Penny pried the dead man's gun from his fingers—a Sig Sauer P220 semi-automatic—and stuck it in her jeans behind her back. She banged through the stairwell door.

"If you get the chance, you might check swimming pool on the level below."

She chose down instead of up and emerged onto a darkened B2. She immediately banged into something small but hard. The object clattered into a stack of others, raising an almighty alarm as they scattered onto the floor. Fiddling with the phone to bring up a flashlight function, she saw she had run into a phalanx of tools: pickaxes, shovels, a jackhammer.

Her phone's glow was too meager for the cavern's dark. She moved carefully now across unfinished cement flooring and through a maze of bigger construction equipment. The bulldozer occupied the middle of the space, a big napping beetle in a tomb of mud and concrete. As she walked behind it, she saw a light in the distance, a cold will o' the wisp. A trap? As she made her way through the inky chamber, her alarm grew. She redoubled her hold on the slender phone because her hands had grown sweaty.

She crossed an open divide to a platform of rising steps— bleachers. She turned to look behind her, her pathetic phone light failing to penetrate the murk, but she had seen enough to guess this place was being molded into Konstantin's ice rink, the stands for his guests to watch the oligarch and his cronies slap pucks into nets. She stepped around the bleachers, the phone's torch guiding her around more builders' tools, and resumed her path toward the light. As she closed in, it appeared to be a single naked bulb strung from the ceiling.

The cement floor abruptly fell away into an abyss. She flapped her arms and withdrew the foot that nearly tumbled into it.

A low chuckle echoed up. "Watch your step, honey."

"W-what?" She squinted into the chasm. The light bulb

appeared to be suspended somewhere above it. As her eyes adjusted to the dim, she made out a shadow below.

"There's a ladder," the man croaked. "Little to your left."

Penny looked there and saw it, a pair of metal curves that bubbled up and descended into darkness. She turned the phone light off, stuck it in her pocket, and moved around the edge to the ladder at her feet.

Don't.

It's a trap.

That voice.

Impossible.

Penny turned and climbed down two rungs, three, and then ran out of ladder. She looked down, had a vague sense of a curving surface, and chanced a light jump. The edge only came up to her chest. She turned and faced the giant concrete basin, descending and widening. At the far end hung the single light, suspended like an omen. The shadow stood a little in front of it in silhouette, upright, legs spread, fading to black.

"Who are you?" she demanded, the cavern swallowing her voice.

"You know who I am."

"...Stack?"

She walked down through the empty pool. The figure didn't move, but as she closed in, she could make out his tight curls, the shadow of his suit's lapel, the prayer beads on the wrist of his outstretched hand. He stank of his own excrement.

"Good to see you, Pen."

"But...I saw you...die."

"Well," he drawled, "either we're both wandering in Hell, sweetheart, or I didn't die."

"If your death on that screen was faked, then..."

278

The missing piece: how Viktor had known exactly where to find her. How he knew the exact suite. How he knew when she'd be at her most compromised with Timur, her most vulnerable. How he'd known where to continue the hunt in Beirut. The wild card in Fuad's deck had been dealt one more time.

"You set me up."

"Guilty," he said.

Emotion overwhelmed her. It wasn't her fault that her sister and her family had been murdered. Not her fault that she'd conspired to rip off the wrong Russian Mafioso. Not her fault that Fuad was dead. Stack's fault!

She pressed the mouth of the Glock against his forehead. "You son of a bitch."

"As you can see, it's worked out for me, too," he said. "Dig my new kicks?"

"What?"

She looked down. His feet disappeared into lumps of con‐crete.

"Oh," she said.

That might explain the bad smell. Stack had been here a while.

"Word from the man is that they fill the pool tomorrow," Stack said.

"If you betrayed me to them, why are you here?"

"I only betrayed you because you were the walking dead. They got the jump on me because they figured out the money went to your *hermana*. From there they had some of their own guys in Russia reverse-hack the chain and eventually... Turns out I was only the second best in the business. And the reward you get for your silver medal is a chance to turn coat so they

279

stop wedging blades beneath your fingernails."

"You were shot," she said, still not comprehending it.

"Lev's dead," Stack said. "You saw him die for real. I just put on an act. Konstantin had promised me a full-time gig with his crew for getting you, but you escaped. I helped him track you down at Fuad's, but you escaped that too. So even though it's Vik who's screwed it up every time, I got the blame, and the concrete shoes."

"They've tried to recruit me," she said.

"Hope you said no."

She nodded, putting a hand on his chest. She was glad his face was covered in shadow. His cocky tone couldn't hide the undertone of suffering or the sense that he had been hollowed out.

"For what it's worth, Penny, I am sorry."

She nodded. "So am I." Penny took the dead assassin's phone and slid it into Stack's breast pocket.

"Who's is that?"

"One of theirs," she said. "I need you to hold onto it for me. Just for a little while."

"GPS locator? I'm your decoy?"

She nodded. "You going to tip them off?"

"No," he said, and she sensed the outline of a grin on his darkened face. "Scout's honor."

She patted his chest one last time. "Good." Penny turned away and headed back for the ladder, breaking into a run. She scurried up and headed around the other side of the edge. Her eyes had adjusted to the dim lighting, but away from the inside of the pool basin it was essentially black.

She heard them before she saw them. One following her tracks from behind the ice rink. The other from the opposite direction, emerging like a ghost.

The one from the direction of the rink said, "Stack, where is she?" It was the driver. His Russian accent was a little more obvious now. A sign of distress.

"Come and gone," Stack called up.

The driver climbed down the ladder into the basin. She could see he was armed with a machine pistol. The man walked a few steps deeper, then swiveled, looking for her.

The other man, the one still in the darkness, said something in Russian. She'd recognize Viktor's hiss anywhere.

"No, she's taken off," the driver replied as he approached Stack. "This was a wild goose chase." He plucked the phone from Stack's jacket. "Come on, mate, what she say?"

"She's a very scared girl," Stack told the driver. "If I were you, I'd secure the exits, bring in more men, and hunt her down. You don't want her escaping the house."

"That's what I said we ought to do!" the driver called up to his boss.

Viktor replied in Russian, softly but firmly.

"She's not here!" the driver protested. "She's probably in the garage."

Viktor's shadow approached the pool. Penny held her breath as he crept closer to where she stood.

The driver moved away from Stack, to climb back up to meet Viktor; they were zeroing in right at her. "Viktor, mate, we got to go now!"

Penny stepped back into the darkness, away from the sole light suspended over the pool, moving so slowly that she barely noticed the wall loom behind her.

Viktor was maybe ten feet away now, skirting the pool's edge, now eight, now seven.

She lowered herself to a chair position, back pressed against the wall, both hands on the Glock. Viktor halted just short of where she wanted him, breaking her line of sight to the light bulb, where she would be confident of hitting him. Anything else would literally be a shot in the dark.

But something had given him pause.

"Fine," the driver said from below. She was far enough away, crouched sufficiently below any line of sight to the pool's interior, that his voice was muffled and faint. But she heard him say, "I'll go down there myself."

Viktor motioned in the dark, raising a hand to signal something. Penny gulped and kept her gun aimed toward the will o' the wisp. He took a step and broke the light. She squeezed the trigger.

Click.

Out of ammo.

Viktor whirled at the noise and light and thunder erupted from his hip. *Brrrrrrrrrrriptttt!* The bullets carved a line into the wall just above her head, covering her in shards of concrete and dust.

She rolled, chucking the Glock, and came up on her knees. The machine pistol spat fire again, but she was out of its line of sight. She pulled out the Sig Sauer tucked behind her jeans, fired but missed.

Brrrrrrrrrrriptttt!

She rolled out of Viktor's line of sight and over the edge into the abyss.

Now the driver down in the empty pool was firing his machine pistol at her, too, but she rolled towards his side and he couldn't swivel his hips fast enough. *Uke* was pure aikido: blending into the attack of the *tori*, receiving the technique, adapting its energy. She disabled him with a wrist lock that torqued his arm while her elbow found his radial nerve. She maneuvered behind him and his body suddenly convulsed as Viktor's bullets raked the pool. She pushed the dead driver forward, the Sig Sauer in her hand. She fired and fired, she saw Viktor's shadow jerk, and his next salvo of bullets erred wide.

She ran to the high edge. Her fall had been controlled, the energy dissipated by the roll, but it had been a six-foot drop onto cement. Things were starting to hurt. She had to ignore the aches and jump to get her hands on the edge. If Viktor hadn't been injured, now would be his moment to finish her.

She hoisted herself up and nobody shot at her.

From what little she could make out, Viktor was gone. But he had left her a gift. Blood on the floor.

"I think you scared him off," Stack called up to her.

She inhaled, exhaled, breathed sense back into her brain.

"Nice shooting, by the way."

"Which way did he go?"

"Hard to see anything," Stack replied. "Vik's a coward, though. He be running."

The garage. Penny wasn't sure how to get there, which meant going back toward the stairwell. She loped around the edge of the pool, toward the unfinished rink, and pulled up short at a pile of tools.

You don't have time for this.

She stuffed the Sig back in her jeans and used her hands to feel the instruments, try to identify them.

This man betrayed you.

With both hands she lifted a long, thick handle. The thing was heavier than she expected.

But I'm doing it anyway.

283

Careful not to strain her spine, Penny returned to the edge of the pool. She heaved it headfirst into the air. The sledge-hammer landed near Stack with a thud.

"Good luck," she called.

"You too, sweetheart."

She ran back, moving as quickly as she dared, Sig in hand. She opened the stairwell door and was nearly blinded by the chandelier light. She took the stairs down. More blood, in bigger splotches, including one shaped like a footprint. Viktor was bleeding down his trousers.

Penny heard it before she saw it. Running into the garage, she saw the bronze Maserati peel toward the exit.

Bam. Bam.

She fired at the oncoming car and spangled the windshield. Viktor turned the wheel hard, the rear of the car fishtailing toward her like a fist. Penny rolled and kept rolling, but when she reached her feet, Viktor put the car into a new gear and raced across the hall. She followed—running, shooting, but Viktor reached the open car lift on the far end and her final bullet sparked on the closing doors.

Out of ammo again. She flung the gun aside and made for the Range Rover Sport. She opened it, pulled Charles's knife from her back pocket and tossed it onto the dashboard, got the keys resting in the sun visor and started the ignition.

"Come on, come on," she seethed, releasing the brake and gunning it for the opposite exit. The remote to the garage door rested in a plastic cup holder. She pressed it as she ascended the curve, hoping the door was opening because she couldn't wait. She pushed the gas and spun the wheel with both hands, defying the centrifugal resistance. The heavy steel door hove into view. It was moving too slowly, but she wasn't going to brake. She bent forward and jammed it. There was a metallic yelp as the Rover scraped the bottom edge of the door and she burst free.

It was dark outside, wee hours. The speedometer said fifty, then sixty, and as she barreled down the meadow lane, seventy. She forgot about the lowered beam at the edge of the parkland and, the car's lights off, didn't see it until she smashed through it. Streetlights, the silent judgment of tycoons' mansions: she peeled a fishtail turn, rubber screeches splintering the night's hush—seventy, eighty, ninety—and aimed the car toward Hampstead Heath.

Another right turn, arcing out to the left-hand lane along-side the heath, heedless of oncoming traffic. There was none, just the bronze bullet coming at her low. They were about to cross paths, but she'd never keep pace once Viktor burst past.

She jerked the wheel right.

* * *

When she came to, she couldn't breathe and all she saw was a blank nebula. It took a minute for her to realize she was choking on the airbag. Penny pushed it away and did a quick check. Plenty of aches, a surfeit of pain, but nothing new, nothing sharp. The airbag had saved her.

She opened the door. The crash had shaken her more than she realized, for her knees turned to jelly and down she went. She caught herself with both palms on hard earth and eased herself to a standing position.

The impact had sent the Rover into the heath, the passenger side wrapped around a big oak. No air bag would have saved her had it been the driver's side flying into the tree.

The knife might have killed her, too, but it had been flung into the rear seat. She eased it out of the cushion.

Stumbling, still working out new kinks, she moved around the car and looked across Hampstead Lane. The Maserati had spun over and come to a rest on its top. What was left of it had buckled like a squeezed accordion. A single taillight flicked on and off, Morse code for SOS.

Viktor must have shot through his windshield. He lay in the middle of Bishop's Avenue. Glass shards glinted in the streetlight like dew drops in the dawn. She limped toward him. From the strange angle on the ground, it looked as though the impact had broken his spine. Viktor looked up at her with his one remaining eye.

And in that eye, she saw fear. A lot of fear.

"Penelope," he begged.

So now what? She felt the sense of emptiness in her gut. Nothing she did to this guy was going to change a thing. It wasn't going to bring back Vivian or Fuad. It wasn't going to restore her life. It wasn't going to make her a better person.

A worse person, maybe.

She regarded the broken, quivering loser on the empty street, and she knew that killing him wouldn't make his ghost go away. It wasn't going to unrape her. He might always be in the mirror, taunting her.

But it was harder to imagine Penelope Lee with a halo and white wings, strumming her harp, just for sparing him.

She crouched beside him. "Killing you would do me no good," she slurred. She showed the knife, and his one eye trembled from that sweating, shivering wreck of a body.

"*Nyet, nyet...*"

She traced the tip along his inert neck, down along the

strange twist of his chest, over the ribs that pointed at un-natural angles.

"Turn the other cheek, right?"

"*Nyet...*"

Down to his pants where the hungry blade sliced, popping the button into the air, opening the zipper. He had already wet himself, if not in an earlier moment of terror, then upon impact. He was doing it again, twitching and stammering as she sliced the elastic band of his boxers.

The words, the ancient words that she had underlined long ago, desiring this day, they returned.

I brooded on this trial, this ancient blood feud
Year by year. At last my hour came.
Here I stand and here I struck
And here my work is done.
I did it all. I don't deny it, no.
He had no way to flee or fight his destiny...

She put her face in his, his fear and blood and broken flesh vibrating with the stuff of life. The one thing of his that remained intact was the partly mended cleft of his lip.

And Clytemnestra sang,

And then I strike him
Once, twice, and at each stroke he cries in agony –
He buckles at the knees and crashes here!
And when he's down I add the third, last blow,
To the Zeus who saves the dead beneath the ground
I send that third blow home in homage like a prayer.

Penny touched his harelip with her tongue.

* * *

287

The sun struggled to penetrate the leaden London sky. The bridge was busy: a few early tourists but mostly people hurrying to work, either to the Tate Modern on one end, housed in the old power station, or to the offices and trading floors of the City, scattered around the soaring dome of Saint Paul's. In their rush to escape the wind cutting over the river no one gave her the slightest notice.

After watching Viktor die, ensuring in his last moments that he knew exactly who was responsible for his torment, she had returned to the rental flat and to the storage company at Saint Pancras Station. She collected her only possessions, the detritus of her existence. Now Penny stood at the Millennium Bridge's apex, taking a quiet moment to admire the fine view. The red backpack was at her feet, containing her cat's lives.

Physically she was a mess. Emotionally...she didn't have a way to assess that damage. It was too soon to think about anything. So many people were dead, her life unwoven. She had wanted to feel like what the Greek play had promised: reveling, reveling in the justice won by her own hand, or in the simple fact of having survived. But she mostly felt wrung out, wondering if she'd ever enjoy a peaceful sleep after what she'd just done.

Maybe her father was alive?

No, that was almost certainly a lie.

But as she regarded the river prowling through the ancient capital, she knew that she wanted the truth. And even though she ought to fear the ramifications of his being alive—a whole new level of betrayal that even Penny couldn't comprehend— she didn't feel apprehensive. Instead, she felt something she hadn't experienced for so long that it required an effort to identify: hope.

The job wasn't done yet.

She withdrew Thérèse Nulty's iPhone and prepared an email to names of reporters she had looked up. *The Guardian, Le Monde, The New York Times.*

This wasn't for Kasym. It wasn't even for Timur, although Penny had decided she might have done it for him after all.

Maybe she would come to regret wreaking vengeance against Viktor, as he lay supine and helpless. Or maybe he had it coming, just like L'Orancourt had it coming.

She attached the sex video, her own face spliced out, and pressed send.

Thérèse was now officially too hot. All trails would lead to her cell phone, and then to her bank account in Paris. The searchers would then hit a wall, because the Chamouns had covered her tracks well. But the longer Thérèse remained active, the more likely someone would unearth the name Penny Lee; the sooner Konstantin would find her. Thérèse Nulty, *au revoir.*

Penny adjusted the iPhone as though she were taking a picture. Lean against the rail, get London Bridge in her sights, and oops! Clumsy tourist, too greedy for the shot. The phone slipped through her fingers and fell into the gunmetal waters of the Thames.

She slung the backpack over her shoulder. Shimura's dojo was thousands of miles away, and there would be no tycoon's Learjet to take her there. Best to start walking.

* * *

Penny Lee will be back...in PENNY BLACK

VI

Next in the Penny Lee series

Read the opening to PENNY BLACK, the second book in the Penny Lee series.

26

Penny Black

She wore no makeup, hid her body in the blocky canvas *gi*, and jailed her black locks in braids, but her face was her face, and maybe Daigo relished the chance to hurt something pretty.

Penny Lee had washed up at Shimura's dojo like a corpse on a winter beach. Knee walking, rolling, grappling, *ai*–merging; separating, engaging *ki*–energy; acting in harmony, *dō*–the way, the truth. Shimura was good at uttering a veneer of sacred words over his pursuit of violence. To hell with truth and the way; Penny just wanted to get lost in the ritual training until she could think of a better place to hide.

Hoisted among snowbound peaks, the compound felt removed from worldly dangers. The snow's hush was a lullaby. She didn't disturb it with anything like a word to the other students. She wanted nothing from them, least of all their gaze. They had nothing to do with her, or so she thought until the new guy, Daigo, made it his business to be her tormentor.

Shimura's style of aikido was aggressive but came with a world view. Daigo just wanted to inflict pain. He trailed her constantly: in the canteen, crossing the grounds. She was the only woman currently in training, and he smelled her anxiety. Penny wasn't scared of him, exactly: the fear he picked up emanated from her more general paranoia. But it egged him on.

She didn't think his hostility was directed at her—at Penny Lee, or any of the other names she might go by. It's just that, when she was unlucky to be partnered with him for the end-of-day practice of *kata*, rote forms, he went berserk, flipping her and slamming her on the mat. The *thwack* caused the students around her to stop and look.

They were about the same height, but Penny was a dryad to his bullish gnome. Daigo swung an ax kick. She scrambled quickly enough and the two regarded one another with new, mutual disgust.

He taunted her with a condescending bow. Tough guy pretending to be nice to the girl. She responded by launching her *tori-shite*, applying a throwing technique, but her thoughts drifted to mustering the right word in Japanese to tell this guy exactly where he could put his—

Swoop. Penny paid for the lapse of concentration when he thrust his hand, fingers extended, to deliver a knife chop. Here she needed *ukemi*, the act of reception, to cover her vulnerability and regain her poise. Her double-handed parry was poor, but not in vain: the man had been aiming at her neck.

He could have killed me. She was as stunned by indignation as she was by the weight of pain from where he had struck her. She fell to her knees and raised her palms to take a pause.

She knew what it felt like to be hunted.

She felt it again, now.

Now all eyes were on her. The two-dozen students, sparring

in white uniforms, ceased their whirls. Shimura's main hall was a wooden, high-ceilinged vault over a lake of cream *tatami* mats. The bust of Shimura's father, at the far end of the hall, regarded her without sympathy.

The sensei was not present in the dojo. Taka, one of his black-belted acolytes, ranked two *dan*, was substituting to take the students through their routines.

Surely, he must have seen Daigo's transgression.

Aikido was meant to be peaceful, the practitioner yielding to an attack rather than meeting force with force, submitting to the reality of nature.

Peace and harmony—yeah, right. When it came to nature, the master hewed toward predators devouring prey. Shimura taught a style he claimed to have invented, *sokei*, 'total', aikido. Most sparring sessions at Shimura's school ended up as a violent carousel.

That's what drew all these men.

But this wasn't sparring time. The dojo, even Shimura's, had rules, especially around propriety, and the newbie Daigo was skirting a line. She didn't want a confrontation; she wanted to train, to breathe, to turn her body into an automaton, and not think about the rest of the world.

But the rest of the world was here, incarnated as this jerk.

Penny snapped her canvas jacket straight beneath its white belt. "Want to fight the *hafu* girl?" She took a step back, clearing space. The neighboring pairs of students had dropped the pretense of practicing to watch the dust-up unfold.

Daigo adjusted his stance, face pinched by malevolence.

She pointed at her chest. "*Hafu.*" Her Asian half was actually Chinese, not Japanese, so she wasn't sure if the term applied to her, but right now the distinction didn't seem to matter.

They circled, the other students backing away to open more space.

"*Yamete!*" shouted Taka: Stop what you're doing!

She relaxed her guard, waiting for Daigo to receive a dressing down. But Taka aimed his little lecture at her. His Japanese was too rapid for her to catch all the words, and his tone was polite and controlled, but she got the gist.

He was kicking her out. Only her.

Penny stared at Taka in amazement. Daigo maintained a discreet silence, head bowed, but eyes tilted upward at her, laughing. It was just as well that her mouth and tongue couldn't form the Japanese words she wanted to spit.

Taka was the opposite of Daigo, with a delicate face and a broomstick neck. He was an amazing fighter, one of only two black-belt students under Shimura's tutelage, the one whom all the other students sought to emulate--the one who commanded their respect. Yet she couldn't mask her resentment towards him. Taka's own expression hardened in response, and she allowed a rebellious thought. *You're the one who paired me with this psycho.*

She took a breath, allowing contrition to relax her features. Taka clapped his hands, admonishing the others for stopping to watch, but he still didn't rebuke Daigo. She bowed to Taka and wove toward the exit. The students resumed throwing one another on the mat, except for one, another newcomer, who watched her go with naked interest. She had noticed him too, earlier in the day, and she had enjoyed returning his gaze, and the way it had prompted him to bury his chin in the cold and be on his way, smiling.

She didn't want his attention now. The pain in her shoulder grew insistent but it didn't compare to the feeling churning in her stomach, the burn of humiliation––and something more.

I've been set up.

She reached the dojo exit, part of her head trying to tell herself to calm down, that she wasn't the victim of a conspiracy, that she had simply screwed up and now she'd have to work her ass off to earn redemption. And the other part of her cerebral cortex, a part that she had come to trust—the deep well of survival instincts—warned her to stay alert.

Behind her Daigo was working solo on the dummy, grunting as his thick arms struck its red oak.

Penny stepped off the dojo's porch into the frozen night. The path led through snowbanks to the center of the compound, where the men's dorms and the canteen leaked soft electrical light. Ice bent the tree branches and froze the leaves, but the wind found its voice whistling through the *torii* gateway that loomed over the complex. Beyond this huddle of buildings, another route meandered toward Shimura's house and the hot spring. But that was not her direction: her path twisted through a rougher patch of darkness to the bottom of uneven stone steps. Above perched the women's cabins.

Female students were relegated to a ledge overlooking the compound. A quartet of single-room wood cabins, once lodgings for hunters, hugged the cliff, with an outhouse clinging to the ledge's corner. There was no electricity, only a hearth and, outside, bundles of kindling. Shimura let the women students shiver out of sight while the men enjoyed hot showers and TV. But for Penny, the solace was worth the hardship, and right now the cabins were empty save hers.

She switched on a battery-powered lamp inside her cabin. The red backpack was still there, hanging from its wall hook, holding her change of clothes. The second-hand, yellowed copy of Homer's *Odyssey* still brightened her rickety table.

She didn't trust anyone with her vital possessions, not even here at Yamamizukan, Shimura's school. The physical man-ifestations of whatever Penny Lee had become—the slender passports, her face in different nationalities; the encrypted phones in their Faraday sleeves; the credit cards with their financial lifelines—were buried beneath the hearth.

She could dig them out, pack her few possessions and escape this frozen tedium. She had felt safe at the dojo, and there was nowhere else to go. Something about Daigo, though, made the haven feel more like a prison.

He reminded her too much of what lay in store, out there.

She coaxed the hearth fire and let drowsiness dull her aches and slow the spinning in her mind. The nights were becoming harder; peace, elusive. Ghosts invaded her dreams, men from the world. An eyeball dangled from a shattered face; another's hands struggled with the guts slithering out of his belly. A hypodermic needle wobbled in the chest of a man with sorrowful eyes. Spies, blackmailers, rapists, murderers. That had been her world.

Not the last ghoul, though: hers had been a world of church bakes, simple pleasures in family, the unearned bliss of ig-norance. Lately this innocent maiden, chunky in her white wedding dress, had infested Penny's nightmares. The ghost didn't protest as her body erupted in a dozen bloody wounds. She just stared at Penny like the avatar of blame.

Sister.

Her sister's murder had left Penny the last of the line. A dead end.

The ghost had no sympathy. She pounded her fist into her palm. A toll. Knocks. Penny woke up.

The knocks persisted.

Penny raised herself from the hearth and its warmth. "Whoisit?" Exhaustion slurred her words and blunted her alarm. Shimura's rule was clear: no men allowed up here.

"Taka. Sensei sent me."

She opened the door and offered a curt bow. Taka was wrapped in a thick robe over his *gi*. A cone of light shone from his industrial-sized flashlight. He couldn't suppress the urge to peek inside her cabin, as if it hid some heavenly pleasure. She moved to block his view of the backpack; better that no one, not even Taka, would even think to ask if she possessed anything up here.

"*Fukushidoin*," she mumbled, using the title for a second-*dan* teacher. "What is it?"

"Come with me please."

"Master Shimura wants to see me?" A decade of on-and-off training here, this was a first.

"Yes, now."

"Can you tell me what it's about?" A futile question; Penny was already pulling on her leather biker's jacket.

She followed Taka outside. His flashlight wasn't much help because his body blocked her view of the illuminated steps. At least he wouldn't notice her shivering, and not just from the cold.

Muscle memory guided her descent. The dojo was dark now but the lights inside the men's dorms were still on. Steep snowdrifts lined the path to Shimura's house.

Hokkaido Island was like a giant Japanese hand grasping at Siberia. Like many of its houses, Shimura's was built for winter: tall and narrow, with a sharp-cornered roof of iron that glinted dully in the moonlight. The slatted windows offered softly glowing lines but no interior view. A motion sensor activated the porch light, illuminating the rusty pickup parked to one side.

The door opened and Shimura's wife exchanged bows with Taka. Plump rolls of flesh and rosy round cheeks seemed to insulate Mrs. Shimura from the chill. She smiled at Penny, eyes crinkling. She was a constant presence at the dojo, driving the pickup to ferry students or supplies, but she otherwise kept to herself, denying the camp any maternal sympathy; the handful of times Penny had bumped into her outside the house, Mrs. Shimura had offered nothing more than bland pleasantries.

Taka and Penny shook the snow off their shoes and left them on the porch.

The house possessed a modern, vaguely Western sensibility with pine flooring and stucco walls. The only obvious traditional Japanese touch was a shrine built into an alcove on one side, raised above the height of the door. Several porcelain miniature deities reigned there behind white paper symbols of lightning. Taka paused to clasp his hands and acknowledge the Shinto menagerie.

Central heating—a revelation. The wife twittered and Penny gladly handed over the leather jacket. Mrs. Shimura gestured to a row of slippers. Penny stepped into the smallest pair and shuffled after Taka, who made it to the end of the hallway and knocked on a door. He was rewarded with a grunt from within.

Taka turned the handle but didn't enter. He was waiting for her, even though he was the senior. Her face must have betrayed puzzlement. "Sensei will see you alone," Taka said.

Penny assembled her composure and entered the room. It was a study. Shimura sat behind a dachshund-shaped desk, his legs crossed beneath it, surrounded by busy bookshelves. A large, square wooden board lay on the table, its surface dotted with white and black stones. Shimura, dressed in a kimono of indigo, was scrutinizing a Japanese text through thin glasses with surprisingly stylish frames. These, plus his lithe figure and full head of black hair, made him look to be in his forties, veiling the sixty-five years he had logged.

Taka, in the hallway, shut the door.

Penny made a deep bow.

"Lee," he said. His voice, at least, hadn't escaped the husky rasp of age.

"Yes, Sensei."

He gestured for her to sit. "How long have you studied at Yamamizukan?" His English was excellent, if heavily accented. From watching Chuck Norris movies, he had once said.

"For almost ten years, Sensei." Penny sat on her heels.

"Ten years of washing laundry, cooking food, raking stones and failing to master the basics on the *tatami*."

She had certainly raked her share of stones. All the newcomers learned obedience and rote movement by tending to the master's Zen garden.

"If this is about me and Daigo, Sensei, I am ready to accept your punishment." She bowed again, touching her head to the floor.

Shimura muttered, "I should have said no to Chamoun-san."

The unexpected comment raised the hairs on the back of her neck. The Chamouns, a clan of glorified pimps in the private espionage business, were the ones who had inserted her into Shimura's school. For self-defense, and to give her a pursuit between jobs that didn't involve snorting coke in a playboy's Lear jet.

301

"Fuad Chamoun held you in high regard." Shimura reached into one of two bowls sitting by the wooden board and, with a satisfying clack, added a polished white stone to the diorama. He seemed to be recreating a game in which white and black stones tried to outmaneuver one another on the board's grid. It was the Asian game of Go. "You are *kunoichi*, correct?"

"I'm sorry, Sensei, I don't know that word."

"*Kunoichi*. Nine plus one. A man has nine holes in his body."

"So a woman..."

"Has nine-plus-one, yes: *kunoichi*."

She waited, wondering where this was going. Shimura seemed absorbed in his text.

He set a stone down on the board. "In feudal Japan, the samurai practiced *shinobi*, deception. An art cheapened by many imitators."

"If you mean spying or fooling an enemy, I guess everybody does it." Under the tutelage of Fuad Chamoun, this had been her vocation. "Governments, big companies, hackers."

"The samurai practiced deception to reach an enemy when he is at his most vulnerable. But it is such times, such places, that are most difficult for a warrior to use *shinobi* against an opponent."

"I'm sorry, Sensei, I don't understand."

He gave her a penetrating look from behind his glasses. "I think you do."

"An enemy is at his most vulnerable when he lets down his guard. When he relaxes or lets himself be distracted."

Shimura grunted, his version of approval, and placed a black stone on the board.

"Such as in the old pleasure quarters," she ventured. "When he was surrounded by courtesans instead of his advisors."

The master ran a finger down his text.

"But then," she continued, "there is no way a samurai or his men can spy on their enemy in such a place. There's no way to reach him without being noticed. Hence...*kunoichi*?"

"Have you read Fujibayashi?"

"No, Sensei."

He stood from the table to kneel by a bookshelf. He lowered his glasses, squinted at the titles, then extracted a volume. "I suppose you don't read Japanese."

"No, Sensei."

He flipped through it. "His *Bansenshukai* is an account of the way of *shinobi*. This volume deals with *in-nin*. Infiltration."

"It's, like, a ninja manual?"

He ignored her question, absorbing a passage. "To translate is difficult." He cleared his throat. "Send *kunoichi* in advance, especially if his castle is well defended and he is difficult to kill. If you are able to enter, let the *kunoichi* guide you to the target. High-ranking men indulge in their sexual desires, so let the *kunoichi* help him give in to his lust. *Kunoichi* is an effective tactic of *yo-jutsu*, art of trickery."

"I understand now, Sensei." So he knew all about her. Shimura had probably known since she first arrived a decade ago, flush from one of her first honey traps, blackmailing some low-ranking bureaucrat with her barely legal call-girl routine. Maybe Fuad had told him, or the master had simply guessed.

"You are right, Sensei. I am *kunoichi*."

He returned to the table and folded his legs. "But your patron, Chamoun-san, is dead."

She held her nerve. "You heard about that."

"Yes. But not from you." The accusation hung over the white and black stones.

303

"Fuad sent me here when I was younger. But for the past several years, I have come to your dojo by myself. I no longer think of my training as related to him."

He growled.

"Fuad taught me discretion," she added.

She had been the Chamouns's courtesan spy, serving a network on behalf of giant corporations—oil majors, agribusinesses, aerospace companies—whose executives were desperate for any advantage. Never work *for* governments, that had been the Chamouns's pledge, but frequently *against* them.

But the last mission had been a failure. More than that: it had become a conflagration of vendettas, hot enough to make a Sicilian blush. From Moscow to Abu Dhabi to Paris, quite a few powerful people would have liked to take out their frustrations on Penny Lee.

This *kunoichi* was suddenly on her own, without master or mistress. Out of moves.

"I don't see any tears of grief." He placed a stone on the board, recreating a game from the text before him. Then he removed his glasses. "You think hiding here will protect you from whoever else is out there?"

"I...it...Please, Sensei, let me stay here to train."

"Have you ever played Go?" He put his glasses back on and resumed looking at his text.

"No, Sensei."

He placed a white stone on the board.

"Then you are of no further interest to me."

About the Author

Jamie Dibs was born in the U.S. (go Phillies!), but lives in Hong Kong with his wife. They have done a stint in Paris and are regular visitors to Lisbon. Jamie's interest in different cultures, world affairs, technology, and history provides the mood music for his stories.

He was born in the Year of the Dog.

You can find serializations of his novels, plus short stories and commentary, at his Substack, "Dark & Stormy". Please support independent authors by giving this book a review on Amazon.

You can connect with me on:
🌐 https://www.jamiedibs.com
🔗 https://jamiedibs.substack.com

Subscribe to my newsletter:

✉ https://jamiedibs.substack.com

Also by Jamie Dibs

Penny Black (book 2 in the Penny Lee series)

Penny Lee, an industrial spy and profes-sional honey trap, has lost her career and all she possesses. She holes up in a remote Japanese training camp to lick her wounds and avoid a long list of enemies – a shelter made all the more appealing by the arrival of David Diya, an antiques dealer she falls for, despite her best instincts.

Shimura, her aikido master, has other plans for her. Reveal-ing his awareness of her past life, Shimura coerces Penny into becoming his assassin: first target, a South Korean tycoon.

The plot goes wildly wrong, leaving Penny at the mercies of an American spy with an interest in artificial intelligence, a Korean scientist gone rogue, and Chinese military officials who know more about Penny's past than she does – and are willing to share what they know, for a price.

Bad Penny (book 3 of the Penny Lee series)

The job seems easy, and maybe even fun: seduce Thibaud Maurel, an aging French movie star, infiltrate his computer, and blackmail him. For Penny Lee, ex-spy on the run, it's a job she can't refuse.

But then there are the menacing Russian bodyguards, a family of gangsters staging a bank heist, a Swedish arms manufacturer, and a young African prostitute with a mysterious link to Maurel.

Penny's return to Paris has tipped off the Chamoun clan from the espionage underworld that she once served and betrayed. Penny should run, but Daliyah Chamoun holds secrets about Penny's family – and learning the truth of her lineage is worth the risk, even the risk of death.

Star Fall People

Immortals walk among us. Slipping into new lives, decade after decade, from Shanghai to San Francisco: Sley falls in love with a mortal; Nadia wants to bear children; Mang amasses wealth and power.

...Until technology threatens their ability to assume new identities. Mang builds a corporation that develops artificial intelligence and turns it into a weapon of mass terror, for if he is to be unmasked, then he must rule.

The world is vulnerable, still recovering from a week-long loss of electronic communication called the Darkout. With Nadia siding with Mang, Sley can't stop the coming catastrophe.

But when Mang's AI reaches sentience, it too becomes like an immortal – with its own idea of humanity's fate.

Gaijin Cowgirl

Working Tokyo nightclubs is easy money for the party-loving Val Benson – until her number-one tipper, Takahashi, a corporate titan with sinister hobbies, reveals a map to gold stolen during World War Two.

Val embarks on an action-packed treasure hunt, from the neon-drenched streets of Japan to the mountainous jungles of Thailand. Snapping at her high heels are Yakuza gangsters; bent cops; rogue CIA agents; and Val's estranged father, a philandering Congressman.

Val is joined in her quest by Suki, a hostess desperate for a new life; Simon, a British kickboxer; and Muddy McKenzie, a washed-up Australian treasure hunter. But as they close in on the gold, can she trust them?

The Blue Jungle (novella)

Gangsters kidnap Naomi Sato, a struggling journalist in L.A.

Their boss thinks Naomi knows what's happened to his daughter.

He may be right: Naomi covers the world of porn.

It's simple. Find the girl before the goons do, and Naomi gets to live – body parts intact.

But the only path to the missing starlet goes through Bobby Feathers, master of sleaze.

And to survive, Naomi has to face a worse terror: herself.